BLOODY BELL

A Samantha Bell Crime Thriller

JEREMY WALDRON

ALSO BY JEREMY WALDRON

Dead and Gone to Bell

Bell Hath No Fury

jeremy@jeremywaldron.com

CHAPTER 1: GIRL GONE MISSING

KATE WILSON DIDN'T ALWAYS WANT TO BE A MOTHER. SHE was just a kid of eighteen who dropped out of high school in pursuit of her G.E.D. *A loser,* her teachers called her. *You'll never amount to anything,* they had said. Kate ignored them all. She didn't need to listen or care because she had always known those things about herself, thanks to her parents.

Her mother was the person who introduced her to the abuse and made her numb to the pain. Her father was distant and unresponsive—a deadbeat, just like they said she was. Though her young skin was tight and smooth, it held the strength of seasoned military armor from a decade's worth of direct hits.

School meant less to Kate than prospects of work and a paycheck she could use to finally move out of the dinky old rundown apartment she shared with her hatemongering mother on the east side of Denver. Though, for Kate, work was in short supply even if her dreams were not.

At the time, Kate was more concerned with weekend parties, girl's nights out, and the sporadic flash in the night hookup with random older boys who thought of her as cute.

She could manipulate them for money, booze, drugs, and still walk away hanging on to what little dignity she had left when it was all over. It wasn't perfect, but it was what it was, and even Kate was smart enough to know that the good times wouldn't last forever. Kate knew she had to get it while the getting was good.

She just never expected it to end so soon.

Kate squeezed the hand she was holding and felt her entire body flex through another excruciating contraction. Her teeth grinded as she clamped her eyes shut. Tears popped free with the force of the pinch. She had never felt anything as intense as what she was going through now.

When her head hit the pillow she could breathe again. A cold damp cloth swept across her heated forehead and time ceased to exist. All she wished was for it to be over and to hold her daughter for the first time. *How many more hours? Would this baby ever come out?*

Her chest rose and fell fast, but not nearly as quick as the thumping of her heart.

Kate's once reckless behavior seemed so long ago. It was difficult for her not to think of those days because she swore she would be a different person after this was all over. After all, it was only eight months ago she'd learned she was pregnant.

"Kate, honey. Drink some more water," a woman's soothing voice whispered in her ear.

Without opening her eyes, Kate pursed her lips and let the woman guide the straw to her mouth. Sucking gulps of cold water down her throat, she felt the liquid begin to cool her core. Without warning, her stomach muscles flexed and Kate was back at it.

Kate's torso lurched forward, she wrapped her fingers around the bar attached to the bed, and latched on for fear of falling over. Feeling stronger than she had ever felt before, she growled and pushed, wanting so badly for this baby to come out.

"We're almost there. On the next contraction, you'll be meeting your daughter," a man's voice said from somewhere behind the bright light.

Kate fell back into the bed and let her mind go back to dreaming. She could hear her heart thrashing, feel the cool slick of sweat coat every inch of her naked body. But all she could think about was how much she'd cried the day she learned she would be a mother.

She could still feel the gigantic pools of tears that had puddled in the palms of her hands that night. She couldn't sleep. Couldn't find peace with herself—refused to believe the news was real. Kate blamed herself, cursed the child that was only a cluster of cells—punching her stomach repeatedly with hopes of dislodging the embryo in her womb—but couldn't place a face to who the father might be. That bothered her most because she took precaution when having sex. Always played it safe, always on the defensive, never wanting to be in the position she found herself in now.

Kate was all alone and deathly afraid of breaking the news to her mother. Her mother would never forgive her, and certainly wouldn't help with the unexpected costs. But today, even though Kate was still without anyone close by her side, everything made sense and she was beyond excited to have a fresh start.

Kate's muscles contracted. Her mouth opened and she screamed a primal noise of warfare that ricocheted off the walls.

"There's the head. Keep going, Kate. You're doing great."

Something inside of her lit a fuse and Kate put everything she had into evicting this child she had been carrying for the better part of a year.

Her inner thighs quaked and she kept squeezing her

muscles until she felt a sudden release. Though more exhausted than she had ever been, she leaned forward and reached for her daughter.

The doctor, hiding behind a surgical mask, held her baby inside his hands and Kate knew immediately something was wrong. The urgency and buzz that had lived in this room for the past six hours was instantly replaced by complete silence.

Kate flicked her eyes between the faces in the room and felt the onset of a panic attack take root. Her lungs squeezed the air free from her body and her veins opened up with anger and fear.

"Why is she not crying?" No one could look her in the eye. When no one answered her, Kate asked again, "Tell me. Why is my baby not crying?"

The doctor stood, still cradling the tiny baby in his latex gloved hands, and nodded to the nurse. The nurse threaded her fingers through a pair of scissors and stepped between the baby and Kate, severing the umbilical cord with one quick snip.

Kate's eyes swelled. She felt the first warm tear roll down her cheek. Kate knew in her heart that her baby was dead but, until someone confirmed it, she refused to accept it. *Why aren't they trying to save her?*

"Someone tell me what is happening." Kate grew angry. "Is she dead?" Her chin quivered with fear. "Tell me. Is my daughter *dead?*"

The doctor flicked his stony gray eyes at Kate. Kate stared into the swirls of disappointment glimmering in his pupils and felt her body shrink inside of itself as if somehow this was her fault.

Everyone watched and waited to hear the doctor speak. He never did. Instead, he remained quiet as a mouse as he turned on a heel and tenderly walked out the door, still holding Kate's lifeless baby inside his hands.

CHAPTER TWO

"THIS IS AWFUL," SUSAN KEPT SAYING. "WE HAVE TO go now."

I slid out from the booth, stood, and turned to the desperate mother still looking to me for help. Her name was Ms. Dee and she had come to me, desperate for help in finding her missing daughter, just before Susan learned that our friend, Allison Doyle, had collapsed and was rushed to the hospital.

Handing Ms. Dee my card, I said, "Send me the details. I'll see what I can do to help find your daughter."

"Thank you," Ms. Dee said softly as she took my card.

I nodded and turned to catch up with Susan and Erin who were stiff-arming the exit and making a run for my car. A ball of anxiety stitched my side but it proved to be only a minor handicap as I rushed to catch up.

This wasn't how today was supposed to end. What had begun as a bright sunny March day was now as dark as the sky with the sun behind the Rockies. There were leftover piles of snow in the shaded areas from the storm that had come through a couple days prior, but there was a definite warmth swirling in the air, bringing whispers of the changing season.

"I'll drive," I called out, digging my heels into the pavement before coming to a full stop at my driver's door. When I wet my lips, I was quickly reminded of the margarita I had drank. Salty and sweet, the news of Allison sobered me instantly.

"You okay to drive?" Susan asked from the backseat.

I nodded and started the engine without hesitation as Erin and Susan buckled their belts. Then I backed out of the tight parking spot and headed north on Blake Street before turning on 18th.

I weaved my car between the tall city buildings, allowing my thoughts to jump from Ms. Dee to Allison. Erin stared at her own reflection in the window, lost in her thoughts, and Susan did the same as we bumped along on our way to St. Joseph's hospital.

"Patty is with her," Susan kept repeating as if needing to reassure herself that Allison wasn't alone. We didn't know what to expect once we got there. All we could do was pray that our friend was in good hands.

Allison's chief of operations, Patty O'Neil, was the one who'd called Susan. None of us could guess why Allison had suddenly collapsed. And it didn't matter. We had each other's backs no matter what and would drop everything to be together as the makeshift family we were.

When we stopped at a red light, I sighed and drummed my fingers on my thigh. I could hear the clock ticking down to zero inside my head. It did little to ease my worries. *Tick tock, tick tock*. Like a bomb I couldn't defuse.

It wasn't just that I wanted to rush to be at my friend's side—which was more important to me than anything—but it was that Ms. Dee's daughter, Cameron, had already been missing for two days now and we were past the critical first forty-eight hours. That was a tough pill to swallow. The odds of finding Cameron alive now decreased with every minute that went by without her. *Where were the police in all this?*

The light flicked over to green and I slammed my foot down on the gas.

My Subaru Outback pathetically lurched forward. That had to be the reason Cameron's mother had come to me—the police missed their chance and Ms. Dee knew she was running out of time. I would have done the same thing if Mason was the one missing. Desperation could work miracles if given the chance.

Handing Erin my phone, I said, "Message King. Ask him if he knows anything about a missing person named Cameron Dee."

"A woman is missing," Erin muttered as she typed up her text message. "Cameron Dee. Heard anything?"

Erin flicked her gaze to me when she was finished. I turned away. I couldn't talk with my mind swimming in perpetual worry. A part of me wondered if I got what I'd asked for. Since the Sniper story, I'd been looking for something to get my juices flowing. What I didn't expect was to get my fix like this.

When we arrived to St. Joseph's, I took the first open space we could find. Together, we moved as a team, sticking by each other's sides until we were able to gain our bearings.

Susan took the lead, Erin and me following close behind. We galloped through the hallways and soon found Patty in the west wing after a quick elevator ride up to the third floor.

"Oh, I'm so glad you weren't far." Patty hugged each of us.

"How is she?" I asked.

"Do they know what caused it?" Susan asked before Patty could answer my question.

"She's up and talking." Patty looked me in the eye as she spoke. Then she turned to Susan. "Still running tests. C'mon, let me show you to her room. She'll be thrilled to know the party has finally arrived."

CHAPTER THREE

THE MOMENT WE STEPPED INTO ALLISON'S TINY HOSPITAL room, she raised her fists in the air and shook them as if she was holding a pair of maracas. We all laughed, exhaling a collective sigh of relief into the air.

"Ali, baby," I smiled when reaching for her hand, "you had us all worried."

Allison's grin was wide when she squeezed my hand. "But Sam, you should have seen how bright the stars were before I fainted."

I smiled but I needed to be reassured she would be okay before I started in on the jokes. "You've been working yourself too hard."

Allison shrugged. "Nothing out of the ordinary. Isn't that right, Patty?"

"I plead the fifth," Patty said from the corner.

Susan and Erin began hammering Allison with their own questions as I let my eyes rake over the curls of IV tubes slithering up her arm like an iridescent snake. It looked bad but she was in good spirits. That eased me.

Erin razzed her about secretly having a love life she hadn't shared with the group. Susan was quick to join in on the jokes. "Not knowing about a pregnancy would certainly explain the sudden dizziness."

"If only." Allison grinned and kept rolling her eyes. "I haven't been with a man in over a year. Really, it's nothing. I was probably just dehydrated." She inhaled a deep breath and blew out a heavy sigh. "I'm sorry for not making happy hour. I was really looking forward to having a margarita or two."

We laughed, reassuring her that we drank hers for her.

My cell dinged with a message, a second one close on its heels. Everyone stopped to stare. "It's only work," I said, feeling a bit bashful.

"And here I thought I was *the* story." Allison chuckled.

I couldn't help myself. It just came out of me. I told Allison about Ms. Dee approaching Erin and me at the Rio and her request to help find her missing daughter. I could hear my own excitement as I spoke, my fingers already typing up the story on my thigh.

"Then what are you waiting for?" Allison's eyebrows pinched, her mood turning serious. "You should understand a mother's agony better than anybody in this room."

I stared into my friend's chestnut eyes and thought of my son, Mason. "I can't leave you."

"I'll be fine." Allison waved me off. "You go find that girl and don't let her mother down."

CHAPTER FOUR

DETECTIVE ALEX KING AND HIS PARTNER, DETECTIVE John Alvarez, were speechless as they stared through their unmarked sedan's windshield, not believing their eyes. They had been called to an apparent double homicide in Congress Park but never expected to see this.

The German Shepard barked and snipped as two Animal Control officers wrestled with the beast. Dragging its thick nails across the pavement toward the back of their van, they tugged, but the dog tugged harder, refusing to go down without a fight. On it went for several more minutes until finally the two officers had the sharp-toothed dog safely contained in the back of their van.

"Let's hope our night is a little easier than that," Alvarez said, opening his door.

King followed Alvarez's lead and stepped out beneath a flickering night sky. There was a chill in the air but nothing he couldn't handle. The two large men approached the two-story Tudor and badged their way past the police line before entering the house where they were quickly pointed to the upstairs master bedroom.

After climbing the creaky Victorian stairs to the top floor, King stepped into the room where a couple lab technicians were already busy working. They combed for clues and collected evidence as King pulled a pair of latex gloves from his sport jacket pocket and slid his fingers inside. The elastic band snapped around his wrist as he swiveled his neck to each of his shoulders, assessing the scene.

At the center of the room, a white couple in their mid-forties lay on top of the covers of their queen-sized bed. They were both fully clothed, their eyes closed, a peaceful expression on their faces. King's gaze drifted down the man's arm to find his hand seemingly purposely draped over the woman's. It was an intimate gesture, suggesting they were married.

King and Alvarez split up—King going to the dresser and his partner to the bed.

At the tall oak dresser, King took note of an expensive looking sports watch on one end and a pair of diamond studded earrings on the other. It was your classic married couple's bedroom—his side and hers with a walk-in closet only feet away. Inside that, clothes and shoes for all occasions. It was clear this couple was comfortable with their finances.

As King side-stepped back to the dresser, he listened to Alvarez speaking to the crime lab investigator behind him. "No forced entry. Nothing reported stolen—valuables left out in the open. And no sign of struggle," the investigator said.

King opened the leather wallet near the watch. He thumbed through various credit cards before matching the victim's name, Keith Brown, to the Colorado issued driver's license inside. Putting the wallet back where he had found it, he glanced over his shoulder and asked himself, "Who did this to you, or did you do it to yourselves?"

Alvarez was still conversing with the officer when King padded his big feet to the bed. There was a half-emptied bottle of scotch on the nightstand marked as evidence. Next to it sat a glass still full of the amber liquid, also flagged by the techs.

King peered down for a closer look.

A lipstick smudge in the shape of a smile was imprinted on the glass rim. A prescription pill bottle was opened. The label was for Vicodin but the imprint on one of the pills inside suggested it was generic.

King turned his focus to the victims. He studied each of their faces, making note of how their bodies were positioned. Both their lips were blue, and what appeared to be dried saliva in the corners of their mouths had King thinking this was an overdose or possible suicide. He glanced to the woman's ring finger, noticing a wedding band—big expensive rock—still firmly locked in place. The scene was too clean for it to be a murder, he thought.

"Anyone know her name?" King asked.

"Keith and Pam Brown." Alvarez relayed what the investigator had shared only a moment ago. King had been lost inside his head, making mental notes of his findings, piecing it all together. "He was a banker and she was an accountant."

"Bankers have more enemies than accountants, right?" the young officer at the door said. His eyes were bright as he glanced between the detectives.

King glared at him from under his brow. Making assumptions was like walking a tightrope. Too risky to chance it.

"How about you make sure no one enters the house who isn't authorized." Alvarez read King's expression and patted the officer on the back. Guiding him to the exit, King went back to studying the bodies.

"What do you think?" King asked Alvarez when it was just them and one lab tech still in the room.

"I think it's a suicide." He side-stepped and pointed over

the bed to the opened prescription pill bottle King had seen on the nightstand.

"Who found them?"

"The young chap you just sliced up with your eyes." Alvarez shoved his hands inside his pants pockets and raised his brows. "Responded to a disturbance call. The call was made by a neighbor complaining about a dog barking. The front door was jarred opened so they came inside and discovered this."

King kept his eyes on the husband's hand perfectly draped over his wife's. The dog would have been a huge deterrent if an intruder did break-in—unless the dog knew who the attacker was. King's thoughts kept churning over every possible scenario. "If the front door was left open, why didn't the dog just leave?"

"Maybe you're underestimating a dog's loyalty."

King cast his gaze to the wooden floor. He could imagine the dog sitting guard at the bedroom door, protecting his owners as they took their last breaths—which then ruled out carbon monoxide poisoning.

"There was nothing else reported." Alvarez's cheeks ballooned as he bounced his gaze around the room. "Only a barking dog."

King straightened his spine and met his partner's gaze. "Anyone speak to the caller?"

Alvarez shook his head, no.

"Ah, my two favorite homicide detectives." Leslie Griffin, the medical examiner, arrived and stepped into the room carrying her supplies.

King and Alvarez quickly briefed her as she readied herself for a night's work. They didn't know much, but shared all the facts with her. She didn't seem to mind. King liked Leslie's approach. She kept it fun, considering the job. Leslie was quick on her toes and was always one to appreciate a good puzzle.

"Suicide, huh?" she said, moving to the nightstand and picking up the pill bottle while eyeing the scotch. "I was kind of hoping for a homicide." She glanced back and flashed a squirrely grin. "But, yes, it has all the makings of a perfect, lovely mutual suicide." She laughed. "Though I won't know for sure until I get these two back to my office and run some tests."

The detectives left Leslie alone to give her more room to work. As they opened up the first of the other two bedroom doors, King was toying with the idea that they could be working a murder-suicide case.

It was a guest bedroom they browsed first and, as they combed through the sheets and pulled back the curtains, King thought back to similar cases he'd worked in the past. Nine out of ten times, it was the controlling and depressed husband or boyfriend responsible for the woman's death. Was Keith Brown one of those men? But besides how the couple lay in bed, nothing else gave him reason to conclude it was anything other than an accidental overdose.

"Let's just call it a suicide and get on with the night." Alvarez scrubbed a heavy hand over his chin.

The men exited the guest bedroom and entered the next through the en-suite bath. King paused at the sink and knew he'd found something of interest.

The feminine scent and beauty products were everywhere. Hair bands, lotions, and makeup. He knew they were about to step inside the bedroom of a teenager girl and, as they did, he moved to where a collage of photos was pinned up on the wall. There, King found his reason for being here tonight.

"They have a daughter." King unpinned a family photo from the wall and thought about Samantha's son, Mason.

Where is she now and does she know her parents are dead? The thought was dreadful.

"Lord, why does it always have to be a family?" Alvarez muttered as he stared at the Browns' family photograph. "All right." He rolled his shoulders back. "Let's see what the neighbor says before we go searching for this girl."

CHAPTER FIVE

THE SKY WAS PITCH BLACK AND THE STREET LAMPS HAD turned on by the time Erin and I left the hospital. Susan decided to stay behind to keep Allison company. The doctors wanted to keep her for observation as they worked to monitor Allison's condition. It killed me that they didn't know why she had collapsed. Despite Allison's cheer, I knew she wasn't painting a complete picture to how she was actually feeling.

"You know Susan is only staying because her boyfriend works here." Erin flashed me a knowing look.

"I know." The corners of my eyes crinkled. "Can you blame her?"

Our sneakers squeaked on the floor as I thought about how great it was Susan had found someone as wonderful as Dr. Benjamin Firestone. Even if he worked crazy hours, I knew they were good for each other.

"So, you going to tell me what all those messages were about back there?" Erin glanced to my phone just as we were stepping inside the elevator.

I punched the lobby button with my finger and watched

the doors close. Some were from my editor, Ryan Dawson, others from Mason, but the only one Erin really cared about was from Ms. Dee. "Ms. Dee was just saying we could stop by."

"It's not too late?"

"I imagine she hasn't been sleeping much since Cameron went missing. She said it would be easier to tell us what happened in person." We stepped out at the lobby floor and headed for the exit. "I think now that we know Allison is all right we need to learn as much as we can about Ms. Dee's daughter. She's already been gone for far longer than what makes me feel comfortable."

Erin clutched her stomach as if suddenly feeling queasy about the situation herself. "Like I'd rather be doing anything else."

I reached for Erin's hand and, when my fingers took hold of hers, we shared a smile. We stepped outside and I called Ms. Dee.

"Samantha, is that you?" she answered.

"Is now still a good time to meet?"

"Yes. Of course." Ms. Dee repeated the same directions to her apartment she'd texted me earlier. "If you have any trouble, call."

Erin co-piloted as I drove east toward the Denver-Aurora line. We mostly talked about Allison, our website, and the future for Erin's podcast. *Real Crime News* was gaining subscribers and our monthly visits were growing. Word was spreading about our work and I was starting to believe that I would soon have no choice but to decide what I wanted more; working the crime beat for the *Colorado Times*, or running *Real Crime News* full-time. Either way, I was certain our website was why Ms. Dee came to us instead of going to a private investigator.

Less than twenty minutes passed before we arrived. The

apartment complex was what I expected. It wasn't fancy—
simple and nondescript. We parked, entered the building
without hassle, and trotted up the stairwell with the bounce
in our step that only came with a new story.

"This is it," I said as we approached the door.

Erin knocked and, not a second later, Ms. Dee answered.
She was still wearing the same purple blouse we'd seen her in
at the restaurant and her straight black hair was neatly done.
Her eyes were puffy and swollen but she forced a smile
anyway.

"Can I get you something to drink?" Ms. Dee moved to
the small kitchen with beaten up wooden cabinetry. "I don't
have much, but a glass of water?"

I politely declined and took in her home. It was impres-
sively small for two adults to be living in. There was a nice
vanilla scent in the air and the furniture, though used and
worn, came from a single collection. "Not meaning to be
rude, Ms. Dee, but I'd like to cut straight to the facts around
your daughter's disappearance."

Ms. Dee swallowed and held out her hand for us to take a
seat at the tiny round kitchen table. It shared the same room
as the foyer and living room, no walls to separate the three.
We took our seats and I asked, "Tell us, when did you last see
or speak to your daughter?"

Ms. Dee's hands were folded on the table in front of her.
There were gold rings on her fingers but I guessed she wasn't
married based on her living situation. Ms. Dee's brown eyes
cast to the ring she spun lazily around her knuckle. "We had
an early dinner here." Her voice was so small I could feel her
pain. "Cameron was quiet that day."

"And what did you two talk about?"

She shook her head and sucked back a deep breath that
whistled as it passed over her lips. "Nothing unusual. I had
just come home from my job at Safeway and she was here

watching TV." She lifted her eyes and locked her gaze on mine. "That was Saturday night and I would always bring home a roast chicken from the deli on Saturday." Her eyes fell back to the table as she grinned. "Cameron left after dinner and that was the last time we spoke."

"Did she say where she was going?"

"Out." Her head shook. "I didn't ask. She's eighteen, old enough to make her own decisions. I assumed she wanted to walk out her back pains."

"What kind of car does your daughter drive?" Erin asked.

"Cameron doesn't have a car." Ms. Dee arched a brow. "Just like her mother."

My stomach rolled as I easily put myself inside her shoes; having a teenager was no piece of cake. "What are Cameron's friends like? And, more importantly, what do they like to do on Saturday nights?"

Ms. Dee dropped her hands onto her thighs. "Cameron's not like that."

"Like what?" I knew Ms. Dee thought I was making assumptions about her daughter, but I wasn't.

"The party stopped for Cameron the moment she learned she was pregnant. I made sure of it myself." Ms. Dee gave a stern look.

"Hence the back pains?"

She nodded and cast her sad eyes back to her hands. "That's why I assumed she stepped out for a walk. The doctor said it was good for her, and I couldn't agree more. All she does is watch TV. It's not good for her or the baby. She needs to move more. Be on her feet."

I tipped forward in my chair. "How far along was she?"

Ms. Dee smiled but kept her eyes low. "Thirty-eight weeks tomorrow."

"Is the father still in Cameron's life?"

Ms. Dee's arm muscles flexed. I could see her body tense

beneath her blouse. She couldn't look us in the eye for several minutes, but when she did, she said, "She did have a boyfriend. His name is Tyler Lopez, but he made sure Cameron knew he had no interest in taking responsibility for the child Cameron and I were both certain was his."

"Tyler denied the baby was his?"

"As if his life depended on it. And I suppose it does. But it's not entirely his fault. My daughter has a thing for bad boys."

"It seems like you resent him."

"Damn right I do." Ms. Dee brought one closed fist to the table. "Cameron's future was looking bright until he came along. He ruined her life."

"Did you tell Cameron that?"

"I did. And, depending on the day, she might even agree."

Erin pushed away from the table and casually perused the room, never once leaving Ms. Dee's sight. "Are you married, Ms. Dee?"

Ms. Dee glanced over her shoulder and answered Erin. "Cameron's father left me when she was three. He wanted more children and I didn't."

I took note of her cheap jewelry and makeup. "When was the last time you spoke to Cameron's father?"

"The day he left," she said firmly.

Erin dropped back into her seat at the table. "Are you seeing anybody now?"

"Why are you asking these questions?" She glared at Erin.

"Because, Ms. Dee, if someone has kidnapped your daughter, chances are good that Cameron knows them."

"You think my daughter has been kidnapped?"

"Do you?"

Ms. Dee's lips parted, her gaze going distant. She blinked and said, "Cameron is a very likable young woman. We tell each other everything." She paused when she heard her voice crack. With tears filling her eyes, she asked, "You think Tyler took my baby?"

"If he wasn't ready to become a father, it could explain her disappearance."

"Oh, God." Ms. Dee covered her mouth with her hand and started crying.

I shared a concerned look with Erin. I wasn't sure we had enough to go on, or even if I wanted to begin searching with so little information. "And you mentioned all this to the police?"

"I have. They haven't told me anything. I'm not even convinced they're looking for her."

I was nibbling on my lip when I felt her hand steal mine. She had working woman's hands. Strong and calloused, much like the strength I saw glimmering inside her eyes. But it was in that mother-to-mother moment I knew I had to at least try to find Cameron.

"Promise me you'll find my baby." Ms. Dee stared and pleaded with her eyes. "Samantha, you're my only hope. Please, you have to help."

I patted her hand and stood. Without making a promise I wasn't sure I could keep, I said, "Let us come up with a plan and I'll give you a call soon."

Ms. Dee escorted us to the door and thanked us for coming as we left her apartment. Erin didn't say anything until we were back at the car. "I suppose if we're going to help her we should first speak with Tyler Lopez."

"It's really the only clue she gave us." I turned the key and flicked on the police scanner. King still hadn't responded to my text from earlier and I assumed he was busy working his own case. "If Cameron wasn't pregnant, I'm not sure I would have agreed to help."

"It won't take long to decide where to place this story. If

it's only good for a brief blog post, fine. But maybe it could grow into something bigger I could use for the podcast."

That was exactly what I thought Ms. Dee wanted to achieve. Have her daughter's story raise hell in the media with hopes of it getting the police's attention to act. Suddenly, the scanner crackled with life.

"Wait," Erin held up one hand and froze, "did you hear that?"

I turned up the volume and, when it came through again, I repeated what I heard, "Double homicide. Congress Park."

"It's worth a look." Erin's eyes sparkled. "Who knows, could be Cameron Dee."

CHAPTER SIX

"Yes, I called about the dog." The neighbor's name was Andy Crowe and his eyes were shifty as they passed between King and Alvarez. "If you were me, you would have done the same."

Andy snarled in the same manner King and Alvarez had seen the Shepard do when taken away by Animal Control. King couldn't help but notice the similarities between Andy and the dog when trying to get to the bottom of what might have happened to the Browns tonight.

"That thing won't shut up." Andy was a dramatic, speaking with his hands, chomping at the bit. "All day. All night. It's a menace and needs to be put down." He stomped his foot for effect.

King listened to the thud echo off the adjacent roof and travel up the quiet street. "How well did you know the Browns?"

"Look, I was only calling about the dog. I didn't expect to be questioned like a criminal."

King exhaled a deep breath and shifted his feet on the step.

Andy's facial expression pinched with a hint of paranoia. "What is going on here?" He folded his arms and let his gaze travel over King's shoulder toward the Browns' house. "This response seems excessive for only having to deal with a dog."

Alvarez jumped in and shifted the conversation before assumptions starting flying off Andy's top shelf. It didn't take long for him and King to get the approximate time Andy called and made the complaint.

"Do you make this call often?" King asked.

Andy stretched his neck like a giraffe going for the leaves at the top of the tree. "Should I call my lawyer?"

"It's a simple question, Mr. Crowe." Alvarez was growing impatient. "We could do it here, or you could come down to the station and make your complaint official."

Andy's eyes volleyed back and forth before saying, "Perhaps more than I should. But the response has never been anything like this. If I knew you were going to send the infantry, maybe I would have let it go tonight."

"Besides the persistent barking of the dog, did you see anything out of the ordinary tonight?"

"Yeah. Take a look around. I'd say everything I'm looking at right now is out of character for this neighborhood. We're working class. We go to work and come home. Then do it all over again."

Alvarez shook the loose coins in his pocket. "What my partner meant was, did you see anything suspicious that might be cause for concern?"

Andy rolled his eyes back to the Browns' house and stared before shaking his head. He was still wearing only a t-shirt and King noticed goosebumps stand his arm hair straight. Andy didn't seem to mind the dropping temperature. When he dropped his heels back to the pavement, Andy scrunched his nose, lowered his voice, and asked, "Are they dead?"

King palmed the small notepad he was holding and

glanced to his notes. "You noticed the dog barking around 7:15PM, halfway through your show." King lifted his eyes. "Did you notice any other activity at the Browns' around that time? Maybe people coming and going, cars parked out front that you've never seen before?"

Andy shivered for the first time. "The Browns all seemed to be swinging friends in and out of their house. It was an active household."

"So, is that a yes?"

"I can't say for sure." Andy's initial defiance was beginning to wane. "I'm not a stalker, it's just that stupid dog interrupts my TV and it really got to me tonight."

King scribbled a couple lines of notes.

"Know if the Browns entertain, like to party?" Alvarez's bottom lip curled as he bobbed his head up and down like a buoy rolling with the ocean's waves.

Andy shook his head.

"From your perspective, would you guess their marriage was healthy?"

"I don't know." Andy shrugged. "I always took them for the type of people who put on whatever face they thought you wanted to see."

"And what face did they put on for you?"

"They smiled but I always assumed they didn't have much good to say about me."

"You didn't like their dog much." Alvarez narrowed his gaze.

Andy's eyes lit up. "Yeah."

"What about their daughter, have any interaction with her?"

Andy pursed his lips and whistled. "A feisty one, that is. Given too much freedom, if you ask me."

"Do you have children, Mr. Crowe?" Alvarez asked.

"No." Andy's eyes rounded into coins as he tucked his chin into his neck. "Thank God."

King's thoughts churned, thinking back to what he'd seen inside the Browns' house, the daughter's room. "What constitutes too much freedom in your eyes, Mr. Crowe?"

"Hung out with more boys than girls." Andy paused. "Not sure what that says about her, but..." He gave a look as he slowly nodded his head. "Mmm-hmm, you catch my drift."

"Did you see her here tonight?"

"Didn't see her here tonight." He drew his thick eyebrows together and glanced to the street. "But something tells me much of their unhappiness recently was the result of the choices Tracey made."

"Tracey?"

"Yeah, the daughter." Andy gave a quizzical look. "Tracey Brown. That's who we're talking about it, isn't it?"

"You think the Browns were an unhappy household?"

"Lots of screaming and yelling and slamming doors these last couple of months. Not to mention that stupid dog."

"Any idea what that was about?"

"You kidding? None of my business. I prefer to stay out of people's lives with hopes they will do the same for me."

King imagined rolling his eyes at the irony of Mr. Crowe's statement as he fished out his business card and handed it to him. "If you remember anything else that you think might be useful to us, give my number a call."

Andy took the card and stuffed it into the palm of his hand. Pushing himself up on the tips of his toes, he asked, "How long until you all are gone?"

King and Alvarez didn't bother to respond as they turned and walked away.

Andy yelled after them, "It doesn't make the rest of us look good, you know."

CHAPTER SEVEN

THE POLICE HAD THE STREET BLOCKED OFF BY THE TIME WE arrived. We stepped out of the car and stood at the hood with our hands in our pockets. The air buzzed with activity and lit up the house in question. Erin nudged my arm with her elbow and jutted her jaw toward the gathering of press already here.

"Slow news night or could this story just be that good?" Erin ran her tongue over her front teeth, debating whether to join them or not.

News vans from all the local stations had their floodlights pointed on their reporters. They had their gear out, mics on, red camera lights flashing. It didn't take long to find Nancy Jordan reporting. I thought it best we join the flock before someone saw us.

"C'mon, let's see what the story is," I said, taking the first step toward my colleagues.

The moment we stepped into the light, eyes flicked in our direction. Microphones were lowered and jaws loosened. It seemed everyone was staring as if they were witnessing a crime—or seeing their favorite celebrity for the first time.

"This is totally weird," Erin whispered under her breath.

I continued walking with my hands in my pockets, pretending like I hadn't noticed all eyes on me. My mind swirled and I could only think that it must have been a while since we'd all wanted to tell the same story because this certainly wasn't the reaction I had expected to receive.

We passed the first crew and their envious eyes followed us to the next.

"It's your reputation, you know," Erin said into my shoulder.

"And what reputation would that be?" I flicked my eyes to the sides.

"Oh, I don't know. Maybe for solving crimes faster than the police."

I rolled my eyes and gave Erin a look of disbelief.

"It's true. But if you're not careful, these same people will soon have no choice but to either resent or envy you."

"And what are they doing now?"

"Deciding which side to take."

"They shouldn't do either." I kept walking. "Don't forget, my success is your success. We're in this together."

Erin hooked her arm through the crook of mine. "But I'm not the one dating a cop."

I poked my tongue into my cheek and glared at Erin. Suddenly, I heard my name being called.

"Samantha!" Nancy Jordan called the moment she saw me coming. "Over here."

I forced a smile. My relationship with Nancy was a series of ups and downs. We were competitors, colleagues, and confidants. We weren't exactly the best of friends, but we were on speaking terms and occasionally helped each other out.

"I was waiting for you to show up to the party." She smiled.

We greeted her and her crew. "Any official statement from the cops?"

Nancy shook her head. "The reports we've received are saying a husband and wife committed suicide." We asked their names and professions and Nancy knew them both. "Other than that, we're still waiting on the juicy details to be shared."

I looked toward the house. Something told me that was it for tonight. There wouldn't be a press conference for a pair of suicides unless they were celebrities—which they weren't. So why was everyone here? There had to be more to it than this.

"This isn't our story," I said to Erin, hoping she would convince me otherwise.

Erin was gazing off in the distance. "Animal Control?"

"Oh, yeah," Nancy said. "The Browns' dog was taken away. Put up a good fight, I heard."

I kept sifting through the crowd. King had to be here somewhere. And as I searched the faces around the coroner's van, I kept thinking there was a secret waiting to be told.

As if reading my thoughts, Nancy said, "I saw Alex at the neighbor's not too long ago."

I closed my fingers around my cell phone inside my pocket and pulled it out. Nudging Erin's arm, I said with my eyes to follow me. We left Nancy with her crew and, without making a scene, I discreetly messaged King again.

I'm at the Browns'. Then I told him where my car was parked in as few words as possible, asking if he could meet us there.

"Samantha." When I heard Nancy call out my name, I stopped and turned. "I hope you share whatever inside secrets you're about to learn." She flashed me a knowing smirk that caused my stomach to flex.

My lips pinched as I turned back around without responding. We moved in the dark, bypassing the herd of reporters that had stared on our way in. My cell chimed with an incoming message from King. *Give me 15 min.*

"You're serious?" Erin asked. "We're just going to leave?"

"Not yet."

"But we're heading back to the car."

"I messaged King. Unless he gives us something good, our focus needs to stay on Cameron."

Erin agreed and we waited at my car without speaking. With our backs pressed up against the side, fifteen minutes passed in silence before I heard footsteps sneaking up from behind. When I turned to look, King latched onto my hips and pulled me into his solid chest. I yelped and smacked the flat of my hand onto his sternum.

"Why do you always insist on scaring the crap out of me?"

King laughed and pecked at my lips.

They were warm and inviting but this wasn't the place to get romantic. We were parked away from the action but he still managed to cover his tracks when sneaking away from the scene.

"Did you get my message earlier?" I asked.

"I'm sorry. I haven't had time to respond." King held onto my hips and lifted his gaze to Erin. "Is that why you're here?"

"We caught the activity on the scanner." I pressed the tips of my fingers into his sports coat.

"Nancy Jordan filled us in on the public details," Erin said.

"Anything else you can tell us?" I asked.

King's hands left my hips and I watched his gaze travel up the block toward the Browns' residence. Red and blue lights flashed in the trees. "Their neighbor, Andy Crowe, called complaining about a barking dog. Apparently, this type of incident happens fairly frequently."

"Is he a suspect?"

"Not at this time."

"But you haven't canceled him out yet either?"

"No. He claims he doesn't know much about the Browns, but his story told me something different."

"We heard it might have been a suicide," Erin said.

"Everything we saw inside says it was." King's eyes were back on mine. "We'll see what the ME comes back with." Suddenly, his cell phone started ringing. "It's Alvarez. He's probably wondering where I went."

I chewed my lip, wondering if I could find a reason to stay.

"Look, I'm not sure there is much of a story for you, Sam. I'm already jeopardizing mine and the department's reputation by meeting with you now."

I knew as much, but why did it seem every reporter in town was here?

"At least not until the lab results come back and we speak with their teenage daughter."

Erin stepped forward and I felt my head float to the sky. "Wait, you're looking for their teenage daughter?"

"Yeah." King's thick brows knitted. "Why?"

"Suspect?" I asked, suddenly finding myself stretching for a connection to Cameron.

"No. Person of interest." King had a suspicious sparkle in his eye that made me question if he'd even bothered reading my text earlier.

"How old?" Erin pressed.

"If I had to guess, old enough to drive." Alvarez called King again. King didn't answer. I shared a knowing look with Erin, thinking this had to be it. "If there is a story here, you'll be the first to know."

"Sounds like the daughter *is* the story," I said as King leaned in to kiss my cheek before leaving. "What's her name?"

King pulled back and began backpedaling away. "Tracey Brown. But if anyone asks, you didn't get it from me."

CHAPTER EIGHT

WE ALLOWED KING'S WORDS TIME TO SINK IN BEFORE WE began speculating if Tracey's and Cameron's cases were somehow related. "But King never said Tracey was missing, just that he wanted to find her," Erin reminded me from the passenger seat.

With one hand on the wheel, I drove, not sure where exactly I was heading. "The women are about the same age."

"And we can choose to chase ghosts or keep with what we know."

I knew Erin was right. Maybe I was getting ahead of myself, making our story bigger than what it actually was. But I couldn't get Ms. Dee's sad eyes out of my head. If we stopped now, tomorrow would be the third day Cameron was missing. This wasn't just about the story. I wanted to help. Make a difference. And hope that the story ended well.

Erin yawned and mumbled, "It's getting late and I still have to edit this week's podcast."

As difficult as it was for me to call it quits, I knew we could pick it up in the morning.

"Sam, this week's podcast is one you have to listen to."

Erin pushed herself up in her seat as if finding her batteries suddenly recharged. "Remember how I told you about that woman who was in a vegetative state?"

I flicked my eyes in her direction and nodded.

"Well, she's pregnant."

My heart kicked up a notch. "I'm listening."

Erin told me the woman's condition, and how no one knew she was pregnant until she was close to eight months along. But the mystery behind the story was how no one could explain how she got pregnant. The story was interesting, if not a bit disgusting considering what had to happen to get from point A to B, but Erin was right, this show was going to explode with the listeners.

"And, get this," Erin's eyes flashed, "I've had some people call in who worked at the facility." She paused to raise both her eyebrows. "And they were willing to go on record."

"Do they know who did it?"

"There is certainly a lot of suspicion around one man in particular, even a couple pieces of damning evidence. But until a judge orders DNA testing, it will remain only a rumor."

Erin had been working tirelessly on this bizarre story out of Pueblo while I had been trying to keep up with both our website and my duties with the *Times*. I hadn't given it much thought until tonight, but I was blown away. I loved Erin's approach of letting the story unfold organically. It kept her work exciting and I knew her listeners were going to love it, too.

I dropped her off at home, promising to call in the morning, and then turned around and pointed my car toward my own bed. My muscles were tired and my head was drifting. I thought about calling Allison just to say goodnight but it was close to midnight by the time I pulled up to the curb in front of my house.

I gathered my things from the backseat and was looking forward to spending an evening alone when I heard my own dog, Cooper, bark from the front window.

Someone was there.

My heart jumped into my throat.

I stopped breathing when I saw the dark silhouette of a woman sitting quietly on my front porch. Her face was hidden in the shadows. *Thank God, Mason was away.*

Cooper stopped barking. His tongue dangled out of his mouth. He looked to me, then back to the woman. I knitted my brows, thinking Cooper knew who the person was.

Gathering up the courage to finally step out, I rounded the car and kept my cell ready to call Erin in a moment's notice. The woman said something and I immediately recognized the voice in the shadows.

"What on Earth are you doing here?" I asked my sister, Heather Garret. I gripped my shoulder strap and ran up to the house. "Why didn't you call?"

"I tried breaking in but I couldn't." Heather dangled the old house key I had given her the last time she was here.

My lips frowned. "I'm sorry. I had the locks changed." King had my place locked down like a fortress since my big Sniper story. I had thought it was a little excessive, but I wasn't one to argue about Mason's safety.

"It doesn't have anything to do with your job, does it?" Heather asked.

"And why would you think that?" I winked and gave her a quick hug before unlocking the front door and kicking it open.

I never mentioned anything about dating King. Heather didn't know. Neither did my mother. Mason was gone at a friend's house for the night but, still, as soon as I stepped inside the house, a bolt of fear shot through me. I froze and looked around. *Did I leave any evidence out that would give away my secret?* Heather wouldn't be able to let it go if she knew I was back on the dating train again. After a decade of no man in my life, she'd given up asking but that didn't mean she wouldn't grill me if given the chance.

Cooper came running with his tail wagging. "Cooper knew who you were, he hasn't forgotten," I said, shutting the door and trapping the heat inside.

Heather dropped her bags and patted Cooper's big head.

It wasn't that Heather didn't know King—she did from when my husband was alive—but things were different now. King was making himself a big part of my life—Mason's, too —but I was afraid of what my family would think of my decision to spark up a romantic relationship with Gavin's best friend. So, I had kept that part of my life a secret for the past six months, and planned to keep doing so.

Heather flicked her gaze up to me. "I was hoping Mason would have been home."

I shed my jacket, hung it on the coat rack, and went on feeding Cooper his dinner. "He's at a friend's house tonight. Which is perfect. You can sleep in his bed." I peeked my head out from the kitchen. "But don't tell him."

Heather laughed her way to the kitchen. "I promise."

"God, it's good to see you." I stopped what I was doing and smiled. "I wouldn't have been out all night if I'd known you were coming."

Heather's smile touched her ears. "I wanted to surprise you."

"Did you tell Mom you were coming?"

Heather's face went deadpan. "No. And please don't tell her, Sam. I don't want her to know I'm here."

CHAPTER NINE

I WAS UP EARLY THE FOLLOWING MORNING FOR A QUICK run with Cooper. Once back at the house, I took a shower and started on my plan of attack to search for Cameron.

Coffee was on, my laptop open, and I scrolled my internet search for anything I might have missed after leaving the Browns' residence last night.

Nothing.

The police still hadn't given a statement on either the Browns' deaths or Cameron's disappearance. I felt bad for Ms. Dee as it seemed like the police department didn't care about what happened to her daughter. I could only imagine her pain.

I paused and stared out my window, debating my next move and how far I wanted to take it.

The sky was turning a brilliant orange and the first of the season's birds were chirping in the trees. It filled me with hope and rejuvenation.

Maybe all the city needed was to be made aware Cameron was missing. I could help. Tell her story. Humanize her without blaming the police for failing to make her disappearance a priority.

Wanting to do my part, I logged into my website—*www.RealCrimeNews.com*—and began typing. The keys clacked and my mind was focused. One quick write-up later, I asked for anyone with any information pertaining to the disappearance to contact the tip line Erin and I had set up after realizing we needed to streamline our approach—especially on big cases such as this.

"Here goes nothing," I said, hitting the *publish* button just as Heather stumbled into the kitchen with a serious case of bedhead going on.

"Morning, sunshine." I smiled from behind my coffee mug.

Heather squinted her tired looking eyes and scratched her scalp with her sharp painted nails.

With her being on East Coast time, I thought she would have woken before me. Instead, it was just like when we were growing up with me always the early bird after the worm. Some things never changed.

"When did you start running?" she asked.

"When did I stop? And how did you know I went for a run?"

"I saw your clothes on the bathroom floor." Heather shrugged it off and went for the coffee.

"I have a busy day of work ahead of me. Mason will probably make his way home around lunchtime." Heather turned and silently questioned me with her eyes. "Spring break," I said, forgetting she didn't pay attention to school calendars. I picked up my cereal bowl from the table and set it in the sink. "Help yourself to whatever you need."

Heather skirted past me and opened the fridge. "What are you feeding Mason? You have so little food. No wonder he stayed at a friend's house." She closed the refrigerator door and glanced to me. "Thanks," she said, her tone dripping with sarcasm, "but I think I'll be going to the store, ASAP."

I let her comment go, knowing I would be leaving soon anyway. "I put an extra house key by the door so you can come and go as you please." When I turned to look at my sister, I knew something was wrong.

"There is that look." She rolled her neck and shook her head. "I knew it would come sooner than later."

"What look?" I said, mildly confused.

"You always have that look when you think I'm about to make a bad decision."

"I'm not giving you a look."

Heather always liked to tell me what to do and had to be right. She'd fight tooth and nail even when she knew she was wrong just to make a point. If there was one thing I honestly admired about my sister, it was that she was relentless when making a stand. But sometimes I wished she would learn to swallow her pride because, right now, I had no idea what she was referring to.

"All right. You're right." Heather showed me her palms. "Something is wrong. That's why I don't want Mom to know I've come all this way."

I kept my lips zipped shut and just stood and stared, hoping she would tell me before I said something I would later regret. "You can tell me. I'm here to help."

"I know." Heather rested her tailbone on the kitchen counter and gripped the edge with both hands. She looked me straight in the eye and said in the most even tone, "I lost my job, Sam."

"So you came here?" Again, I struggled to make sense of her rather odd response to jump on a flight west.

"Yeah. I was thinking about looking for a job here, in Denver."

I didn't know what to say. Could I live so close to my

sister? Or anyone in my family, for that matter? It had been so long.

"Don't look so happy," she teased me.

"It's not that," I said, thinking about my own recent struggles. "It's just that I've been waking up daily wondering if today would be my last day working for the paper."

"What are you saying?" Heather dipped her chin. "I shouldn't move here?"

Feelings of disappointment sagged my shoulders when my sister said nothing about my own personal challenges. It was typical Heather to be blind to anybody but herself. "You know I would love to have you near," I said, choosing to take the higher road.

"Good." Heather swiped her coffee mug off the counter and moved to the machine. Pouring herself a cup, she said, "Because I'm serious, Sam. I want to move here." She curled her lips over the rim and slurped back a hot sip. "Live close to you and Mason."

"Mason would like having you close."

"You could use me, too, you know." She quirked a single brow. "With the luck you've been having."

"And what kind of luck is that?"

"The luck of constantly finding yourself in trouble."

"I'm just doing my job."

"But that's just it. I'm worried about you. If anything were to happen—"

I turned my back and pretended to wash my coffee mug. "Nothing is going to happen to me." Even I didn't believe the words rolling over my tongue. I turned back and faced my sister. "But why can't you tell Mom?"

"I don't want her to worry. Once I find myself gainfully employed, I'll tell her everything. I promise."

A rush of cold air swept inside the house. I turned to the front door to find King stopping mid-step, a guilty look lowering his gaze. He and Heather shared a confused glance before they both rolled their round eyes to me.

I tossed my hands up, realizing now I had no choice but to let my sister in on my own secret I had hoped to keep quiet for just a little while longer.

CHAPTER TEN

"WELL THIS IS AWKWARD." HEATHER MADE A FACE AND pointed her eyes to the floor.

"I should have told you," I said, knowing she'd already figured out my relationship with King. It was too early in the day for just anybody to be stopping over.

Heather nibbled her bottom lip as I turned to look at King. "Alex, you remember my sister Heather."

King kicked off his shoes and made his way into the kitchen. "It's good to see you again."

"Been a long time." The corners of Heather's eyes crinkled. "Are you still a detective?"

King pulled back his sports coat—the same one he was wearing last night—and flashed his badge. Heather whistled, pretending to be impressed. "Seeing anyone special?"

King flicked his gaze to me, clearly wondering how much he should tell.

"I'm only teasing." Heather fell forward, laughing, and gripped his arm to keep from falling over. "You two can tell me the story later. I'm sure it's a good one."

My lungs released the air I had been holding as I watched

them get reacquainted. They shared a few more laughs before Heather excused herself.

"You two can have the floor," she said. "I have to shower and get ready for the day." Her eyes rolled to King. "I'm looking for a job."

"Is that right?" He tilted his head and gave a nod of approval.

"And if I can find one," Heather was light on her toes, "I'll be moving here."

King flicked his eyes to me. "And living with you?"

"In this small house?" I looked to Cooper. "That's up to him."

Cooper wagged.

"Anyway," Heather spun around with a smile, "I'll give you guys some privacy to speak about my surprise visit and how great it would be for you to see me every day."

Heather trotted to the back, singing, and I asked King if he was hungry. He was, so I began making him breakfast from the same ingredients my sister turned her nose up at.

"Allison is in the hospital," I said, setting a cup of black coffee in front of King.

His eyes locked on mine. "I hadn't heard."

"I should have mentioned it to you last night but your hands were already full."

"I wish you would have said something."

I briefed him on what happened and how the doctors were keeping her for observation and additional testing. King listened intently, but I could see the exhaustion in his eyes. "You were out all night, weren't you?"

King gave a single nod as he wrapped his lips around the rim of his coffee mug. "We're still calling it a suicide, in case you're wondering."

"And what about the daughter, have you managed to find her?"

King reached for my hand and locked eyes with mine. I knew he could see it in my eyes. The way they twitched with questions I wanted to ask—the ones that had been rattling around inside my head all night.

"What is it?" he asked. "Don't tell me you found Tracey and spoke to her already."

I knew he was only teasing, and we both chuckled, but I still felt my spine curl as I cast my gaze deep into the wood of the table. "No."

"Then, what is it?" His thumb stroked the back of my knuckles as he reassured me he was speaking to me as my boyfriend and not as a detective speaking to a member of the media.

I swept my eyes up to his. "Does the name Cameron Dee sound familiar?"

King stopped stroking his thumb. "I'm so sorry, Sam. I completely forgot about your message. Is that what this is about?"

"Yes, but I'm not mad that you didn't respond to my text." I squeezed his hand and smiled. "Cameron's mother approached me yesterday and requested I investigate her daughter's disappearance."

"Did the mother go to the police?"

I nodded.

"And?"

"That was over forty-eight hours ago now, and nothing."

King leaned back in his chair and wiped a rough hand over his face that was in desperate need of a shave. "That's why you're interested in Tracey Brown."

I nodded again. "Cameron's mother only came to me because she had no other place to go. If you know anything that can help me find her—"

"It's not my area, Sam."

"So you don't know anything?"

"I wish I did." He sighed. "But I'm Homicide. Remember?"

"But you're looking for Tracey. Maybe she can lead us to Cameron."

"We're only looking for Tracey to deliver the news of her parents' deaths." King tipped forward, bringing his elbows to the table with him. Hunching over his half-empty cup of coffee, he murmured, "What makes you think Cameron's disappearance has anything to do with Tracey?"

I shared what Erin and I knew about Cameron, thanks to Ms. Dee. But King was right; we had nothing other than their disappearances only days apart to link the two girls. Learning about them only hours from each other had me jumping to conclusions I had no other reason to make. I was better than that. "Did you ever learn Tracey's age?"

King stared for a moment before saying, "Seventeen."

"Cameron was 18 and still living at home."

"If Tracey is in fact missing," King balled a hand into a fist as he spoke, "and these two cases happen to relate, how does it explain Tracey's parents' deaths?"

"I don't know." I swallowed the dryness down in my throat. "But maybe if we find one girl, we'll find the other."

CHAPTER 11: BORN DEAD

THE SURGICAL MASK BILLOWED OUT FROM THE GUARDIAN Angel's face with each exhale of breath.

The 5lb 2oz baby girl lay beneath an incubator, warmed by the heat lamp. She was swaddled in pink and had a matching cap. The room's lights were dimmed as she took what would be her few breaths of life.

Since birth, her health had quickly deteriorated, and the Guardian Angel knew that the baby wasn't going to make it.

Alone in the room, the Guardian Angel worked to the sounds of a beeping heart monitor and the hiss of an assisted breathing machine. He knew he needed to hurry, gather as much data as possible before the end came.

He didn't have much time left.

The Guardian Angel worked alone and hadn't visited the mother since taking her daughter away from her. No assistant had come to check on either of them—all of them assuming that since the baby had been born dead, she would remain dead.

It had been a miracle he'd managed to get the little girl's heart to beat at all. But it was a Band-Aid solution to an overly complicated problem—a problem with no solution. The Guardian Angel knew as much but, more importantly, he knew that there was little sense in saving the child at all. Even if it was a child he'd nurtured since conception and had big plans for, it was a little too late. The life the little girl would live wouldn't be worth the constant suffering he was certain she would face.

The Guardian Angel drew blood, collected measurements, and thanked the little girl he'd called Mystery for being so cooperative. She barely cried, never once opened her eyes, and stirred only when her pumping blood gave her enough energy to do so. It was the sweetest, but saddest, part of his research.

Once he finished, he took his data and samples into his office on the other side of the wall. Arranging his desk, he labeled a plastic bin and folder—*Mystery*—before lowering himself into the ergonomic chair at his computer.

Curling his fingers over the keyboard, he entered his password—a lengthy one full of characters no one would be able to hack—and glanced to the clock. It was nearly 9AM and he was surprised he'd been working through the night without a single break. Though tired, he would get by.

He flicked his eyes back to the window, gazing at Mystery.

The ventilation from the air ducts above hummed as he thought about the girl's mother and what he would say to explain the death of her daughter—if there wasn't something better he could say than what hadn't already been said.

The Guardian Angel blamed himself for what had happened, but he would never admit it. Even if it was something that should have been prevented; if only he had gotten his formula right. Somewhere along the chain, he had missed a step or the technology went astray. He didn't know which, but the Guardian Angel was determined to not let it happen again.

There was too much on the line—both riches and fame—
to quit now. He wasn't about to give up and walk away. There
was more work to be done. More tests to conduct. This was
only the beginning.

As soon as the desktop loaded, an instant message notif-
ication popped up on his screen. The Guardian Angel took
his eyes off of the little girl and read the message.

"We got her and are bringing the egg back to the
nest now."

CHAPTER TWELVE

SUSAN YOUNG STIRRED AWAKE AND IMMEDIATELY THOUGHT of Allison. Rolling to her side, she reached for her cell phone perfectly placed for convenience on her nightstand. Blinking the sleep out of her eyes, she squinted as the bright screen lit up.

Nothing from her friend.

Susan supposed no news was good news, but she still couldn't go without sending Allison a quick message. Even if all she wanted to say was that she was thinking of her, it would be worth having Allison know she wasn't alone.

After the message had been sent, Susan rolled onto her back and stared at the ceiling.

She knew Allison was hiding her fears. She couldn't blame her friend for pretending like her hospital stay was nothing more than an annual checkup. But an overnight stay was nothing short of concerning.

The bare-chested man next to her reached for her hand. Susan smiled without looking. A warm bloom spread across her chest. The toe-curling sensations she experienced last night buzzed among the leftover scents of romance lingering in the air.

Susan stayed with Allison until Benjamin went home after his shift last night. She felt guilty for leaving her alone while she trotted off to spend a night wrapped in Benjamin's arms but Allison knew that was what she was doing—all the girls knew it—and encouraged her to do it, too.

Benjamin offered to go back to his place, but Susan wanted to be home. Benjamin didn't argue, knowing they would be playing the same games no matter where they ended up.

Susan faced Benjamin and nuzzled her face into the curve of his neck. He lifted his head, threaded his fingers through her hair, and pulled her to his lips. Susan closed her eyes and felt the electricity spark.

"Everything all right?" Benjamin asked her. "You seem a little tense."

Susan let her eyes sway inside of his. "I'm just thinking about Allison."

"She was kept for further evaluation. It's standard proce-dure in cases like this." Benjamin smiled and tugged on Susan's bottom lip with his thumb. "Her doctors only want to make sure that nothing serious is hiding beneath the surface."

Susan dropped her gaze, retreating inside her head, hoping he was right.

Benjamin hooked a strand of Susan's hair behind her ear and added, "With your friend experiencing blurry vision and passing out, it's possible she's a diabetic."

Susan hoped not. But she knew it was better this way. It was still hard to see a friend having to confront such chal-lenges with so many unknowns.

She slid out from under the covers, pushed her feet through a pair of fleece sweats lying on the floor, and moved to the closet, reaching for a t-shirt. Flipping through her clothes, she knew Allison wouldn't want to see her mope.

"Are we still planning to be out the door by 10?"

Benjamin was still in bed, appreciating the rare chance of having a late, lazy morning. "Maybe a little before, if possible. I'd hate to arrive too late."

Susan turned back to her clothes, thinking about the conference Benjamin had invited her to attend with him. She hemmed and hawed, unable to make a decision on what to wear. "I know nothing about this conference other than you booked an expensive suite with an incredible view for us to stay in tonight."

"And you need my opinion on what to wear." His voice was playful, if not flirtatious.

Susan glanced over her shoulder toward Benjamin. "That would be most helpful."

Benjamin's eyes hooded. "Something sexy."

Susan rolled her eyes. "Let me rephrase. What can I expect from this conference? Is it a black-tie event, or business casual? And would it be appropriate of me to drum up business, or am I only allowed to hang off your arm to make you look good?"

Benjamin laughed. "You're thinking much too hard about this. The mood is laidback, educational, but you should dress however makes you comfortable and if you can snag a few clients along the way, more power to you."

Susan loved how loose Benjamin made her feel. Unable to make a decision, Susan chose to pack two options and make the final decision once they arrived at the hotel.

"Tell me again, who are you looking forward to hear speak?" Susan asked as she packed, quietly asking herself again if maybe she'd be better off skipping.

"His name is Dr. Glenn Wu and he is a leading scientist in the biotech industry."

Susan gave him a questioning look. "Are you sure this conference is something I'll enjoy?"

Benjamin left the bed in only his boxer shorts and padded across the carpeted floor with intention in his eye. "You'll be blown away by the advances you'll both hear and see today." Benjamin wrapped Susan in his arms and peppered kisses down her neck. "I promise there will never be a dull moment."

Susan reached behind her and touched Benjamin. "I don't doubt that."

CHAPTER THIRTEEN

"FIND WHO?"

Heather's voice surprised me. She came out from the back of the house, dressed in jeans and a sky-blue hooded sweatshirt, combing her wet hair. I barely looked in her direction out of fear of wondering how much of my conversation with King she'd heard before making herself known.

King stared into my eyes before standing.

I wasn't entirely sure if he was subtly asking me to write a story for the paper to help lure in Tracey Brown, or if he truly thought she would show up on her own. We hadn't gotten that far in our conversation and I wasn't about to ask now. Not in front of my sister.

King was at the sink washing his coffee mug, thanking me for the quick pick-me-up, when Heather flipped her gaze back and forth between King and me. "Hello?"

My sister's call fell on deaf ears.

"Are you sure you don't want to stay?" I asked King. "You can keep my sister company, make sure she doesn't get herself into any trouble."

"Hardy har har." Heather moved to the stove and plucked

the crumbs of leftover egg from the pan and tossed them into her hungry mouth. "We all know that you're the one who travels down troublesome gulch, Samantha."

"Thanks," King said, "but I'm in desperate need of a hot shower and a quick nap." He glanced down his front. "Not to mention a change of clothes."

I knew King wanted to catch at least a couple hours of sleep before going back to work, but I thought I'd offer anyway. I stood and walked him to the door. He took my hand and leaned in for a small kiss goodbye. I closed my eyes to soak in his sunshine, holding onto his hand for as long as I could, uncertain when we would see each other again with our crazy work hours. Something told me it wouldn't be long, but I never knew for sure.

"I'll call you later," he said as he reached for the doorknob.

I could feel Heather's eagle eyes staring from the kitchen as I nodded. "And will you look into that thing we discussed?"

"If I find anything, I'll let you know." He squeezed my hand and let go. "And tell Mason I still want to take him for a hike in the mountains this weekend."

"You may need to remind him. Spring break has him sleeping until noon and staying up past midnight."

King gave a slight smile of nostalgia. "I remember the days."

Cooper trotted to the door with his tail wagging. He nudged his head against King's thigh, needing a quick pat before he left. Then he was out the door, leaving Cooper and me in the window to watch him drive away.

"You know you don't need to protect me," Heather said.

I pushed Cooper down and retrieved my cell phone from the charging cable. "I know that," I said, dialing Erin. Heather held my gaze as I pressed my phone to my ear.

"Then why do you insist on keeping secrets from me."

"We were just discussing work." Heather crossed her arms over her chest and gave me a look of disappointment. "It's nothing really."

She didn't believe me. I could see it in her eyes. She wasn't entirely wrong, either, in her thinking. Cameron's story had the potential to be the biggest one I worked in quite a while, and I didn't want to let it go to waste.

"How long have you two been dating?"

I wasn't surprised at the question. She knew that I'd been keeping our relationship from her as soon as he walked in. King and I didn't hide our affection this morning, but this really wasn't the conversation I wanted to be having.

"Not long," I said, wishing Erin would pick up the phone.

"And you didn't bother to tell me before things got awkward?"

"What is there to tell?" Heather stared and I stared back. "Besides, it looked like you two were having fun getting reacquainted."

The line clicked over and I felt the excitement of not having to tell Heather any more than I already had rush through my opened veins.

"Sorry, Sam," Erin answered. "I had my headphones on, working the podcast. This story has my skin crawling." I thought back to what Erin shared with me last night in the car and found myself shivering with disgust.

"You got time to help me track down Tyler?" I asked as Heather rolled her eyes and gave up on me. "I could use a wingman."

"Are you kidding me?" Erin's voice jumped up an octave. "Anything to take my mind off the creep who got this woman pregnant."

"Good." I smiled. "I'll see you in fifteen."

CHAPTER FOURTEEN

FIFTEEN MINUTES LATER, ERIN WAS IN MY CAR ASKING ME if I had a visitor in town. "I heard them on the phone and it didn't sound like Mason or King."

"My sister, Heather, arrived yesterday," I said, flicking a quick glance in her direction.

"Why didn't you say anything?"

"Because I didn't know she was coming."

I told Erin how I found my sister waiting in the cold on my front porch late last night after I had dropped her off, and how Heather's visit was a complete surprise.

"Well, that's exciting." Erin's fingers drummed on her thigh. Her eyes were covered in mirrored lens sunglasses. "I bet Mason is thrilled to have his aunt in town."

"He doesn't know." I reminded her Mason was on spring break and had spent last night at a friend's.

"When is the last time you saw her?"

"It's been awhile," I said, thinking about Heather's reason for being here. I told Erin about it.

"And you think the job stuff might not be the only reason she's here?"

I couldn't shake the feeling that maybe there was more to it than what Heather was saying. "She didn't even tell our mom, and specifically asked me to not tell her, either."

"Maybe she's embarrassed," Erin mused.

"Our mom isn't like that," I assured her. "There is nothing to be ashamed about. It's just a job."

"Unless she can't support herself financially."

We turned onto Federal Blvd and headed north. The traffic was cooperative and moved at a steady pace as I allowed my thoughts to drift to my own financial struggles. My bank account was permanently low and I was only one disaster away from losing it all. I tried not to let it get to me, deciding it best to believe that everything would work itself out in the end. But if Heather had already met her financial breaking point, I'd find a way to support her until she was back up on her feet again. After all, she was family and family always came first.

I turned the wheel on W 52nd and thought about how Heather had always been spontaneous, always considered herself right—even when she was wrong—and her history of failed relationships. She had partied hard in college and made some bad decisions along the way. Though I never held any of that against her, I just hoped that she wasn't here because she was in some kind of trouble.

"King stopped in for breakfast." I flicked my gaze to Erin. "He still hasn't found Tracey Brown."

Erin twisted her spine and pushed her shoulders back against the car door. She lifted her sunglasses high on her head. The crease between her eyebrows deepened as she stared. "Any theories as to where she might be?"

"He says the department isn't ruling her parents' deaths as a homicide, but I know King isn't accepting it until there's definitive proof."

"King doesn't think that Tracey killed her parents, does he?"

I shook my head no. "If he does, he didn't make that clear to me. From how I understand it, he's hoping Tracey could shed light on why her parents might have taken their own lives."

"But she's still missing." Erin turned her gaze forward. "Seems odd, doesn't it?"

"And that's why I asked King about Cameron."

"Did he know anything?"

I shook my head. "Not his case. Though we did talk about treating both cases as one until something tells us we shouldn't. He wasn't keen on the idea but I can't seem to separate the girls. They went missing about the same time and are almost the same age. He didn't convince me to keep them separate so I'm not."

"I guess that's all we can ask of him."

"Let's just make sure we get Tyler to talk, because until one of these girls is found, I'm going to keep assuming they're both missing for the same reason."

The house, not far from my own, was tucked one block off busy Federal Blvd on W 52nd street. We curbed the car and shut off the engine. Together, we stared at the house, assessing it from inside the car.

It was a bit bigger and a little nicer than the neighbors it shared a block with, and the lawn was in decent shape, too. That surprised me. It wasn't something I would have expected from the boy Ms. Dee described. Then again, maybe the health of the grass had more to do with the season than the actual people taking care of it.

"Is that his?" I asked, jutting my jaw at the jet-black Range Rover parked in front of us.

Erin nodded. "As long as the DMV's records I pulled up are still correct, it looks like our guy is home."

I pulled the keys from the ignition, stepped out from the car, and snapped a few photos of the vehicle with my phone before turning to the house. The neighborhood was quiet, minus the occasional muffler roaring down Federal. We followed the concrete path up to the house and knocked on the bright red door.

Surprising both of us, it opened not more than a second later.

The young man's eyes squinted into the bright outside light. Inside, the house was dark, the curtains drawn. He wore a muscle-man tee which clung tight to his skinny frame. His head was shaved to the skin and he looked at Erin and me with deep suspicion.

"Can I help you?" he asked.

A pungent smell swirled past us from inside. "We're looking for Tyler Lopez. Is he home?"

His gaze bounced between us. I peered past him and took note of the expensive sound system and electronics surrounding the large curved-screen TV.

"He's not home."

Erin rolled her eyes to me. "Any idea when he might be back?'

The young man shook his head.

I glanced back to the Range Rover we knew was registered in Tyler's name. "Can you tell us where we might be able to find him?'

His half-mast eyes flashed as they roamed down our chests, taking us in like we were pieces of meat to be sold at the butcher shop. Suddenly, I caught whiffs of alcohol seeping from his pores.

"Look, you should have known what you were getting yourself into when hooking up with Tyler."

Erin's eyebrows shot up. Then she started to laugh. "Oh,

no honey. We're not girlfriends and have no affiliation with him. We just want to ask him a couple of questions."

"Why don't you try calling him?"

I put my hand on Erin's arm before she could respond. "I would," I said, "but I lost my phone and his number was on it. Maybe you could give it to me?"

The young man shook his head and smirked. "Or maybe he didn't give it to you all." He paused to stare. Then his brows pinched. "What's this about?"

"We want to ask him about his relationship with a woman named Cameron Dee."

The man started laughing again. "So you caught him with another woman. Is that it?"

Erin narrowed her eyes with disgust and a whole lot of annoyance. "We're not his girlfriends."

"We're hoping you know her," I said, keeping my voice firm but friendly.

He tilted his head to one side. "Who?"

I couldn't decide if he was serious. "Cameron Dee."

"Look, Tyler is a player. He has a different girl on his arm every night of the week. I can't keep up and I don't think he can either." A woman's voice was calling the man back inside. I tried to see her face but lucked out. "I'll let him know you stopped by."

He shut the door in our faces before I could give him my card.

"Well that was a complete fail," Erin said.

When I turned back to the car, I told Erin that Regis University was only a couple blocks away. "We should see if Tyler is a student and if maybe the girls were, too."

"Sure, why not. Anything to not have to talk to this jerk again."

Once back at my car, I barely had my door cracked open

when an unmarked sedan pulled up behind us. I recognized the make and model as well as the man who stepped out.

Detective Bobby Campbell leaned his weight into his opened door and smiled. He had his eye on Erin and I watched him remove his aviator sunglasses away from his face so he could get a good look at her soft features.

I tucked my chin into my neck, debating whether he was about to spit or ask her out. "He's not here, in case you're wondering," I said, saving Erin the embarrassment.

Detective Campbell shifted his gaze to me and put his sunglasses back over his eyes. We knew each other from me working the crime beat. He was part of the Major Crimes and Investigations Unit working cases of domestic violence, including kidnapping—which I assumed was the reason he was here.

"I'm sorry, who are we talking about?" He played coy with me.

"You don't have to play dumb with me, Detective. We both know why you're here."

"And does it have to do with why you're here as well?"

"You can knock if you'd like, but your boy isn't here."

"Why don't you leave the detective play to a professional, Ms. Bell?"

My cell rang and interrupted us. I pulled it out of my pocket to check who was calling.

"That's why I'm here." Erin rolled her shoulders back and smiled at Campbell. "To keep things professional."

Detective Campbell chuckled as I answered the incoming call from my editor at the *Times*. "What's up, Dawson? I'm kind of in the middle of something."

"Sam, drop what you're doing now."

I stared at Campbell, wanting to ask him about Cameron. Knowing him, he wouldn't tell me anything, but it was still worth a try. And I would have, too, if Dawson didn't steal my attention away from what I was doing. "I'm listening."

"That suppressed case we've been watching," I could tell Dawson was excited by the way he was speaking, "well, it just opened up and is on the docket for 10AM."

I could see Dawson's squirrely grin through the phone as I flicked my wrist and checked the time—9:42.

"This is the big break we've been waiting for," Dawson kept going. "I need you to see what this judge is hiding and why the court wants to keep these cases hidden from public view."

I watched the clock tick to 9:43 and stared as if I had the powers to make it magically go back one hour, just to allow me enough time in the day to complete all the tasks I wanted to get done.

"This has the potential to be big, Sam." Dawson's voice nearly cracked with interest.

"Dawson, that's in less than 20 minutes." I couldn't make it. Not this time of day. *Don't make me do it, I'm onto something here.*

"Then I suggest you hurry."

CHAPTER FIFTEEN

ALLISON DOYLE WAS WORKING ON HER LAPTOP WHEN THE door to her room opened after a quick knock. She lifted her eyes off the computer screen with hope that one of her friends had come to keep her company again.

She arched one eyebrow as she watched a strong set of thighs cross the threshold. Her head floated up to the ceiling with sudden interest. *Who could this be?* Her eyes drifted up his torso and she felt her heart beat faster as she grew anxious to see who her visitor was. Then his face appeared and Allison exhaled a breath of air.

"Please tell me you're here with the release papers," Allison said.

Doctor Daniel Pico chuckled and lowered Allison's chart down to his side. He had a stethoscope dangling around his neck and a pager attached to his belt. He was easy on the eyes but the attraction stopped there.

Allison appreciated his casually opened collar and well fitted slacks, not to mention the cute dimples that appeared every time he grinned. It helped ease the pain of having to endure her unexpected hospital stay.

"You really should be resting," Dr. Pico said, eyeing her computer.

"When you work for yourself there is no such thing as vacation." Allison smiled. She had already been here longer than she would have liked and she was growing impatient. "So, what time can I expect to leave today?"

Dr. Pico's eyes flashed as he stared. "I don't have a time yet."

"Then what are you keeping me for?" Allison's expression pinched. "I feel fine."

The doctor set a gentle hand on Allison's shoulder. "You look exhausted."

"You try sleeping in a hospital bed and you'd feel exhausted, too."

"Ms. Doyle, I have both good and bad news." Dr. Pico reeled his hand back to the bed rail and paused for a brief moment to watch Allison's lips press firmly together. "Which would you like to hear first?"

Allison twisted at the hips and set her laptop on the bedside table next to her. She sipped from her juice box to quench her sudden thirst and released the muscles in her neck. Her head hit the pillow with a solid thump. Then she sighed.

Looking the doctor directly in the eye, Allison said, "I'd like to begin with the bad."

Dr. Pico never looked away as he delivered the news. "The bad news is we don't know exactly why you collapsed or why your vision has been blurry."

Allison drew her brows together as she lifted her head off the pillow. "If that's the bad I can't wait to hear the good."

The doctor smiled. "The good news is you're not diabetic."

"So that's it?" She lifted her chin. "I'm good to go?"

Dr. Pico broke his locked gaze with Allison and glanced to

her laptop. "I was hoping the cause of your dizziness and low blood pressure was only due to stress."

"I'm sure that's all it is." Allison spoke in a bubbly tone. "I'm fine. I told Patty that, too, after I collapsed but she insisted I come here."

"It's a good thing she did." The doctor's eyes were back on Allison's. "Stress can lead to other complications if left unchecked."

Allison rolled her eyes. "Really, this isn't anything new for me," she pleaded, making her case. "I like working under pressure. Sure, I could eat out less and walk more, but time is tight."

"Let me listen to your heart."

Allison agreed and Dr. Pico helped her sit upright. Placing the stethoscope on her heart, he listened to it beat steadily.

"Any chest pain recently?" he asked.

"Only after eating too many tacos," Allison joked.

The doctor moved the tool to her back and listened to her breathe. "Any joint pain?"

"I'm forty, Doc, and we've already established I don't exercise enough. You don't have to rub it in." She laughed. "The pain is something I could do without, but I'm not going to let it slow me down."

"And fatigue is nothing new either, I assume?" Dr. Pico plucked the stethoscope from his ears and looked Allison directly in the eye.

"No. Nothing new." Allison could see the serious look he was giving her but, despite it all, she fought to keep the mood light. "Coke and Red Bull get me through my days." Then her expression pinched. "Why are you asking me all this?"

Dr. Pico took one step back. "Because I'd like to run a few more tests before I release you."

"I'm not a lab rat."

"No. You're not." He grinned.

"Check for what?" Allison felt her limbs go cold. Her blood had slowed and she could feel that this was much more serious than she'd originally thought. She was too afraid to say the word cancer, but that was what she was thinking.

Allison held her breath as she watched the glimmer in Dr. Pico's eyes dull. He broke more bad news to her and, as he explained his hypothesis and the tests he wanted to conduct, Allison felt a bubble close over her head. All she could hear in that moment was the sound of having her head submerged underwater.

It couldn't be. What did that mean?

Her heart beat, but she didn't feel alive.

Dr. Pico's words looped around the track as if stuck on repeat. It was all she could hear. She didn't know what his words meant or what was going to happen to her. All she knew was that things would never be the same.

CHAPTER SIXTEEN

"ERIN, IN THE CAR NOW," I BARKED, SUDDENLY FEELING pressed for time. She gave me a funny look like I was crazy. "I'll explain in the car, but we have to go. Now."

Erin lunged forward and yanked her car door open.

"Leaving so soon?" Campbell frowned, equally as confused as Erin. I was certain he was questioning what was said on the call he saw me take—who it was and why it was suddenly more urgent than anything else we had going. "Is it something I said?"

"Do be in touch if you track down Tyler," Erin called out to Campbell before lowering herself into the car. He shook his head and watched as we sped away. Erin turned to me with a twisted forehead, curious to what was happening. "Wait, this isn't about Tyler, is it?"

I had no choice but to take Erin with me. I was thankful for her keen sense to pivot in my sudden urgency. "No. This isn't about Tyler or Cameron Dee."

"Then what is it? I'm starting to question where your priorities are."

"That was Dawson on the phone," I said as we rushed downtown to the courthouse. "After the Sniper investigation, I discovered something I wish I hadn't."

"Why are you just telling me about this now?"

I tightened my clamp hold on the steering wheel and focused on weaving in and out of traffic in my rush to make it to the courthouse in time. "Several months ago, I brought it to Dawson's attention," I said, beginning to fill Erin in on what was happening, "and each time we tried to dig deeper into what was actually going on, we were met by more road-blocks and more jaw-dropping surprises neither of us could believe."

Erin's eyes were round saucers as she stared and waited for me to reveal more. "What are you talking about?"

I must have been giving off a buzz of annoyance for having to step away from Cameron Dee's story because Erin was anxious to hear why this was important enough to break our original plans. I understood her confusion. It was the last thing I wanted to be doing, but also knew I had no choice in the matter.

"There are over a thousand court cases across the state purposely being hidden from public view," I said, applying the brakes and stopping at a red light.

"What, like concealed behind judge's orders?"

"Exactly." I flicked my gaze to hers. "Orders that can remain in effect for years. We're talking felonies, too. Not just traffic tickets."

The light turned green and I set the wheels in motion.

"Any idea why?" Erin asked.

"My initial guess..." I paused long enough to collect my thoughts, "the courts know that there are fewer eyes on them now that journalists are dropping like flies."

"The checks and balances are being eroded," Erin mumbled. "But you don't sound convinced."

"I'm not." My heart knocked fast against my ribs and I kept stealing glances at the clock. We weren't going to make it in time. "That could certainly be half of the reason—"

"And the other half?"

"The newsroom's new location. Where we were once positioned directly across the street from City Hall, we're now far enough outside of town to make it impossible to pop in conveniently at any time of day."

"And the judges are taking advantage to cloak their courtrooms in secrecy?" Erin shook her head as if thinking it was too farfetched to believe.

"Most of the requests are coming from either the prosecution or defense." I flipped on my blinker and merged lanes. "The judge is simply granting them their wish."

"As if by design, without journalists, corruption can flourish."

"It's only my suspicion that's why," I assured her. "I have no proof to back it up."

"It makes sense. Without good reporting, the public remains in the dark." Erin's ponytail whipped across the back of her shoulders when she turned to look at me. "How long has this been going on?"

"Far longer than you would believe." We were almost downtown and traffic was completely congested. I had five minutes before it would be too late. "Even the judges' reasons for supporting the orders are shielded from public scrutiny. No one is acknowledging the suppressed cases exist."

Erin looked ahead. "Shady."

"Completely suspicious." Stuck in gridlock, it was stop and go, leaving me no other option but to keep traveling toward my destination while hoping for a miracle. "Especially considering many of these cases are already closed and the convicted are potentially serving lengthy prison terms. All this information should be made available to the public under the Open Record Law, but they're not. And how the law is currently written in the state of Colorado, this is all perfectly legal."

"All without anyone double checking to see if their shuffle through the legal process was fair." Erin's voice fell flat as if she was thinking of the innocent and unknown faces sitting behind bars who had slipped through the cracks of an overly complicated justice system.

Erin was starting to see it for what it was. It was troubling enough to know entire files were disappearing, but a public courtroom operating in the dark was unimaginable. The more I thought about it, the angrier I got.

"So who are these defendants?" Erin asked.

"That's just it. No one but the court knows." I felt my body tensing. "We know nothing. Not the names of the defendants, the charges they faced, or even the identity of the judges who closed them. The only way of knowing any of that is by staking out the courthouse every morning and waiting for the docket to arrive just to learn whose proceedings were scheduled for that day. It all has to happen before the case is even tried."

"And without the manpower, that would never happen."

"Exactly. Who has that kind of time to waste?"

"But you'd think the judge would have to give a reason for making that decision."

"There are many reasons a judge might suppress the details. Could be a case that had waited years to go to trial. Could be gang related, or involve a minor. But as soon as the trial is over, we might never learn the details of what went on to lead a person to conviction."

"Unless you were there..." Erin's words trailed off.

We didn't have time to park. Even with us rushing over, I was already late. Instead, we pulled up front with Erin jumping behind the wheel and me galloping up the front steps and into the courthouse. Security slowed me up and by the time I reached the courtroom, the doors were already closed. They'd already moved on to the next case.

CHAPTER SEVENTEEN

THE MORNING WAS QUICKLY GETTING AWAY FROM THE Guardian Angel, and so was his work. He'd changed out of the lab coat he'd been wearing since yesterday, showered at the office, and was putting on his suit jacket and tie, readying himself to leave, when he received word from the front desk that his patient had arrived.

"Excellent," he said to himself. "Impeccable timing."

He glanced to his watch as he stepped out of his office. While all he'd like to do was go home for a quick nap, he didn't have that luxury. He had to quickly take care of his responsibilities so he wasn't late to his next commitment.

He traveled beneath the bright florescent lights, holding his chin high as he whistled along to the beat of his dress shoes clacking against the linoleum floor.

Live and learn, today is another day, he sang to himself as he felt his spirits rise.

Outside Room 3 he stopped to grab the patient's chart. He quickly read over it. Everything was lining up, the initial data showing positive results.

The Guardian Angel felt his heart stall.

He picked his head up and let his gaze go distant as he filed through his thoughts.

Behind his eyelids, images of Mystery, the baby, flashed.

A sharp pang of regret stabbed his side. This chart was the same as Patient #1 before things went so terribly wrong. Mystery had since passed, as was expected, and the last thing the Guardian Angel wanted was to experience a repeat of last night.

He took a couple deep breaths and refocused his eyes before opening the door to Room 3. Putting on a friendly face, he felt the color come back to his cheeks as he greeted the young woman staring at him, bright eyed and innocent. She lay in bed with her dirty blond hair tied up in a messy knot, looking as if the pregnancy was beginning to catch up with her.

"Hello, darling," the Guardian Angel greeted her. "How are you feeling?"

The young woman cradled her pregnant belly with her left hand while she massaged her noticeable baby bump with her right. "Tired." Her voice was flat and sounded exactly how she described her mood.

He lowered himself to the stool beside the bed. "Are your mornings getting any easier?"

"The queasy feelings come and go."

"And are you continuing to watch your diet?"

"I crave French fries like there's no tomorrow and eat like a pig." She laughed. "But, yeah, other than that, I'm just peachy."

The Guardian Angel grinned. "Let's take a look at what the baby is up to, shall we?"

The patient agreed and lifted her shirt to reveal her stomach. The Guardian Angel fired up the ultrasound machine, squirted a cool slab of lube on her skin, and turned to the monitor. Together, they listened to the baby's heart beat soundly. The swishing sound filled the room and they both shared a smile. "Sounds excellent."

Relief swept over the woman's face.

Over the next half-hour, the Guardian Angel took the baby's measurements and snapped a couple dozen images. Everything was looking great and when the baby kicked, he was thrilled.

"Would you like to know the gender?" he asked.

The young woman stared at the monitor. She couldn't take her eyes off her child. It was the look of a first-time mother. A variety of emotions glimmered inside her eyes. The Guardian Angel had seen the same look on all his patients—they were all first-time mothers. There was fear, excitement, and a roller-coaster of ups and downs that came with knowing her life would never be the same again.

"If it's a girl I was thinking of naming her after me," the woman said in a soft voice. Then she rolled her head and looked the Guardian Angel in the eyes. "But, no, I think I would like to keep it a surprise."

"Always exciting." His smile was brief. He cast his gaze down and frowned. "I'm afraid there was something in the charts that has me concerned."

The woman's lips parted as she stared.

"Nothing to worry about. Honestly. But I'm going to suggest you stay here," he paused to gauge her reaction before continuing, "for further testing and observation."

"That's why they called and picked me up?"

The Guardian Angel nodded. "Yes."

"Tell me. What is it?"

He inhaled a deep breath and sighed. "It's just that our tests show a high possibility of a premature labor."

"But I'm not even at 30 weeks yet."

"Yes, I know. But if anything were to go wrong, I wouldn't

want you to be far. It can be a serious condition. For not only your baby, but you as well."

The woman's brows knitted as she blinked and cast her gaze to her belly. "Then at least allow me to call my parents."

The corners of the Guardian Angel's lips curled upward into a tight, knowing grin. "I've already left a message with them."

Suddenly, the door burst open behind them. "I'm sorry to interrupt," said the nurse. "But there's an emergency."

The Guardian Angel stood. "Which room?"

"Room 1."

The young woman watched in horror as she propped herself up on both elbows. She asked what was happening but was ignored. The emergency unfolding in Room 1 took precedence.

Without saying a word, the Guardian Angel hurried from the room and ran down the hall. Bursting inside, he knew immediately that his patient was experiencing a tremendous amount of pain.

"Something isn't right," the woman cried. "It hurts." She flopped around on her bed in agony. "It hurts so bad. Please. Do something. I can't take it anymore."

The Guardian Angel turned to the nurse. "Up her dose." He looked to his watch again, knowing that he didn't have time to monitor his patient himself. He had somewhere else to be and had to leave her in the very capable hands of his nurse.

"But—"

"Just do it!" he snapped. "If she dies, this will be on you."

CHAPTER EIGHTEEN

I WAS BACK BEHIND THE WHEEL DRIVING NORTH ON OUR way to the newsroom when I started thinking once again about Cameron Dee. Whatever happened in the courtroom wasn't as important as Cameron. At least, that was what I told myself in a lame attempt to justify my failing to come through for Dawson.

We were so close to finally sitting in on one of these mysterious hearings and I had blown it. It made me sick to my stomach to think we might not get another chance. Today had been nothing but a tug-of-war between which story was more important. I wasn't sure how Dawson would react to my shortcomings, but I prepared myself for the worst.

Erin and I entered the building without saying much. Though she wasn't employed by the paper, she took the liberty of treating my desk as her second office when we were together. It was a way to kill the monotony of always working from home, but mostly it was because we never took on a big story without the other at our side.

Computer keys clacked and phones rang as smells of reheated lunches drifted through the air.

Erin had given up on me leaving the paper, and Dawson hadn't brought it up since the Lady Killer case months ago. But that didn't stop me from flirting with the idea of throwing in the towel and risking it all on the gig Erin and I had going.

When I glanced to Erin, a part of me thought she enjoyed being back in the newsroom—even a pathetic looking one like this. Erin looked like she belonged. Long strides, she had her game face on. Even if it was only half the environment it used to be since the *Times* was bought out by a New York Hedge Fund six months ago and was forced to relocate from across City Hall to North Denver; it was still a newsroom. I knew Erin was too proud to admit it. Even to me.

My colleague Trisha Christopher made eye contact and I immediately warned Erin about the unsettled weather heading our way.

"Christ, what do you think it will be today?" Erin mumbled as we both avoided eye contact with hopes of having Trisha move on.

"Sam! Sam!" Trisha called. I cursed under my breath. "Wait up."

I didn't bother slowing. Trisha caught up to us by the time we reached my desk. There was no place for us to hide.

"You got something for me?" I asked.

Trisha rooted her hands on her hips and worked to catch her breath. "Heads up. Dawson is having a day. Don't ask why, but I think it might have to do with another round of layoffs coming."

I rolled my eyes and turned to face my desk. "Thanks, Trisha."

I heard her trot off and, as soon as we were alone, Erin said, "That woman is going to kill herself with stress before she even has the chance to be fired."

Erin's comment made me laugh. Six months ago was when

pink slips were being handed out like Valentine's cards. And though we had never personally met the faces behind the board now controlling the destiny of our paper, if what Trisha said was true, their reputation among the staff would only get worse.

"I just hope that the new owners can someday convince me that they had a better plan for the *Colorado Times* than simply squeezing it dry."

"That's a little optimistic, don't you think?" Erin kicked her feet up on the desk. "They'll do what they do with all the papers they acquire. Downsize and keep downsizing until the last penny drops into their bank accounts and good journalists like yourself are left scrambling to find a new career."

I heard what Erin was saying; could read between the lines. But was our website to the point of supporting both of us financially? Erin made it work but she didn't have a teen boy to support, either. Something about sticking it out at the paper kept my juices flowing. Maybe it was pride, or just the security of a paycheck. Either way, I wasn't about to quit.

Sifting through my piles of notes, I fired up my laptop computer and stole an empty chair from a nearby cubicle before checking my emails and listening to the messages that had come through our tip line.

"Anything?" Erin asked when I cradled the phone back in its home.

"Nothing solid."

Erin reached for the receiver. "I'll call Regis University. Ask if either Cameron or Tracey are, or have ever been, students."

"Don't forget to include Tyler on your list."

Erin scribbled a note on a sheet of paper. "I'd also like to track Cameron's father down, hear what he has to say about all this."

I agreed with what Erin was doing and appreciated her

no-nonsense approach. "I've got to go talk with Dawson," I said, flipping on the police scanner before leaving.

I headed to the coffee maker, hoping that would be enough to cheer Dawson up. When I arrived to the break room, I found the machine off. It wasn't even plugged in and the boxes of K-cups were empty.

"Well, darn," I said, thinking how nobody was picking up the slack. I wondered if I should be the one to take charge. But who could afford it on our bleak salaries and with the persistent threat of a mass layoff looming over our heads; it hardly seemed worth it.

I glanced toward Dawson's office in the corner. I really could use Allison's tech assistance about now. If only we knew who was in Cameron's social circle, then maybe we could find her.

My side cramped with guilt.

I should have called Allison, just to check up, but I knew she would understand.

I turned my attention back to the coffee cups and went ahead and made two cups anyway. Sugar, cream, a stir stick— everything but the actual coffee—before taking them into Dawson's office.

I knocked on his open door but he didn't react. He just kept on working like I wasn't there.

Floating across the floor, I set the cup of sweet cream down on his desk. "Got you a coffee," I said.

Dawson kept on working. "When I tell you to do something, I expect you to do it," he said without taking his eyes off his computer screen.

I stared into my own cup of white sugar and pursed my lips before lowering my bottom down to the seat across from his desk. My sad attempt of a joke was lost.

"The hearing was canceled," I said. Dawson's fingers stopped typing. "No reason given. We didn't miss anything today. But who told you about the hearing on the docket anyway?"

He pushed back from his desk and stared out of the corner of his eye. "I have my sources."

"Anyone I know?"

"It doesn't matter."

He was right. I didn't care. "Is it possible they knew I was coming? Because if you were a judge wanting to keep his courtroom secret, wouldn't you abruptly cancel the moment you learned a reporter from the *Times* was planning to attend?"

"I'm not speculating on any of this." Dawson pulled his elbows into his sides, swiveled his chair to face me. "I just need eyes and ears in on one of these proceedings to know why they insist on suppressing the details." He reached for his empty cup and, after peering inside, gave me a confused look.

I raised one brow and answered with a silly grin. *Maybe the joke wasn't dead after all?*

Dawson set the cup down without a single laugh. He didn't even mention it. "Tell me you have something."

"Trisha is warning everyone to stay clear of you today, but couldn't tell me why. Care to comment on that?"

Dawson's gaze was unwavering and I could see it in his eyes.

"How many this time?"

"Thirty percent." His voice was as depressed as the current mood of the entire staff.

"We're already less than one hundred strong."

"I know." He reached for the coffee cup without thinking. "Which brings me to my next point. You might want to stay off your website this week."

"Dawson," I pinched my eyebrows and gaped, "you know that's not possible."

His eyes pleaded with me. Just this one time to swallow my pride and keep my head low. "At least until the list is finalized."

"Am I on the list?"

A pause hung in the air. "I don't want them to have any reason to can my best reporter."

With my body overheating, I said, "I appreciate the warning, but it's not just me who runs it."

"I know." He ironed his hands over the tops of his thighs. "But your name is all over it."

I flicked my gaze over his shoulder and landed on a signed Denver Bronco football. "Did you hear about the couple found in Congress Park last night?"

Dawson nodded once. "Suicide, right?"

"That's the verdict right now, but they had a daughter and the police still haven't been able to track her down." Dawson tipped forward and folded his hands on top of his desk. I knew I had his full attention. "Well, another young woman about her age is missing, too. Her mother came to me. Specifically asked me to look into it."

"And what did you find?"

"Haven't found anything yet." I gave him an arched look.

"Is there a connection between the two?"

I was glad he asked. After King tried to keep the two cases separate, it was validating to have Dawson jump to the same conclusion I had. "Something is going on. Girls don't just disappear. I can't say for sure that these two cases are related, but I think this might be my story."

Dawson shook his head. "Sam, you're not a private investigator."

"Maybe I should be."

"You're a journalist. A damn good one."

I saw little difference in the two but I wasn't going to argue with Dawson. Trisha was right, he was in a mood. I nodded my head like the good servant I was, doing whatever it took to get back to my desk and out the door to continue my search for Cameron when suddenly Erin flew into Dawson's office, panting.

"He's on the phone, Sam." She gripped the door to keep from falling over. Her chest rose and fell as she worked to catch her breath. "Tyler Lopez called your desk. You have to go speak with him now."

I jumped to my feet and together we ran to my desk with me asking, "Did you get him to talk?"

"He'll only speak with you."

We barely hit the brakes when reaching my cubicle and I slingshot my way to the phone, taking a couple deep breaths before picking up the receiver and clicking Line 1. "Hi Tyler, this is Samantha Bell."

Silence hung on the line for a moment before he said, "I didn't have anything to do with Cameron's disappearance."

CHAPTER 19: WORTH KILLING FOR

DETECTIVE KING'S VEHICLE WASN'T EVEN PARKED WHEN HE knew his chance for sleep was ruined. His partner John Alvarez was sitting on the top step of his house, basking in the morning sun with a crinkled brow and permanently stamped scowl.

"I was just about to contact Search and Rescue to come looking for you," Alvarez teased as he met King by his car. "Where the hell have you been? I've been trying to reach you." He lifted the second espresso he was holding and offered it to King.

King stared at the coffee before flicking his gaze toward his house. All he needed was an hour. Sixty minutes to rest. It was all he could think about since leaving Samantha's, but it was hopeless now. He took the espresso and said, "What is it?"

Alvarez furrowed his brow. "A patrol unit located what they think is Tracey's car."

King's heart jolted him awake. "And what about Tracey? Did they locate her, too?"

Alvarez's eyelids drooped. His sagging shoulders said it all.

King pinched the bridge of his nose and rubbed his eyes. "Where?"

"Thirtieth and Downing."

"All right." King tipped his head back and followed Alvarez to his car. He downed his espresso in record time and remained quiet as he stared out the window thinking about Keith and Pam Brown while Alvarez drove.

The more time that passed without locating Tracey, the grimmer her disappearance became. He thought about the missing person Sam had mentioned to him earlier and was anxious to find Tracey. He didn't want Sam to be right, but something told him she was. Sam was *always* right. These two girls were missing for the same reason

Ten minutes later, Alvarez turned into the RTD Park and Ride lot and killed the engine. A pair of uniformed officers was already on scene. They greeted the detectives and were quick to give an overview of what they'd found.

"Plates match the DMV record and the car is registered to Mr. Keith Brown."

"Any signs of the girl?" King asked.

The officer shook his head and gave King an eager look. "The car hasn't been stripped or nothin'. Parked and left."

Alvarez had his hands rooted on his hips as he looked around. "As is the case with all these vehicles."

"True," the officer agreed sheepishly as King took in his surroundings.

The white sedan was parked in the back of the lot, far from the lamp post. It would have been a dark spot to park at night, and certainly not a place he would want his own daughter to have chosen if he had one. But when was Tracey here, and why? Or was it even her who parked the car at all? There were no signs pointing to her being here, and that concerned King.

Dropping to one knee, King ran his finger over the vehicle's emblem. It was a 2017 Honda Accord and had been kept in good condition.

He thought about the Browns and his growing doubts about their deaths being a suicide. It would have been easy to say it was, but with Tracey nowhere to be found, and this car finding its way here on the same night Keith and Pam Brown died, King was highly suspicious that something bigger was at play. But he didn't know what exactly it was.

"It's not unusual for people to park their cars here overnight and come to pick them up in the morning," King heard the young officer say.

King lifted his gaze up to the man. "No, but what's odd is why Keith would have left his car here on the same night he and his wife were found dead inside their house."

The crease between the officer's eyes deepened. "Tracey is a suspect, right? That's why you're looking for her?"

King shot up to his feet and got in the officer's face. He felt his cheeks glow red when he asked, "Why would you say that?"

"I heard they were killed," the officer stuttered.

Alvarez put a hand on King's shoulder. King relaxed and stepped back. "You said the car was registered to Keith Brown?"

The officer nodded.

"But we don't know who parked it here." King moved back to the vehicle. "And just so we're clear, the Browns' deaths haven't been ruled a homicide."

The officer stood ghost face and frozen as he watched the detectives begin to work.

Alvarez had his gloves on when he moved to the passenger side door. He tried the handle. To both their surprises, the door opened with ease. "Left unlocked."

King stared, his thoughts churning. "Who leaves their car unlocked?"

"Locking doors only keeps the honest people out."

King turned to the officer. "Did you open this vehicle at any time before we arrived?"

He shook his head, no. King tapped on the driver's side window after finding that door locked. Alvarez reached over from inside and unlocked it. King immediately checked to see if any of the other doors had been left unlocked. None. Strange.

"What do you make of that?" Alvarez asked.

"Bad luck."

Alvarez opened the glovebox and dug around. "I'd consider it good luck. Now at least we have a chance to maybe find out who parked here."

King checked the center console. He found pens, paper-clips, and a tire pressure gauge. Nothing that could point him to Tracey—or to anyone else. Twisting around in the front seat, King reached to the back. Tucked between the seats, he pulled out an Olive Garden uniform. Unfolding it on his lap, he found the name tag and paused.

"Look here," he said, angling the name tag toward Alvarez.

"Well, I suppose that confirms it." Alvarez stared at Tracey's name.

"I guess it's safe to say this *is* her car."

"Registered in Daddy's name." Alvarez reached beneath his seat and hesitated mid-action. A second later, he pulled a half-empty prenatal vitamin bottle out from beneath. "Now this just got interesting."

King stared. "She was pregnant."

"Maybe this was what started all the yelling and unhappiness in their house like Andy talked about."

King exited the vehicle and said, "It's time we put out a BOLO for Tracey Brown." Alvarez had followed. They both ignored the questions coming from the officer. "Let's also see if we can track down which Olive Garden she worked at. The sooner we find her, the better." Alvarez nodded. "And we need to move fast. If this is a missing person's case, the clock is ticking—especially if she is carrying a child."

Suddenly, the uniformed officer's radio crackled to life.

Both detectives hit the brakes and turned to listen.

"Location 7800 Smith Road. Female, approximately 17 years of age, brown hair, unresponsive. All units in area are requested to respond."

King shared a knowing look with his partner. Tracey's image immediately popped into his mind. "Sounds like it could be Tracey." They both jumped into action.

Piling into their cruiser, Alvarez popped the clutch and sped off, saying, "There is only one way to find out."

CHAPTER TWENTY

Not more than thirty minutes later, we were sitting down inside a Starbucks offering to buy Tyler Lopez a latte. I wanted to learn how he knew Cameron was missing.

Erin glanced over her shoulder from the counter.

Tyler Lopez was better looking than I'd imagined. He wore a stallion black leather jacket with pressed slacks and bright white sneakers. His hair was slicked back and there was a cool calmness about the young twenty-two-year-old that completely shattered my stereotype of the man who I thought I'd be sharing a coffee with.

"You have a nice smile," he genuinely said.

Tyler was confident, too. But I wasn't going to let any of that fool me into forgetting he may have had his hand in the disappearance of Cameron.

"Why did you call?" I asked as soon as Erin was back with the coffees.

Tyler nodded a quick thanks to Erin. Stroking his paper cup, he said, "To clear my name."

"And why do you think you need to clear your name?" I asked, wondering if he had spoken to Detective Campbell.

Tyler gave a cockeyed look. "Cameron has disappeared and I'm naturally the first suspect."

"You knew she was missing?" Erin sat upright.

"I heard." Tyler unzipped his jacket, slung his left arm over the back of his chair, and stared. His t-shirt read @GetHighWithTy. It was about the only thing I didn't like about him up to this point.

"And who did you hear that from?" I asked, sweeping my gaze up from his shirt and into his eyes.

He was elusive in his answer. He was probably home when we visited his house. He could have either overheard us talking to his roommate or his buddy told him everything we said. Perhaps Tyler had even spoken with Detective Campbell. But, if that were true, what did Campbell say and did he tip him off to why we were looking for him? I wasn't sure about anything today, but I knew one thing was certain: Tyler had more than enough time to prepare his answers before meeting with us.

"My roommate told me." The sound of his voice never wavered. "But what you don't understand is that Cameron and me, we were never a thing."

"Her mother seems to think differently," Erin said.

Tyler flicked his eyes to her. "Of course she would." He brought both his elbows to the table and hung his shaking head over his steamy cup of coffee as if needing time to think through his response.

"What do you mean by that?" I asked.

He swept his eyes up and stared from beneath his brow. "Look, the baby wasn't mine."

"How can you be so certain about that? Was there a paternity test done?"

Tyler leaned back and sprouted an arrogant grin. "I always wear a jimmy hat."

"That doesn't prove anything." Erin shook her head and huffed a hot breath of disgust.

"Look, Cameron was as much of a slut as I am. We had fun but we weren't exclusive. She showed up to a few of my parties and we hooked up but that was about it. She never could stand the fact that she was one of many women I was sleeping with."

My stomach flipped and now both Erin and I were on the edge of losing our breakfast. But I remained professional in my inquiry. "Her mother said you two had a rocky relationship, that you were a bad influence on Cameron."

Tyler laughed hysterically. "When it comes to Cameron's mother, it was never about her daughter. It was always about her."

I stared and tried to make sense of what he was saying. Before I could come up with my own conclusion, Tyler fleshed it out for me.

"Ms. Dee is one of those moms who wanted to go back in time. Like they regretted their earlier years and wished they'd done more than they had. She saw the fun we were having and now she was making up for it. A mid-life crises, I guess." Tyler shrugged. "She wanted Cameron to have that baby more than anything."

"More than Cameron wanted it?"

Tyler nodded.

"Why is that?"

Tyler leaned forward, dropped his voice down to a whisper, and looked deep into our curious eyes. "Because as soon as Cameron gave birth," his dark eyes glimmered, "then Ms. Dee could have me all to herself."

CHAPTER TWENTY-ONE

KING AND ALVAREZ RUSHED ACROSS TOWN WITH THEIR lights flashing. Neither of them spoke the entire ride, though King knew they both firmly believed that the victim could very well be Tracey Brown.

Alvarez maneuvered between vehicles—many of which pulled to the side of the road, but not all. The description of the victim matched and King was certain he was going to find her dead.

King's muscles were tight. His stomach clenched with anxiety. He tried not to get ahead of himself, but the further his day went on, the harder it became not to think that maybe Sam was right and Tracey's and Cameron's cases were somehow related.

As soon as they arrived, Alvarez slammed on his brakes and King hit the pavement running. He badged his way through the police line and stared at the ambulance parked near a half-dozen cruisers with their lights flashing blue and red. No one was in a hurry and that could only mean one thing. Then he saw Leslie Griffin already working the scene, confirming what he feared. It was too late. The victim was already dead.

King's world spun as he approached the cobalt blue Kia Optima. Both front doors were opened, only Leslie poking around inside.

This can't be Tracey, he thought as he approached. *Why would she be in this car?*

King couldn't see the victim's face but he couldn't get past the car's location. Tucked into a dark, inconspicuous corner of the Walmart parking lot, he was surprised anybody had found the woman at all.

His steps were slow as he approached the vehicle from behind. Colleagues greeted him but he couldn't hear them. The blood in his ears was thrashing too loud, his heart hammering hard against his chest in a steady echoing thump.

Slowly, he padded closer, stepping forward to gain a clear view of the victim's face.

He wanted to find Tracey Brown more than anything, but not like this. He needed her alive—needed her to tell him her theory of why her parents would want to kill themselves.

One step closer and King stared into the victim's soft features. His lungs released and stars flashed bright across his vision. Weak in the knees, King turned to look away, thankful it wasn't Tracey.

"You all right there?" Leslie lifted her gaze to King.

King opened his eyes, shaking off his anxiety before turning to face the medical examiner. "Has the vic been identified?"

"Kate Wilson."

King wiped his face and stepped forward. He pulled a pair of latex gloves out from his back pocket and slid them over his fingers, feeling his sweat cool his core.

"I estimate the time of death not more than six hours

ago," Leslie shared. "I can give you a better time after the autopsy. If there is one."

"Cause?"

Leslie lifted the woman's left arm and pointed to the track marks bruising around a large vein. "Overdose. The syringe was still dangling off her arm when I found her."

"Heroin," King said softly.

"That would be my guess." She lowered the vic's arm "But that's not the most interesting piece of information." Her voice was light with excitement.

King arched a brow.

"Kate recently gave birth."

King knitted his brows. "I guess she didn't do it here?"

Leslie shook her head. "No sign of that."

"Gave birth, then went to get high." King couldn't believe it.

"Not exactly. I won't know for sure until further examination, but I'd estimate her birth to be somewhere in the window of the last seventy-two hours."

Leslie lifted the hem of the victim's shirt and showed King signs of stretch marks across her belly. Leslie then pointed out the stains on the victim's shirt from milk leaking from her breasts.

"No sign of the baby," Leslie spoke calmly, "and it doesn't appear she gave birth in the car, either." Leslie looked around the seats. "There would have been quite a mess if she had."

King hovered overhead, lost in his thoughts. The drug epidemic was out of control. It seemed like every day it was hitting closer to home. Too many lives claimed, too many victims left to clean up the mess from those who died. When he blinked, his thoughts drifted to the woman's baby and how it would now join the other thousands of orphans growing up without its mother. Suddenly, Leslie surprised him.

"Oh, Detective," her gaze locked on King's, "by the way, the deaths of the Browns seems suspicious...I found fentanyl in their systems. I'm ruling it a homicide and will conduct a toxicology report for Kate, too." She rolled her eyes to Kate's face. "Wouldn't be surprised if I find the same in her. Seems like a bad batch is sweeping the streets these past couple of weeks. We have to make sure whoever is spreading it is behind bars. Only one way to do that—take them down—and this is the first step."

"Another overdose?" Detective Bobby Campbell came out of nowhere and joined the circle. "Who's to blame? The dealers or the users? That is the question."

King didn't share Campbell's amusement. "Was she a case you were working?"

"Indeed, she was." Campbell bent forward and put his face directly over Kate's. King stared at Campbell's behavior in bewilderment. Campbell sprang back on his heels and continued, "She's been missing for the last two months." He stuck his hands in his pockets and rocked on his heels. "She was considered a runaway."

"But you didn't think she was?"

"Can an eighteen-year-old really run away?" Campbell flashed an annoyed look to King. "Her parents are worthless, poor, and split up. Kate grew up without either of them really giving two shits about her." Campbell flicked his gaze to King. "So I'm told. It's the same saga, different name."

"Leslie says Kate recently gave birth. Know anything about that?" King asked.

Campbell raised his brows and stared at the side of Kate's face. Then his round head started to bob. "Makes sense." He flicked his gaze to King. "I was told she was seven months pregnant at the time of her disappearance."

"Who reported her missing?"

"Oddly enough," Campbell paused, "her mother." He rolled his neck and stared at the side of Kate's face. "I guess she had a change of heart, realizing the good she had only once it was gone."

King couldn't stop thinking about the baby, how he and Alvarez had found prenatal vitamins inside Tracey's car only a short while ago, and how Sam also happened to be looking for a young woman who was known to be pregnant. Could it be that someone wasn't targeting the women, but rather their babies?

"Does Kate share any similarities to any other cases you're working?" King asked Campbell.

Campbell stared at King out of the corner of his eye. "Tracey Brown's name hasn't come across my desk. I assume that's who you're referring to since I heard the BOLO go out."

King nodded, not wanting Tracey to get lost in the shuffle, like what seemed to have happened to Cameron Dee.

"I'll look into it, but no." Campbell looked away. "Not that I can think of."

"Are you sure about that?"

"Yes, Detective. I'm sure," Campbell said through clenched teeth.

"Because there is a name I'm thinking of that you might be familiar with."

Campbell arched a sharp brow and continued to stare.

"Cameron Dee."

Campbell's skin flushed as he narrowed his gaze. "Your girlfriend put you up to this?"

"What do you know?"

"What I know is," Campbell squared his shoulders with King's, "Samantha Bell has a way of impeding important police investigations." His pupils narrowed to tiny pin pricks. "And if I were you, I would tell my woman to stay in her lane before she crosses a line she can't uncross."

King inched closer and balled his hands into fists. "Is that a threat?"

Campbell gently pretended to pick lint from King's sport coat. "Let's just put it like this." He lifted his eyes and locked them with King's. "If Samantha botches just one more of my investigations by alerting the suspect that we're on to them, then I'll make sure she's not telling the stories, but *is* the story."

CHAPTER TWENTY-TWO

SUSAN YOUNG ENJOYED A LEISURELY MORNING WITH Benjamin. It was a nice change of pace for them both. They stopped for brunch on their way to the Boulder Medical Convention and Susan's head was still light from the Bloody Mary she had drank.

Once arriving in the city of Boulder, they checked into the hotel suite and had a porter deliver their luggage to their room. The views were exactly as Benjamin had promised. Large floor-to-ceiling windows with sweeping views of the magnificent Flatirons.

The scent of rose hung in the air and promised a night of romance ahead. Susan had decided on a cherry red shoulder sheath dress to match Benjamin's elephant gray three-piece designer suit. It was a splendid combination and one which was sure to turn heads.

"You look stunning," Benjamin said to Susan as he took her into his arms.

Susan tipped her head back and smiled. "You're not so bad looking yourself." Their lips pressed together and Susan felt her body melt into his. "But I would hardly call this," she tugged on his suit, "laidback and casual."

Benjamin's chuckle vibrated her core. He lifted his sleeve and glanced to his silver wristwatch. "We better get going so we don't miss Dr. Wu's keynote."

They took the elevator down to the lobby and strolled through the hotel hallways, making their way into the conference room. They checked in at the door with the event organizer and together they entered the room filled with hundreds of guests. Heads turned their way and whispers started. They were the best dressed couple in the room.

Once inside, the air buzzed with excitement. Susan could feel the allure quake in her bones and it was contagious. Everyone was smiling, looking forward to the speech from Dr. Glenn Wu, speculating on whether it would live up to the hype.

The more Susan learned about the man, the more eager she was to hear Dr. Wu's grand announcement. Biotech wasn't exactly her arena, and wouldn't have been something she sought herself, but today's announcement promised to be nothing short of spectacular.

Dr. Wu had promised his findings were revolutionary—so large it would forever change the course of human history. It was a tall order and Susan only hoped that she wouldn't be let down.

Benjamin had explained this all to Susan over brunch, but hearing it and seeing it were two different things. Now, Susan felt ashamed for thinking this could have been a conference she could pass up. She was more excited than even her date.

She had her arm in the crook of his as they meandered through the knots of people. Benjamin was recognized by many and he took the liberty of introducing Susan to everyone they stopped to greet. He impressed Susan, and when they found a rare chance alone, Susan commented on the Big Shot doctor he was. Benjamin laughed and played it cool, remaining humble in his small moments of celebrity.

An announcement came over the loud speakers.

The chatter dimmed to a soft murmur.

Benjamin turned to Susan, squeezed her hand, and smiled. "It's time."

They found their seats close to the stage and Susan was blown away by the spectacle. It was a show of entertainment and, once again, shattered Susan's expectations. Music played loud overhead and a video flashed on a large screen in front of the room. It was a mini-documentary on Dr. Wu's work as a research scientist and the incredible work he had achieved over the years of his successful career as a leading geneticist.

Susan watched intently while holding onto Benjamin's hand. Soon, the video finished with a crescendo of instruments and the lights flashed the entire room bright.

"The moment you have all been waiting for has finally arrived," a man's voice boomed from the speakers. He was nowhere to be seen. The stage was empty, but his voice was strong. "This afternoon you will hear from the man himself, Dr. Glenn Wu."

The crowd erupted into an explosive applause. A spotlight found the tall, slender man by the name of Dr. James Andrews as he strode onto the stage. He had a big grin on his face and walked with confidence.

"What Dr. Wu is doing now has only been dreamed about as science fiction," Dr. Andrews said.

Susan shared a look of thrill with Benjamin.

"His work will be praised. It will be criticized. News cycles will continue to debate the ethics of what Dr. Wu has accomplished, but nothing will stop the progress he has made." Another roar from the crowd. "Others will follow his lead, but he will always be the founding father. So, without further ado, I am proud to introduce to you the man who is rewriting the course of human history. Dr. Glenn Wu!"

CHAPTER TWENTY-THREE

We watched as Tyler left with an attractive college-aged woman tucked under his arm. She had arrived just when things were getting juicy. It was as if Tyler had planned his escape before he'd even arrived. He was smart enough to be that cunning. We didn't catch her name, but it was clear Tyler's promiscuity made both Erin and me gag.

"Is Tyler so cocky that he thinks Ms. Dee wanted to sleep with him, or were they really having an affair?" I was thinking out loud and wasn't even sure Erin was listening. Either way, I didn't want to believe what Tyler said could be true. Until I had proof, though, I couldn't discredit his statement.

"And that right there is why I remain single," Erin said, still staring at Tyler through the window. "Men like him give the good ones bad names."

"C'mon. Let's go," I said as soon as we saw Tyler drive away in his Range Rover.

Standing, I paused a brief moment to appreciate the luck I had in finding King. He was a great man, a man with integrity, and I was sure I wouldn't be dating anyone if he hadn't found his way into my life.

Erin followed me to the door. Sliding her sunglasses onto her face, she said, "I think we need to clear some things up with Ms. Dee. If she was sleeping with Tyler, it would give incentive to push her daughter out of her life."

I stiff-armed the door and exited the shop. The lovely scent of coffee was replaced by the fresh smells of spring. I soaked up the sunshine, knowing this story was about to get ugly.

"If Cameron found out her mom was fooling around with Tyler—or even thinking about it—why would she want to stick around?" I asked.

It was the one recurring thought I had—the only thing that made sense. Something told me we were only given half the story by Ms. Dee, and that disturbed me more than I cared to admit. Why even bother seeking our assistance if she wasn't going to give us the complete truth?

"God knows I would have left if my mom did something like that." Erin opened her car door and lowered herself inside.

When I did the same, I said, "But if Cameron did leave on her own, you would think she would have told someone." I started the car and began driving toward Ms. Dee's house.

"Are we wasting our time by speaking with Ms. Dee again?"

"It's possible. But it's the fastest way to the truth," I said, wishing we had more evidence to go on. All we had was Ms. Dee's word and the brief crossing of paths with Detective Campbell. But Campbell talking to Tyler was only an assumption, and I didn't work off assumptions.

It wasn't long before we were parked in front of Ms. Dee's apartment building. It appeared she was on her way to work. I couldn't believe our luck. The timing was perfect.

"Ms. Dee," I called out to her after having stepped out from behind the wheel. "Do you have a minute?"

Ms. Dee dug her heels into the sidewalk and gaped. I watched her glance up the block as if debating whether or not she wanted to speak to us at all. I was taking note of her Safeway work uniform when she said, "I'm late for work and really can't miss the next bus."

If I hadn't seen the inside of her home, I would have thought she was purposely trying to avoid having to speak with us. But I believed what she said and could almost see the look of terror hiding in her eyes with the possibility of missing the next paycheck if she didn't report to duty. I'd been in her shoes, was still there. Though something told me she was in a far worse position than even I could understand.

"We can walk you to your stop." Erin didn't wait for a response, taking off after Ms. Dee.

I galloped close behind and was quick to catch up. Not wanting to waste time by beating around the bush, I said, "Ms. Dee, we spoke with Tyler Lopez."

She didn't slow her stride or shorten her gait. "And does he have my daughter?"

"Ms. Dee," Erin matched her quick pace, "were you having an affair with Tyler Lopez?"

Suddenly, Ms. Dee slammed on her brakes, stopped, and sneered. "Is that what he told you?"

A black woman lowered her cell phone and listened from a nearby stoop. A rusted-out truck rumbled past and drowned out our voices. "He also says that the baby isn't his," I said.

Ms. Dee's eyes flicked over to me. "Of course a man-whore like that would deny it."

Her tone was full of attitude and I couldn't help but notice how Ms. Dee seemed resentful of everything we were telling her. I could imagine it was hard to take, but it was also important we covered our bases, knowing that we were presenting the facts. *Maybe what Tyler said could actually be true?*

Ms. Dee's posture tensed. "Did you forget that I came to you for help?"

"And we're still trying to find your daughter," I reminded her, remaining cool even in the presence of the ticking time bomb I could feel about to go off.

"Really?" She pinched her brows and stared. "Because it seems like you're accusing me of something."

"Why didn't you hire a private investigator?" Erin asked.

Ms. Dee snapped her fiery gaze to Erin. "If you haven't noticed, I don't have much money."

We were losing ground and this was turning personal. I didn't want to make this about finances, only wanted to know what happened to Cameron and if we could still help. But we needed the truth, even if it was hard for Ms. Dee to swallow.

"You must understand the reasons we're asking you about your relationship with Tyler," I said. "We can't help if you're not being completely honest with us."

The sound of the bus's brakes hissing filled the air behind me. Our time was about up.

Ms. Dee stared as a wave of anxiety rolled beneath my collar.

Then she narrowed her gaze and backpedaled away. "I thought you were better than the detectives, Ms. Bell. But now I see I made a mistake in thinking you were someone I could trust to find my daughter."

CHAPTER TWENTY-FOUR

Ms. Dee climbed onto the city bus and we watched as it sputtered away in a thick cloud of black exhaust. Erin rolled her gaze over to me. "Should we follow her?"

I thumbed my ear, worrying about the current path we were on. I wanted to believe that Ms. Dee was only anxious to get to work, not that she wanted to push us away. But her words stung and left me asking myself why I should care at all.

It was clear Ms. Dee was stressed. With everything that was going on in her life, I didn't doubt the burden of guilt riding on her shoulders. I tried not to take her jab at me personally, but it was easier said than done.

"No," I finally told Erin and headed back to the car. "This time, we're on our own."

Erin followed but I wasn't in a hurry to turn the car on. I didn't know where to go next or what to do. My head was spinning, trying to make sense of what little information we had to work with. Did Tyler have a hand in Cameron's disappearance, or were we getting played by Ms. Dee?

"If Ms. Dee was in a romantic relationship with Tyler," I

whispered my thoughts out loud, "that could explain Cameron's disappearance but not Tracey's."

Erin was biting the inside of her cheek, filing through her own thoughts of confusion.

I wanted there to be a link between Cameron and Tracey but, so far, there was nothing but my suspicion. Maybe that was all there ever would be.

My knee bounced with anxiety as I thought about King.

It would be so much easier if there was a connection. Just one piece of evidence to lead me to one of the women's whereabouts. I couldn't let this go. There was a story hiding somewhere and the pressure in my head squeezed harder.

Erin was looking at me when she asked, "Why do you keep thinking there is a link at all between the two cases?"

My hand pressed against my gut when the black woman from the stop knocked on Erin's window. I turned the key so Erin could power down her window.

"Can we help you?" Erin asked.

"I heard you talking to Ms. Dee." The woman's golden eyes bounced between Erin and me. "You're not wrong, you know."

I leaned over the console. "What aren't we wrong about?"

The woman gave me a knowing look. "I've seen them together."

Erin tucked her chin into her neck and rolled her eyes over to me.

"The age difference between them is what fuels gossip magazines." The woman's eyes glimmered.

My eyebrows pulled together as I stared into her magnificent eyes. "You've seen Ms. Dee with Tyler Lopez?"

The woman nodded. "He drives a black Range Rover. It's always bumping that loud music when he's around." She frowned and shook her head with disapproval. "We're all talking about it behind her back."

"Does Ms. Dee know this?"

"Can't say for sure, but she's smart enough to pick up on the clues." Her lips pinched as she nodded her head. "I told all this to the detective who came by yesterday, too."

"You spoke to a detective?"

She nodded.

"Do you remember the detective's name?"

"Campbell." She flicked her gaze to Erin. "I remember because of the soup."

"What did he ask you?" Erin asked.

"He was asking me questions about Ms. Dee's daughter, Cameron. She's missing, you know." The black woman nodded her head once. "Hasn't been seen for three days now." She shook her head. "Shame."

I gripped the steering wheel with my left hand, suddenly feeling nauseated. Staring ahead, I couldn't stop my frustration at Campbell from reddening my cheeks. He seemed to be treating this case like Cameron's life didn't matter. I wondered if it was because Cameron was poor and came from a black neighborhood.

"If you asked me, I'd say that Ms. Dee used her daughter to meet Tyler and then stole him away from her."

"Why would you say that?"

"Because Cameron was the first to bring the boy around, and Ms. Dee was the last to see him go."

"When was that?"

"The last night I saw Cameron."

"Three nights ago?"

"That's right. The two of them were together. Ms. Dee and Tyler Lopez."

Erin was giving me a look that said we had finally found the evidence to prove Tyler's statement was true. I couldn't believe it. My stomach flopped like a pancake. I told the woman that we were looking for Cameron, purposefully leaving out the detail that we were recruited by Ms. Dee. She couldn't tell us much more than what she'd already shared, but she promised to call if she witnessed anything unusual that we could potentially use to help find Cameron.

"If I see that boy around here again, you'll be the first person I call." She glanced to my card and swept her gaze up to Erin. "And if you need a statement from a witness, I'd love to volunteer if it means getting on your podcast."

Erin patted the woman's hand on her door. "I'll keep that in mind."

The woman pulled away from the window with a bright grin spreading to her ears when I received a message from Dawson about an apparent homicide on the north side of the city.

My heart lodged in my throat and there was nothing from King. That had me worried.

Why was Dawson the first to be telling me this? Did he know who the victim was? Could it be Cameron? There were so many unknowns I couldn't help but feel like Dawson had purposely kept his message short to hide the facts from me.

We left our new star witness on the side of the road and raced across town. The scene was already unfolding by the time we arrived. Investigators were shedding their suits and the coroner's van was closing its doors when I spotted King from afar.

His face was pale, his spine curled with exhaustion.

It didn't take long for us to join the herd of reporters trying to learn the victim's name. No one knew. Only that it was a young woman, which had me thinking it could easily be Tracey or Cameron.

"They're keeping their lips tight on this one," a colleague said just as I saw Nancy Jordan step out from behind her news van.

"Any idea why?"

"We can only speculate." He shrugged.

When King spotted me, he immediately strode in my direction. My lungs released their tight squeeze and I inhaled a wish of hope. I held his eyes inside of mine and watched him lower his chin. A dark cloud formed overhead and all I could hear was the sound of my heart beating. I knew immediately something was wrong.

"Sam," he covered his mouth when he spoke, "you need to leave now."

I blinked and felt my body heat rise. I gave a slight head shake and said, "Is it her?"

King tilted his head to his shoulder and sighed.

"Tell me. Is it Cameron Dee?" I flicked my gaze over King's shoulder and saw John Alvarez and Bobby Campbell staring into the back of King.

"You have to leave, Sam. You're not welcome here."

I kept shaking my head, asking myself *why?*

"Trust me."

King's hands reached for my shoulders but I quickly swatted them away. I stared into his eyes as I breathed fire through my nostrils. Alvarez and Campbell were still staring and I knew that King's request for me to leave had something to do with our run-in with Campbell earlier.

"Are you telling me to leave or is someone else?" I couldn't see it being Alvarez making the request. King wouldn't allow it. But Campbell? He had the venom to play dirty.

"No one is getting anything right now." King kept his voice low and to the point so that only I could hear. "You won't miss a beat. I promise."

"But this is my beat," I argued.

I felt the air around me freeze. Erin was clever enough to distract nearby reporters to keep them from eavesdropping. Something was clearly bothering King and I wished I was in a position to ask. But I couldn't. Not here. Not with Nancy

Jordan staring at the back of my head from across the way. I could almost feel the glimmer of amusement I knew was in her eye as I was singled out by the man who was supposed to have my back no matter what.

"Sam, please." King's gaze softened. "Make this easy on all of us and just go before someone makes a scene."

Erin looped her arm through mine. "C'mon, Sam."

I rooted my feet into the ground, wanting to make a stand. I stared into King's eyes and felt my arms begin to shake. Why was he doing this? Had our professions finally collided and come between us?

"Let's not risk losing our only good source at the department," Erin murmured into my ear.

She was right. King would explain later. I'd make sure of it. But before I retreated off into the sunset, I narrowed my gaze and made sure King saw the storm of anger swirling in the pin pricks of my eyes. When I knew he understood what I had waiting for him, I snapped my neck and walked back to the car with my chin held high, acting as if his words didn't bother me at all.

CHAPTER TWENTY-FIVE

ALEX KING RAN A LIMP HAND OVER HIS HEAD AS SAMANTHA Bell strode out of his reach. Staring at his feet, his heart was heavy with guilt. He wanted to tell her why she couldn't stay, but this wasn't the place. There were too many eyes watching and ears listening. He could only hope that she would come around and understand that this wasn't personal—strictly business.

King rubbed the nape of his neck, feeling his shoulders knot with sudden stress.

It was a combination of the Browns' deaths and now Kate Wilson's, but it was also the complication that came from dating a reporter.

Sweeping his gaze up, he caught sight of Samantha pushing her way through the line of gawkers. They were staring at the scene, all wondering when they—the police—would give a statement about what happened and who died. But, like he told Samantha, no statement would be made. Not today.

"It's for the best," King heard a woman say.

He turned his head and found a sympathetic Nancy Jordan staring with clasped hands at her waist.

"For you both, really." Her red lips smirked. "The conflict of interest is shockingly apparent."

King's Adam's apple bobbed in his throat with agitation. Spinning on a heel, he refused to let Jordan's comments get to him. His relationship with Samantha was certainly complicated, but it wasn't a mistake. That much he knew.

Pushing his thoughts aside, King met up with his partner.

"Campbell is an asshole," Alvarez said. And King agreed.

They knew Samantha was one of the few reporters they could trust to do the right thing. Samantha's previous marriage to one of their own, Gavin Bell, meant that even a decade after his death, she was still seen as family.

Detective Campbell glared from near the victim's car. The crime lab team was packing up and preparing to leave the scene. Kate Wilson's body was already zipped up and in the wagon by the time Lieutenant Kent Baker arrived.

"Detectives," Lieutenant greeted the men. Alvarez caught their superior up to speed. "Was Kate Wilson part of this growing group of women that's suddenly gone missing?"

Alvarez nodded his lowered head. "Detective Campbell said she was."

"And where is Detective Campbell? Is he here?" Lieutenant's brown eyes scanned the area.

"I'll go find him, sir." Alvarez went to find Campbell and, when he did, King turned to Lieutenant.

"The victim recently gave birth." King's voice was low and even.

Lieutenant's eyes rolled over to King's. "And do you know where the baby might be?"

King shook his head. "Not sure the baby is even alive."

"Christ, Alex. Why does it feel like we have a crisis on our hands?"

An image of Keith and Pam Brown flashed in the front of King's mind. He stood chewing his tongue, looking for the right words on how to share his theories without mentioning Samantha by name.

"Because we do," King said in a raspy voice.

Lieutenant cocked his jaw and stared as Campbell waddled his round haunches into the center of their little pow wow. He greeted Lieutenant and avoided eye contact with King. Lieutenant asked him questions about Kate Wilson and Campbell said, "Kate was considered a runaway. I don't believe she was kidnapped."

"Then what about Cameron Dee; is she a runaway, too?" King asked.

Campbell narrowed his gaze and kept his yap shut. Lieutenant stood firm and watched the two detectives have a pissing contest, hoping the answers he was looking for would soon reveal themselves before a real fight broke out.

"The medical examiner will look for evidence to suggest Kate was sexually assaulted," King swept his gaze back to Lieutenant's, "but I would be surprised if she'll find any."

"And why is that?" Lieutenant asked.

"Because of her recent birth. It's the same story with Cameron Dee and the Browns' daughter, Tracey." King's gaze rounded the circle of men. "They were all about the same age, and all assumed to be pregnant."

"Tracey Brown is pregnant?" Campbell sounded surprised.

"We found a bottle of prenatal vitamins in the car we recovered earlier."

"What are you suggesting, King?" Lieutenant interrupted. "That this is about the babies?"

King turned to Campbell. "How far along is Cameron Dee?"

Campbell's brow furrowed. "Thirty-eight weeks."

Lieutenant exhaled a hot breath and scrubbed one hand

over his mouth. "Which means the clock is ticking." He turned to Campbell. "Where are you at in your investigation with Cameron Dee?"

"Working a couple leads, but the trail goes cold just as I think I'm close to finding out what's happening. Kate vanished without a trace, and, so far, it seems Cameron did, too."

King stood there thinking about Tracey. Gone without a trace. Disappeared into the night, never to be seen again. He was frustrated with Campbell's lack of progress. He wondered why he seemed to be one step ahead of Campbell when tackling each missing person's case—and why he wasn't treating this like a crime had been committed. Because of Campbell's incompetence, King blamed Campbell personally for Kate Wilson's death. If only Campbell would have put in the extra hours the case deserved—if only he took the call seriously—than maybe Kate's story would have been written differently.

"The examiner has ruled the Browns' deaths a homicide," King said when locking eyes with his commanding officer.

"I heard." Lieutenant sighed and sounded annoyed by the conclusion. "And you know what that means."

King lowered his brow and nodded. "I believe I do, Sir."

"In case you don't, let me break it down for you. I need you to dig deep, Alex. Find out everything you know about who might have wanted the Browns dead. Learn who their friends were, if they had enemies, and everyone the couple socialized with. Not just anyone can get their hands on fentanyl. Someone targeted them. Either a bad batch of heroin or a lethal dose of fentanyl."

"You can count on me, L.T."

"I'm serious. Leave no stone unturned. Look into their work life and file through their financials. When you're finished, report back to me when you learn who might have benefited from their deaths. I don't have to make a case for murder on a low-level street thug for peddling fentanyl. We need them off the streets."

King understood crystal clear. And he knew just where to start.

"And, while you're at it, let me know who might have also had their eye on Tracey and if the young woman was worth killing for."

CHAPTER 26: LOOKS LIKE MURDER

TRACEY BROWN'S EYES POPPED WIDE OPEN IN A MOMENT OF sudden panic. Her lungs expelled short wheezy breaths of air as she listened to her heart drum against her chest. The room was pitch black. It was impossible to see anything other than the little green and red lights flashing like stars on a moonless night.

Propping herself up on both elbows, her sweaty back peeled off the bed sheets as her memory slowly came back to her. She couldn't be sure if she had been dreaming or if her nightmare was real.

She remembered receiving the call. Being told where to meet. Getting picked up by the clinic's nurse before being taken here—to a new location she had never been before.

Tracey reached for the television remote and flicked the screen on. Instantly, its light flooded her small room and provided the visual to calm her dark imagination.

Her hand pressed against her womb. A little smile sprouted on her lips at the thought of her baby. She had lost track of time. There were no clocks in the room, no windows either.

Tracey's thoughts soon traveled to the outside world.

She thought about her friends, work and what her boss would say when she didn't show up for the dinner rush. Most of all, she wondered why her parents hadn't come to visit.

Tracey wanted to go home. Get out of this cramped room that smelled as sterile as it felt.

The parallels between her baby confined to her womb and herself trapped inside this small room were ironic.

The endless cycle of TV and movies wouldn't be enough to keep her entertained for the next two-plus months while the doctor who referred to himself as Cherub monitored her pregnancy. But Tracey didn't want to lose the baby. She had changed everything since learning she was pregnant. Her diet, her lifestyle, and she was even taking the prenatal vitamins she was instructed to consume religiously.

Tracey's eyes slowly rolled to the wooden door.

Doctor Cherub never came back after the sudden emergency that interrupted her initial evaluation. Tracey didn't know how long ago that was, but she couldn't stop the cries she heard coming through the walls. They lived on in her head.

The temperature in the room plummeted to what felt like arctic levels.

She continued to stare at the door, wishing she had her cell phone with her. They had taken it when she arrived, along with the clothes she was wearing. Now, she was wearing only underwear and a bra beneath her clinic issued gown. She felt completely naked. They gave her a blanket to keep warm, but it was nothing like the one she had at home.

Her heart slowed to a hypnotic beat.

The walls began speaking to her—coming back to life from the cries of a woman still echoing inside of them. The terror. The pain. The agony even Tracey could feel. It was all there as if a prologue for what was to come in her own life.

When a shiver moved down her spine, Tracey lowered herself back down onto the bed and cradled her baby inside her hands, terrified of the plank she would soon be forced to walk.

Her eyes watered and it didn't take long for the first tear to fall.

Loneliness consumed her. She felt abandoned by her own family and soon regretted not being a better daughter. Tracey blamed herself for bringing shame to the family. It was never her intention. She wished she could go back and make things right—change the course of her life by making one different decision. But she couldn't, and that was the worst feeling of all.

Soon, Tracey was in the fetal position with an endless stream of tears pouring out of her eyes. Her body shook and no one came to save her or comfort her from her own self-destruction. She had several weeks before she delivered her baby into this world. She wondered how she was ever going to make it to the end, or if she even wanted to.

CHAPTER TWENTY-SEVEN

Dr. Glenn Wu lowered the microphone away from his face and stepped to the side.

Behind him, the large screen played a video of a couple—Bryan and Meghan Johnson—who had been part of his original clinical trials. It was meant to be the climax of the speech and Susan still had goosebumps on her arms.

Susan's spine was straight as an arrow and her mind was swimming with possibility. She listened intently and couldn't wait to hear more. Dr. Wu had taken her on an incredible journey already, but now, here was proof that his research went beyond theory and was being applied to real world situations.

The rows of spectators around Susan had also been silenced with disbelief and awe. They were equally as enthralled as Susan. So far, her expectations hadn't only been met, they had been taken to the moon.

Meghan Johnson was a thirty-six-year-old woman and spoke to the audience as if she was in the room with them. Holding her husband's hand, she told the story of her difficult journey to becoming a mother. Miscarriages and complication after complication stole her best years from her. While they consulted with IVF clinics with hopes of eventually conceiving, Meghan's own sister received the news of a gene in their family DNA that increased the risk for cancer in Meghan's future children.

"That's when we first heard of Dr. Glenn Wu and what he was doing with CRISPR technology," Bryan said into the camera.

"It was a simple decision." Meghan turned to her husband and smiled. "We had already accepted that the only way to become parents was through in vitro fertilization, so when asked if we would like to get rid of the potentially cancerous gene," her eyes glimmered with excitement as she nodded, "we said yes."

Susan turned to Benjamin. His eyes were narrow. She knew he was deep in thought, forming an opinion on the extremely powerful technology already being applied to a select few patients willing to accept the risks.

"We allowed Dr. Wu and his amazing team of doctors to edit the DNA in our embryo with hopes of eliminating future suffering for our child." A tear pooled in the corner of Meghan's eyes as her little boy came running into her arms. They introduced him as Little Mikey, and Susan felt an empathetic lump form in her own throat. "Mikey here is about to finish first grade and there are still no signs he has the cancerous gene." Meghan smiled, hugging her little boy. "All thanks to Dr. Wu."

The video faded out and Dr. Wu took center stage once again.

The roar of applause shook the walls like a freight train passing by.

"As you can see," Dr. Wu spoke into the mic, "with this new technology, we are not only able to cure disease, but to stop it before it even has a chance to take root."

People stood and clapped, cheering for Dr. Wu as if he had just won the Super Bowl. Susan shot to her feet, her mind blown. CRISPR technology was going to revolutionize the world through advanced medicine. There was no doubt about it in her mind.

Dr. Wu waved one last time and finally disappeared backstage.

Susan, along with hundreds of others, continued to stand and clap—cheering as if demanding an encore to his performance.

She felt optimistic about the future, like anything was possible after hearing what Dr. Wu was already able to accomplish. There was nothing to be feared, nothing that couldn't be done.

Benjamin turned to face Susan and she stole his hands inside of hers, thanking him once again for inviting her to this event.

"It wasn't anything like I imagined," she said.

But the look on Benjamin's face told Susan he was feeling a little more reserved about what Dr. Wu was doing than she felt. He was looking into her eyes when suddenly he saw them round into large saucers of surprise.

Benjamin turned and found Dr. James Andrews calling him over from the aisle.

"You know him?" Susan threaded her fingers through his and latched onto his arm.

"We've met once before." Benjamin led Susan across the floor, keeping his eyes locked on Dr. Andrews's unwavering gaze.

"Doctor Firestone, I knew I had spotted you from the stage." Dr. Andrews held his hand out and firmly grasped Benjamin's. "Now, tell me, what is a surgeon like yourself doing at a biotech conference?"

"Dr. Wu has made enough headlines this past year and a

half for even me to want to come and see him."

Dr. Andrews threw his head back and laughed. "Yes. Yes. The press has been fantastic, haven't they?"

Benjamin introduced Susan, and Dr. Andrews shook her hand. "And what were your thoughts on the show, Ms. Young?"

Susan's face still beamed a candy apple red. "Incredible."

"Isn't it, though?" Dr. Andrews leaned closer and lowered his voice so that only they could hear him. "But what you saw doesn't even scratch the surface of what the technology is capable of doing."

Benjamin widened his stance and gave a small but fake smile that only Susan caught.

"Would you like to meet with him?" Dr. Andrews swiveled his head back and forth on his skinny neck.

Benjamin lowered his gaze to Susan. Her eyes sparkled with honor as she nodded in absolute pleasure. "If that wouldn't be an inconvenience." She smiled. "I would love to meet him."

Dr. Andrews's laugh cracked the air between them. "Don't be silly. Dr. Wu is always interested to know what others think about his work. He would be delighted to hear what you have to say. Who knows, maybe he could even help you or someone you know."

Suddenly, Dr. Andrews's cell phone buzzed with a text message.

Susan watched his face pinch as he dug out his phone and glance to the screen. After quickly reading the message, he swept his eyes back up and frowned.

"I apologize, but I must make this call." He pulled two VIP passes from his inside coat pocket and gave them to Benjamin. "Here, take these. If anyone asks, tell them I gave them to you."

Dr. Andrews closed Benjamin's fingers around the tickets,

patted his hand, and quickly ran off into the crowd, leaving Susan and Benjamin sharing a look of utter bewilderment.

"We can't accept these," Benjamin told Susan as soon as Dr. Andrews was out of earshot.

"Give me one good reason why," she retorted back.

"Because they are reserved for Dr. Wu's donors." Benjamin flapped the passes like a fan.

Susan's expression pinched. She cocked her head and stared with sudden confusion. "But I thought—"

"And you would be right. But I don't want anybody to get the wrong impression. This isn't why I came."

Susan turned her head and stared at Dr. Andrews who was still busy talking on the phone. She couldn't help but wonder if Benjamin had been purposely singled out as a publicity stunt. If he was, he was certainly not the only one.

"Don't you see what is going on here?" Benjamin whispered in Susan's ear. "Dr. Wu brought us all under one roof to hear his big announcement. And now that he has us all here, it looks like we support what it is he is doing."

Susan turned to face Benjamin, whispering, "But I thought you did?"

"I'm not sold yet," Benjamin said just as Dr. Andrews came back.

"Unfortunately, I have some bad news," Dr. Andrews said. "It appears Dr. Wu had an emergency and had to leave before the meet and greet."

Susan's shoulders sagged with disappointment. Her head was still spinning, trying to make sense of what Benjamin had just shared with her. She wondered if he was right, if it was just a big publicity stunt to drum up some free PR for Dr. Wu. But what was Benjamin seeing that she wasn't?

"It was very kind of you to offer." Benjamin handed the passes back to Dr. Andrews. "Perhaps next time we'll have better luck."

CHAPTER TWENTY-EIGHT

THE TELEVISION FLICKERED IN THE LIVING ROOM. MASON was laid out on the couch watching the Colorado Avalanche game with Cooper curled up beside him. I was glad he was home, safe beneath my roof, but I was still fuming from the way King treated me earlier.

Setting my pen down on my notepad, I leaned back from the table and turned my attention to the television. I kept waiting for Breaking News to interrupt the game and Nancy Jordan's face to pop up on the screen to deliver the information King blocked me from hearing.

My muscles were tense and I couldn't stop wondering why he pushed me away. We had an understanding—a professional agreement—and he broke the vow.

The Denver Police knew who I was—knew that they could trust me to deliver the facts straight without sensationalizing the story for my own gain. I'd been a trusted ally for long enough, but something changed—and I knew it wasn't me.

I felt my skin crawl as I tried to focus my thoughts on anything other than who the victim might have been. Until I knew, I vowed to continue marching ahead as if nothing had changed.

The house was warm and there were still a couple slices of pizza left in the box. It was a cozy March night. And when I checked the time—7:38PM—I started thinking once again about the missing women whose stories we were trying to piece together.

I cast my gaze to the note cards Erin and I had pinned up on the wall behind me. It was a timeline of events—who knew what, and when our victims were last seen. We still didn't have a clear direction to travel, but we weren't giving up.

Suddenly, a feeling like I should have heard from my sister by now hit me. "Mason, did Heather say where she was going?"

"Just said she was going out," Mason answered without looking.

Heather's stuff was everywhere. Two pairs of shoes by the door, a couple of coats hanging on the rack, and a pile of what I assumed to be dirty laundry tossed in the hallway outside the bathroom door. She was certainly making herself comfortable, I thought as I flicked my gaze to Erin.

She looked up from her computer, tucking a loose blond bang behind her ear. "I should call her," I murmured. "Just to make sure she's okay."

"Yeah," Erin breathed.

With knots forming in my belly, I left the table and retrieved my cell phone from my work bag.

Heather didn't know Denver like I did, and I wasn't sure she knew anyone besides me in the city. *Where did she go? Was she looking for a job already?* It was possible she had only gotten lost and was trying to get back home.

I didn't know what to expect.

It wasn't like we had talked about whether she should

check in with me or how late she was going to stay out. I didn't care, and certainly didn't want to place any kind of rules on how she should live her life while visiting. It was these missing women that had me worried about Heather.

I hit the call button and pressed the phone against my ear, suddenly remembering that I'd never called Dawson back. There was no way I could let him down for a second time in one day. I was betting on tomorrow bringing us both better luck than what we experienced today.

The line continued to ring. I paced my way back to the table and peered over Erin's shoulder.

She was on her computer pouring over Tyler Lopez's Instagram feed, cringing at the insensitive crap he posted. He was easy to track down thanks to the t-shirt he was wearing— @GetHighWithTy. A simple internet search and voilà.

"What does any woman see in this guy?" Erin must have felt my presence because I knew she was talking to me.

I retreated into the back corner of the house, finally giving up on Heather answering my call. I bit the inside of my cheek, seriously beginning to think the worst. Where could she be? Why did she insist on keeping me in the dark?

A thought struck when I glanced to my phone.

It could work, but not without Allison's help. We needed her more than ever. Before sharing my idea with Erin, I put a call in to Allison. She didn't pick up either, though I left her a message saying I was thinking of her. It just wasn't my night.

"So, I was thinking," I said as I headed back to the table, "if we could triangulate the location of Cameron's cell phone —" I came to a dead stop and felt my jaw drop to the floor.

Erin stood blinking with guilty doe eyes. Mason giggled and then we all burst out laughing. Somewhere in the short time I was gone, Erin decided she would play dress up and was now wearing Heather's clothes. She pranced around pretending to be my sister and, though they had never met, I couldn't stop laughing.

"You were saying?" Erin batted her lashes at me. "Were you looking for me?"

"That's not funny."

"Then why are you laughing?"

I stifled my laugh. Once we all calmed down, I told her my theory. "Maybe we can find Cameron by tracing her phone."

"We don't have those kinds of resources." Erin shed my sister's clothes when her own phone started ringing.

"No, but maybe Allison does."

Erin answered her phone and retreated into the kitchen.

I took Erin's spot at the table, feeling much lighter after our moment of laughter. It was a nice change but didn't last long. I was soon back to work and feeling tense all over again.

As Erin talked in the back, I continued pouring over my notes, drawing lines, trying to connect the dots before turning back to Tyler's Instagram feed. I scrolled and scrolled until finally stopping on a video I knew Erin hadn't seen.

Was I seeing it right?

I blinked rapidly and finally had the courage to hit the play button. The screen came to life and I couldn't believe what I was seeing. I only looked away when the front door to my house opened and Heather came home.

CHAPTER TWENTY-NINE

ALEX KING WAS ABOUT TO GIVE UP WHEN HE BUCKLED HIS seatbelt for the third time. For the past hour, he and Alvarez had been zig-zagging across the Greater Denver area trying to track down the specific Olive Garden where Tracey Brown had worked. Having struck out a third time, the effort and energy wasted was testing King's resolve. They were running out of options.

King's cell phone rang. He answered. It was Leslie Griffin calling from the medical examiner's office. "As soon as I got Kate on the table," Leslie spoke into King's ear, "it was clear she may have died of an infection related to childbirth."

"Not fentanyl?" King asked, somewhat surprised.

"Oh, I'm sure that was in her system, too," Leslie said, reminding King about the syringe they found dangling off Kate's arm. "I'm running tests as we speak. But what I want to know is whether Kate injected the substance into her system herself, or if it was given through an IV. Having just given birth, she was probably in a hospital recently."

King kept one hand on the wheel, navigating the vehicle through habit. "You mean administered by a doctor?"

"That's right, Detective." Leslie spoke with confidence. "And if I can prove that it was administered by IV, then Kate died of negligence. Not an overdose."

King's chest was heavy as he breathed out a deep sigh. He thanked Leslie for the call and relayed the message to his partner.

"Damn," Alvarez said softly. He turned his attention out his window and watched the world go by for a moment before adding, "And I was hoping she was just a junkie loser."

The complication of Kate's death was still pounding in King's head. If Leslie was right, Kate didn't only die from negligence, but that meant her body had been dumped and staged to look like she had overdosed.

When King didn't respond, Alvarez turned and faced his partner. "But now you're telling me that we're chasing a sick predator with a fetish for pregnant women."

"Not just a predator." King flicked his gaze in his partner's direction. "But a doctor."

"Now I've seen it all." Alvarez ironed the heels of his palms down his thighs. "But who would want only the baby?"

A river of white headlights flickered across King's face as he let his thoughts go to work. Staring at the red taillights shining from the car in front, King said, "Could be someone running a baby black market?"

"What? Like for organs?"

"Maybe." King rolled his neck and looked Alvarez in the eye. "But I was thinking adoption."

Alvarez pushed himself up in his seat as if struck with a sudden thought. King turned onto a new street and began heading north at a steady clip.

"Didn't something like that happen twenty years ago?"

King could only vaguely recall the case.

"Yeah. Something like that did." Alvarez's memory was coming back to him. "And the bastard who was running it got caught, if I remember correctly. But unless he was released from prison, I doubt it could be the same dude."

King's mind wouldn't stop. He had thought of everything, and he kept coming back to how a baby black market made the most sense—whether it be adoption or organs. But who was running it, and why? And where were they keeping these babies after they discarded their mothers?

Several minutes later, King pulled into another Olive Garden and parked near the front entrance. They entered the restaurant to the same smells of garlic and pasta as they had smelled in the others. His stomach grumbled as he joked, "If we get nothing here, we might as well stay for dinner."

"Sounds good to me." Alvarez stepped up to the hostess whose nametag read Beth and asked about Tracey.

There was immediate recognition in the young woman's eyes. King stepped forward and asked, "When was the last time you saw Tracey?"

"Yesterday." Beth's voice was small. Her eyes bounced between the walls with nerves. "She was supposed to have been here by now."

"She was on the schedule for tonight?" Alvarez and King shared a look.

The woman nodded. "Our manager is pissed. Seemed like everyone called in sick and we're short everywhere tonight."

"Wait, Tracey called in sick?"

"I don't know." Beth shrugged. "I just assumed she did. All I know is she's a no show and her job is toast if she's not dead already."

King's heart stopped and he lowered his voice. "Why would you say she's dead?"

Beth stared with doe eyes as she swallowed hard. "Her parents were found dead, right?" When King didn't answer, the woman continued. "I heard what happened. Everyone has."

"And what are *they* saying?" Alvarez wondered, directing his gaze to her colleagues.

The hostess glanced around nervously. "That Tracey was the one who killed them." When both detectives gave a look, Beth corrected herself. "Not literally. Just that she was a tough girl to work with—a *bitch*."

King looked around the restaurant. He studied the staff of waiters and line cooks he caught glimpses of in the back. Middle class citizens of all races were sitting down and enjoying the night. *Is this where Tracey met her kidnapper or murderer? Was that even what happened to her?*

"Has Tracey ever missed work before?" King asked.

"No." The woman answered honestly. "It has me worried about her."

"Have you mentioned this to your manager—your worries?"

Beth shook her head. Her brunette bangs swished across her forehead.

"Is there anything else besides what happened to Tracey's parents that has you worried for your colleague?"

Beth's gaze was pointed to her toes and her movements were short jerks of nerves. King couldn't help but feel like there was something she wasn't telling them.

"What do you think, Alvarez? Take her down to the station and make her statement official?"

The woman's head shot up. "No. I need this job. I'll get fired if I leave."

King gripped the edge of her podium and tipped his big body forward. "Then tell us what you know. What was going on in Tracey's life to make you worried?"

"You must know something we don't," Alvarez followed up.

Beth glanced behind her. When the coast was clear she

said, "About six months ago, Tracey found out she was pregnant."

"Did anyone else here know about it?"

Beth shook her head. "Not right away. I shouldn't have even known. It wasn't like we were close. But I caught her puking in the bathroom and she spilled it all to me. She couldn't tell her parents. They would kill her if they found out. Tracey wasn't convinced she was even pregnant at first, so she went to a clinic and it was confirmed. She was devastated."

"And you know for a fact she kept this from her parents?" King asked, his mind quickly speculating that Tracey found a way to kill her parents by making it look like a suicide.

The woman didn't inspire confidence. "Eventually they found out. Her parents wanted her to get an abortion."

"And what did Tracey have to say about that?"

"I don't know the details of what was said, but Tracey made it sound ugly. The last thing she wanted was to terminate the baby. Even if she was terrified with the prospect of becoming a mother, she couldn't do that."

"How did her boyfriend react to the news?"

Beth flicked her eyes to King. "She doesn't have one."

King pursed his lips in thought.

"At least, she never mentioned one to me." Beth dipped her head and wiped her nose. "This is awful," she choked back the threat of tears. "If only her parents had supported her and she didn't go looking for help."

"Where did Tracey go looking for help?" Alvarez asked.

Beth's watery eyes were locked on Alvarez. "Tracey knew that the money she made here wasn't going to be enough. She wanted to do this on her own—prove to her parents that she didn't need them."

"So what did she do?"

"There was an ad online promising medical care and money to single, first-time mothers." Beth flashed a quick look of hope. "It was like her prayers had finally been answered, but now," her voice fell to a whisper, "I'm not so sure."

CHAPTER THIRTY

MY LIPS WERE DRY AS I BREATHED THROUGH MY MOUTH. I had made a moral judgment as my thoughts scrambled to understand what I was watching.

I played the short video clip again.

Heather stood over my shoulder watching it along with me. When the short clip finished, she told me to play it again. And so it went for three straight loops before I'd had enough.

Heather dropped into the chair next to me. My jaw was still dangling loose as I stared wide-eyed and shocked into silence. My sister was equally as quiet when she set a white packet on top of the table. I thought nothing of it and we shared a look of disbelief—horrified that this video had garnered as many 'likes' as it had.

"You know that woman?" Heather asked me.

I turned back to the computer and stared. "We've met."

Erin was off the phone when she joined us. "Listen to this..." Her words trailed off when she saw both Heather and me staring at her computer screen. She stepped forward and looked to me for answers.

Without a word, I played the video for her.

"Is that Ms. Dee?" Erin gasped.

"And Tyler," I said, staring at Tyler emptying a bottle of champagne over a topless Ms. Dee. They were at some night-club and were being cheered on by the surrounding crowd.

"If we doubted Ms. Dee's neighbor before," Erin's eyebrows were raised, "I guess this confirms what everyone has been saying."

"Everyone but Ms. Dee," I said.

Tyler wasn't lying. It wasn't his ego speaking, either. Clearly, he and Ms. Dee had a history that was not only confirmed by her neighbor, but also here, online for the world to see.

My stomach flipped—the greasy pizza threatening to come back up. We had the proof we were looking for and now we needed to learn why Ms. Dee insisted on keeping this piece of information from us—besides the obvious embarrassment that came with it.

"When was this dated?" Erin tipped forward on her toes and squinted her eyes.

I looked her in the eye. "A month before Cameron went missing."

"Eight months pregnant." Erin dropped onto her heels.

"And you know who I haven't seen a single photo of in Tyler's Instagram feed?"

"Cameron," Erin said in a toneless response.

I nodded.

"What is everyone looking at?" Mason asked as he made his way over to us.

"Just work stuff," I said, closing out the browser before he could see. "Did you get enough to eat? There's still more pizza in the box."

Mason opened and closed the box without taking a slice as he passed by on his way into the kitchen.

Tipping my head back, I turned to Erin. "You were saying?"

"Oh, right." Erin danced on the tips of her toes. "So, I just received a call from a couple who was listening to my podcast tonight—you know, about the woman who got pregnant when she was in a vegetative state?"

"What?" Heather's brow furrowed.

Erin was brief, telling her she had to listen to the episode to understand the complete story, and continued, "Anyway, the woman who called, her name is Kristi Patterson, and she has a story for us to hear."

"What about?"

"She didn't go too deep into the details, wanting to save it for when we meet in person—which, by the way, we are doing tomorrow and I told her you would be coming along with me."

"Okay," I said, but I wanted to hear what had Erin so invested in this story. "But we're kind of busy here, can't this wait?"

"Apparently, she and her husband had IVF almost four years ago and now suspect they might have received the wrong embryo." Erin paused but my thoughts were too scattered to form a response. "She called me because they thought the time might be right for the world to hear their story—for us to investigate whether their suspicions are true."

I agreed, only to satisfy Erin's wishes, but not before making a stipulation of my own. "As long as we don't miss our chance to confront Ms. Dee about this video of her and Tyler, I'll be happy to tag along." I immediately thought of Dawson and his warning for me to stay off the website this week. There was no way—especially if he wasn't giving me an exclusive to publish in the *Times*.

Heather had been quiet as we talked. The only times I knew my sister to be silent were when something was wrong.

Flicking my gaze in her direction, she was biting her fingernails and had a distant look in her eyes. It was then I realized she was staring at the white packet she'd come home with.

"What is this?" I said, reaching for the packet.

Heather slapped her hand down on it before I could inspect it myself.

Erin jumped with surprise.

The air between my sister and me zapped an electric buzz of familial intensity as I stared my sister down in a duel for the packet. Erin didn't know what to do or say, but neither I nor my sister were ready to surrender.

A knock on the door sent Cooper running to the front of the house.

We didn't budge.

Mason bounded from the kitchen and finally Heather managed to reel the packet into her chest when I took my eye off the prize, wondering who was at the door.

"It's nothing that concerns you." Heather stood from the table and disappeared into the back with her mysterious packet.

I heard King talking to Mason before I swiveled my neck around to see him with my own eyes. His gaze flicked to me. A small smile curled the corners of his lips as if offering some kind of peace treaty. Then he shifted his focus back to my son when I gave him nothing in return.

A ball of fire spun deep in my core. I closed my eyes and focused on my breathing. I wanted to remain angry at him just to prove a point, but he was too good with my son to keep me from forgiving him for what he'd done.

Slowly, I backed away from the table and marched up to him.

"You don't get to come here and act like what you did today wasn't wrong!" I slammed the flats of my hands into each of his breasts, surprising the entire room, including myself.

Everyone stopped what they were doing and stared bug-eyed, completely staggered by my reaction. Mason gave me one look and retreated back to the couch. He knew better—had received this treatment himself before. Erin continued to stare and Heather was back in the room to see what was happening.

"Sam," King's voice was low and direct, "I'm here to make peace."

"Then you better be quick."

King scrubbed a hand over his face. "Her name was Kate Wilson and she recently gave birth."

My heart stopped and my blood ran cold. I opened my mouth and quickly snapped it shut. I blinked my eyes in an attempt to refocus but I couldn't get past his eyes, hating him for making it seem so easy.

I glanced to the couch. "Mason, go to your room."

Mason frowned. "What did I do wrong?"

"Just go." I folded my arms across my chest and continued to hold King's gaze inside of mine. "There is something I need to say to King that you can't hear."

Mason flicked off the television and stomped his way to his bedroom.

I didn't want him to hear about my work—listen to the ugliness in the world that surrounded us. Mason wasn't stupid. He was one of the least sheltered teenagers I knew and had experienced too much of the ugliness we were fighting. But I would continue to protect him every chance I got.

"So it wasn't Cameron or Tracey?" My voice was low, calm, as I began lobbing questions at King.

"No." King lowered his chin. "Detective Campbell said he

had been assigned to Kate's case." He told me everything Campbell shared with him at the scene of the crime. "Then I got a call from the medical examiner tonight. It's her belief that Kate didn't die of an overdose but maybe due to an infection she got after giving birth. But that she also suspects fentanyl to show up in her system and that it could have been administered by a health professional."

I listened to King, hung onto every word. No matter what I did, I couldn't get my body warm. It was as cold as our investigation. "Was the baby with her?"

King's eyes hooded as he shook his head. "Alvarez and I got to talking." He swallowed hard. "The way Kate was found made it look like suicide. But with the possibility of the drugs being administered by a doctor, we started wondering if there's a black market going on."

My stomach twisted. "What kind of black market?"

I could see the pain in King's eyes. This was almost worse than the school shooting we'd experienced five months ago. "Best case: stealing babies and giving them up for adoption."

When he didn't continue, I asked, "Worst case?"

"Harvesting their organs."

I couldn't speak. I remembered the moment Mason was placed in my arms and my heart went out to these young women getting caught up in something that was ruining—and ending—their lives.

"There's more," King finally said. "We found Tracey Brown's car."

My neck craned with disbelief.

"We found a bottle of prenatal vitamins inside."

I held a hand over my mouth and felt my eyes prickle with tears. "She was pregnant?"

He nodded.

"That makes three," Erin said close behind me.

Heather was smart enough to keep her mouth shut, but I knew she was listening just as close as the rest of us.

"But you haven't found Tracey?"

"Only her car."

"Are you pinging her cell phone? Tracing her credit cards? Why can't you find her?"

"Sam, the department is doing everything they can to locate her." He sighed. "And Cameron, too."

I pressed my palm against my forehead and went on blaming Campbell for his slow response to each of these cases. I believed King was doing everything in his power, but not Campbell. "Then why does it feel like Campbell doesn't give a rat's ass?"

King rocked slightly before saying. "Sam, not everyone in the department likes how you're conducting your work."

"Good," I snapped. "Then I'm doing my job."

King nodded in agreement. "And, just so we're clear, I have your back."

"Really? Because it didn't seem like it earlier." My chest heaved as an intense heat finally warmed my body.

"That's why I'm here now."

"To tell me how to do my job?"

"Quite the opposite, actually."

"What do you mean?" I didn't want to argue. It was wasted energy when we should have been working together.

Erin must have seen something I hadn't because she stepped forward and said, "Let him speak, Sam."

King walked us to the table and told us everything. That he and Alvarez spent the evening tracking down Tracey's place of employment; speaking in great length to her colleague; and how her now dead parents disagreed how best Tracey should go forward with her pregnancy. It was all helpful information, and even Heather joined the conversation after promising nothing we said tonight would leave the house.

"But if her parents had the means, why did Tracey try to do this without their help?" Heather asked.

"Your guess is as good as any of ours. It might be something we never know."

"We'll know because we'll find Tracey," I reminded the table—rejuvenating our sense of purpose. I was sharing a knowing look with King when the house line started to ring.

Ignoring it, Erin swept her gaze off the table and asked King, "Do we know if she had been seeing a doctor?"

King shook his head. "But, according to Tracey's colleague, Tracey responded to an online ad that promised medical assistance and money. I'll be looking into it in the morning, but now you know where we're at in our investigation."

I mouthed a quick thank you and smiled. It wasn't about exclusive stories or self-interest. We helped each other in order to speed up the investigation with hopes of solving the crime before another was committed.

"Cameron Dee was short on money, too," Erin reminded me.

"Did she respond to an online ad?" King asked.

We didn't know. Erin ran one hand over her head. "Not that we're aware of."

The phone finally stopped ringing when Mason stepped out from the kitchen. "Mom, it's for you."

"Not now, baby."

"It's Allison."

I sprang to my feet and hurried into the kitchen with my heart racing. "Hey girlfriend. You home yet?"

Allison chuckled, but I could hear she wasn't her usual self. "It's bad news, Sam."

I felt every fiber in my body tense with fear. "Did they find out why you fainted?"

"No. But they found something else." Allison sighed and was quiet for a long pause. "Come by tomorrow and I'll tell you all about it."

CHAPTER THIRTY-ONE

THE GUARDIAN ANGEL SLAMMED HIS CAR DOOR SHUT, HIT the lock button on his key fob, and hurried inside the office. He stripped off his sport coat along the way and was hanging it on the rack when the nurse met up with him.

"How far along is she?" the Guardian Angel asked.

"Eight centimeters." The nurse hesitated, the look on her face frantic.

The doctor didn't bother putting on his lab coat. Instead he requested to see the patient's charts. This was an emergency situation and a decision was going to have to be made quickly.

"Sir, the baby is breech," the nurse said after handing over the charts. "We've tried everything to get it to flip, but I'm afraid all our efforts have failed."

The Guardian Angel felt his heart stop. This was something he hadn't heard. The situation was far worse than what he'd been told on the phone. "How is the mother?"

The nurse's face was pale—not a good sign considering the luck they'd been having. "Not well."

The Guardian Angel stood there as the walls began

closing in. His vision tunneled. He was living out his worst nightmare. He hadn't expected two of his patients to go into labor so close together. He and his team could handle it, but it was never his intention to happen that way.

It felt like his feet had melted into the floor.

He was still reeling with the effects of last night. It was a tough blow to his ego—having lost both baby and mother—and he was determined to not repeat his mistake.

"We must do everything we can to save the baby," he said firmly as he marched to the patient's room.

"Sir," the nurse followed him one step behind, "she's asking for her mother."

The doctor stopped at the door and turned to face the nurse. He studied her expression and didn't like what he saw. He was gone only for a few hours and it now seemed that the entire operation had turned belly-up the moment he left.

"And what did you tell her?" he asked.

The nurse kept rubbing at her lips. The doctor knew this couldn't be good.

The pressure was mounting—the clock ticking, a bomb close to detonating.

There was too much on the line to trash everything they had worked so hard to achieve. He could see the light at the end of the tunnel. Everything he'd set out to accomplish was now within reach—he could feel it.

"Speak, dammit!"

The nurse found her footing and stammered, "It happened so fast. We still don't know how she did it."

"Did what?" The doctor's muscles flexed beneath his shirt.

"The patient stole a cell phone and made a phone call."

The Guardian Angel's eyelids snapped wide open. A cold breeze swirled around his ankles.

The nurse was still blabbering on, speaking to the floor,

with her palms opened wide when a sharp pain in the doctor's chest reminded him that he was still alive. His chest rose and fell as quickly as his blood pressure.

"She what?" The Guardian Angel breathed fire.

"It was only one call that we know about before we caught her," the nurse's eyes watered with fear, "and that's when everything made a turn for the worse."

The Guardian Angel turned and faced the wall. He rubbed the nape of his neck, conjuring up the worst-case scenarios to help come up with a game plan on how to deal with the situation. Alarm bells were ringing inside his head and everything was signaling for him to jump ship and get out before the whole thing went down—but he knew he couldn't. He still had a baby to deliver.

"We have to keep our heads on straight here."

The nurse's nods were short little bursts of frantic energy.

"Let's get the baby out safely and then decide what to do next." The Guardian Angel quickly told her the plan and, when she was ready, they entered the patient's room together.

Inside, the temperature was warm and the energy was much calmer than the doctor anticipated. Though his head still felt like it was trapped between a vice grip, he played it cool—always cool when working under immense pressure.

The patient's eyes were closed. She was between contractions.

The Guardian Angel stepped up to the patient's bed and gently stroked her cheek with his thumb. His gaze traveled the length of her naked and sweaty body draped with a white sheet. Suddenly, her eyes opened.

"Focus on me," the Guardian Angel said as he heard the nurse work behind him to assemble the pieces of their plan.

The woman turned her head but her gaze was distant. Her hair wet and matted to her forehead, her body limp with exhaustion.

"We'll get through this together," he told her. "You're doing great."

"I can't," the young woman cried.

The doctor hooked the woman's chin with his finger and brought her eyes up to his. He smiled. "You can."

"I can't feel the baby."

Suddenly, the Guardian Angel felt his heart stall for a moment. The data populating the screen assured him the baby was still alive but they needed to get her out ASAP.

"Your baby is doing just fine," he told her.

The woman's face contorted through another contraction. Her body tensed and he coached her through the incredible pain, knowing she was without medication. By the time it was finished, the woman's eyes were closed and she was resting once again.

The nurse tapped the doctor on the shoulder. The Guardian Angel turned and took the equipment into his own hands. He slid the mask over the patient's face, saying, "Don't worry, this will all be over soon."

CHAPTER THIRTY-TWO

IT WAS STILL DARK WHEN I WOKE THE FOLLOWING morning. Without thinking, I extended my arm and reached to the empty spot in the bed next to me.

A hollowness cratered in the center of my chest.

It was where King should have been. I wanted him to stay the night and seduce me with pillow talk, stay wrapped inside his arms through the duration of the night. I didn't have to tell him to go, that it wasn't appropriate for him to stay. He already knew and made the decision himself.

Burying my face into my pillow, a groan of regret escaped from somewhere deep inside of me.

King was right as much as I wished he wasn't. My house was already too busy with my sister in town and Mason constantly in and out of the house because of spring break. Even if King stayed, we wouldn't have had the privacy I would have wanted—that I *needed*.

I flopped onto my back and stared into the popcorn ceiling.

It was impossible to forget our work responsibilities or

the names and lives at stake. King never mentioned Campbell by name, but he made it clear he was the source of my new problem with the DPD.

When my eyes closed, I touched my lips.

They still tingled from the kiss King left me with after I had walked him to his car. I promised him I wouldn't publish anything until the department scheduled an official press conference and I had someone besides him to quote as my source. It was an easy promise to make, considering it would ease some of Dawson's worries as well.

Killing two birds with one stone—my specialty.

Kicking the covers off, I planted my feet to the floor and left my bed. I thought about going for a run, but decided against it. I was too anxious to see Allison—hear her big news —and wanted to get to her as soon as possible. There was no time to waste.

Allison's call had kept me on edge. Though she didn't say what exactly the doctors had found, I knew it wasn't good. My imagination ran wild and, as I conjured up every scenario I could, one thing remained true; her hospital stay reminded me how fragile each of our lives truly were.

I slid a shirt over my head and stomped my legs through a pair of jeans as I reflected on my own life and the loss of Gavin. It was so easy for us all to get caught up in the moment and take our good health for granted when we were really just chasing our goals and racing to the finish line of each day. I regretted many things, but I swore to myself my relationship with Allison wouldn't be one of them.

I was braiding my hair and tying it off when I entered the kitchen on a mission to brew my first pot of coffee. Suddenly, I came to a dead stop at the sight of Heather's packet perfectly forgotten in the center of the kitchen table. She must have taken it out again last night after everyone had left or gone to bed.

The room spun as I stared and considered my options.

I heard Cooper jump off the couch, the sounds of his nails clacking his way to me. He nudged his head against my thigh and let his tail wag back and forth.

I took one step forward and felt my heart threaten to explode.

I couldn't help myself. I needed to know what the big secret was and why Heather insisted on keeping it hidden from me. It was so strange the way she had been acting. My curiosity only grew the more I thought about how protective of it she was. *Was this a setup? Would my sister purposely leave this out knowing I would open it? Why hadn't she opened it?*

I glanced to the front room where I knew Heather was sleeping and held my breath.

My ears perked as I listened.

Silence.

Finally, the suspense of not knowing killed me and I took the plunge.

I pinched it between my fingers and quickly opened it as I fell into a seat at the table with a soft *thud*. My eyes darted from left to right and I felt the blood leave my face as I thumbed through the pages.

Surrogacy... earn between $45K - $75K...

I made note of the clinic's name—North Denver Reproductive Medicine—and address, and I kept shaking my head, whispering to myself, "No. No. No. Why would you do this?"

"Oh my *god*!"

Heather's voice came out of nowhere and made me jump to my feet. We stared and I didn't say a word. She had caught me red-handed—guilty as charged.

I was still holding her papers in one hand when she lunged for them. "You're going through my things now?"

"You can't be seriously thinking of doing that?" Heather was in deeper shit than I thought.

Heather's movements were frantic as she hurried to shove the papers back inside the envelope. "Why not?" she snapped without bothering to look me in the eye. "I can help a family bring a life into this world."

It sounded like the biggest load of BS I had ever heard. My eyes widened and my body language caused Cooper to get excited. "That's no job," I said. "It's a Band-Aid solution to whatever financial difficulties you're in. Besides, don't they want women who've had kids before?"

Heather's mouth slackened as she glared.

A moment of awkward silence passed before I asked, "How deep of a hole are you in?"

Heather dropped her head into her hand. She closed her eyes and pinched the bridge of her nose.

Were my assumptions right? "There are other solutions."

She swept her head up. "It's not only about the money."

I couldn't even begin to imagine what else there might be. My thoughts flickered between which route she would go— would she just need a turkey baster or have an embryo implanted. But I didn't have the guts to ask. All I could say was, "And what if you become attached to the baby? Because you will. I guarantee you will."

Heather's eyes began to water as I realized how much I sounded like her always telling me what to do and how to feel. My shoulders dropped and I sighed, questioning if I was getting too far ahead of myself.

"I have nothing, Samantha." She shook her head and looked away. Her tone, completely deflated. "And I certainly don't want to keep working in a dead-end profession that leads me to nowhere."

My neck was still ticking hard when I said, "And where do you think this will lead you?"

Heather was still staring at the packet.

"Babies kick themselves out after nine months. Then what will you do? It's another dead-end that will come far faster than what you're imagining now."

"With this," Heather pointed to the packet and turned to look me in the eye, "I'll have freedom to explore."

I snorted as I huffed out my disbelief. "You think you'll be traveling while pregnant?"

Heather rolled her eyes at me. "Explore my passion. I want go back to school—and finish this time." She jabbed her finger at me. "And before you start judging me, I want you to know that I've thought this through. This time it will be different. I'm older and more driven and know what I want." She jabbed the packet with the tip of her index finger. "This will pay for school, and it will also give me access to health-care which I wouldn't otherwise have."

My arms were crossed and I still wasn't sold on the idea. "Did you not hear anything we discussed last night?"

"What does that have to do with this?"

Flashes of Cameron and Tracey shined bright behind my eyelids as I asked, "How did you even learn of this?"

"Online."

I tossed my hands up. As if she needed any more proof of why this was a bad idea.

"This is different," Heather insisted. "Despite what your job may convince you, not everyone in this world is a monster."

I could only answer her with a look.

"I'm not pregnant, in case you're wondering."

"Not yet!" My hands were trembling. I fell into the chair and didn't say anything for a long pause. I finally spoke. "Will you at least explore other options before committing to this?"

Heather reached for the packet and left the kitchen. "I knew you wouldn't understand."

I couldn't stay here. Even if it was my own house. I didn't have it in me to enjoy just one cup of coffee. Slowly, I stood and turned off the machine. I gathered my things and headed out the door, telling my sister, who was sitting on the couch hugging her knees to her chest, "Tell Mason to call me if he leaves the house."

CHAPTER THIRTY-THREE

THE CAR BOUNCED ON ITS WHEELS AS I DROPPED MY BIG butt behind the steering wheel. The early morning nip in the air didn't even register. Heather never said anything on my way out and I still couldn't believe she thought being a surrogate was a good idea.

"She could barely commit to herself," I muttered to an empty car. "How does she think she could go nine months carrying a baby and feel free?"

I asked myself all these questions, suspecting that my sister hadn't thought of any of them. This was all assuming there weren't any complications along the way. Being pregnant was anything but a walk in the park; so much could go wrong.

A thin layer of ice covered my windows and hid me from the chance of being seen. I felt safe to freely explore my thoughts, bad-mouth my sister's decision, and get it all off my chest before I met up with Erin. Finally, I turned on the car and cranked the defrost.

Reaching behind the seat, I closed my fingers around the scraper and stepped out. I moved fast to clear the windows, hating the sounds of plastic over ice on glass. It gave me the same prickly scalp as nails on a chalkboard—the same irritation my sister inflicted upon me.

Once back inside the car, I checked my cell phone out of habit. I'd missed a text message from King.

Dreamed about you last night.

It was cheesy but I appreciated knowing we could not let work come between us.

See you soon. I hope... was my reply. And that was the truth. Whether it be case-related or not, Heather was my reason for my need to escape.

A short drive later, I was knocking on Erin's front door. It faced east and basked in the morning light. The sky promised calm weather and scattered clouds. I heard the lock click over just before Erin answered.

"Is it eight already?" She squinted into the sun.

"I'm early," I said, stepping inside her cute little house.

"I'm just finishing getting ready. You're not in a hurry, are you?"

"Take your time." I kicked off my shoes and meandered my way to the bookcase.

"There is a pot of tea in the kitchen if you're interested," Erin called out from the bathroom just before I heard the blow dryer turn on.

I scanned the shelves of fiction, theory, and philosophy just waiting to find a bestseller Erin had secretly written but never told me about. I could see her hiding something big like that—*the unassuming and wickedly smart woman sleuth, Erin Tate*—there was still a lot about her life I didn't know yet.

Soon, I moved on and kept moseying around.

Erin's house was not too different than my own. Similar in size, but you wouldn't know it. It didn't feel as cramped. It was only her living here. She had no big dog shedding hair, no kids, no boyfriend, and certainly no sister to drive her up the walls. It was nice to freely roam without tripping over a random left out shoe or dog chew. As I padded my way into her office, I continued dreaming of how great it would be to have a house to myself.

Erin had converted the spare bedroom into a home office. She had her desk for writing, and another for recording her podcast. It was perfect. On her writing desk, I caught myself staring at a familiar image.

It was a printout of Keith Brown and, when I fingered my way through Erin's notes, I liked what I was seeing. She was attempting to piece together what happened to them and why.

Could it really be suicide? Was homicide the right ruling if their deaths were the result of an overdose?

Because of King, we knew the medical examiner's office had ruled their deaths a homicide, but charges hadn't been filed by the district attorney's office. It was up to us to figure out if anyone besides a drug dealer from the street to was to blame.

"He seemed like a piece of work from what I gather." Erin joined me in looking into the eyes of Keith Brown. Tracey had the same eyes and nose as her father. We needed to find her. "I keep playing the hypothetical and asking myself, if the Browns were murdered, what did they know that someone didn't want them to share?"

"King said it might not be about the women," I reminded her as I lay the image back on her desk, "but the babies."

Erin shuffled through another stack of papers. "About that. I searched into the early morning trying to find anything resembling the online ad King said Tracey responded to."

I gave Erin an arched look.

She shook her head. "I found nothing."

I fell into her swivel chair and took my lower lip between

my teeth, listening to my brain grind its gears. It was going to be another long day. I could feel my head already beginning to throb.

"So I started putting together a list of family practice doctors, mid-wives, and OB-GYNs. I'm at a total loss of who would only target babies and leave the mothers to die."

"Not only to die, but to stage their deaths to make it look like a suicide. But we only know Tracey responded to an ad. Not that Kate did. Maybe Kate was totally separate from Tracey. Maybe Tracey's ad was on the up-and-up." Even as I said it I knew it couldn't be true. There had to be a catch if she was offered money and medical care.

"Anything from the tip-line?" Erin asked, not pressing my weak theory.

I shook my head. "There is something I didn't tell you."

Erin drew her eyebrows together and paused.

"Dawson told me to stay off the website this week."

"What? Why?" Erin's eyes flashed with annoyance.

"More cuts are coming to the newsroom and he doesn't want to give anyone reason to can me."

Erin folded her arms over her chest and shifted her weight to one leg. "You're not going to do it, are you?"

I cast my gaze to my knee caps and shrugged one shoulder. "You want me to get fired?"

Erin rolled my chair to the side and booted up her computer. Her fingers clacked on the keys and she navigated to a specific webpage with her mouse. "Look here, Sam. This is the ad revenue our website has generated in the last month."

I stared at the impressive number. "Just last month?"

Erin nodded, her eyes sparkling. Six months ago when I met Erin, we immediately hit it off and decided to combine forces—me handling the digital publishing side of things and her on the podcast. We quickly found our audience and had been growing our platform since.

"Our best month to date." Erin smiled. "It's working, Sam. We're making money."

"But it's not there yet." I stood and moved to the opposite wall, knowing what she was showing me wouldn't be enough to support us both.

"I'm working a couple potential clients to sponsor the podcast and, if I close the deal, that will add another significant chunk to our monthly earnings."

I couldn't look Erin in her eye. The paper was the only thing I truly ever wanted—besides Gavin. And when he left, it was all I had. The paper gave me a life outside of being a mom. It supported soccer practice and daycare for Mason. It was my entire community. I loved that what Erin and I were building with *www.RealCrimeNews.com* was growing, but I wasn't comfortable making the leap to going full-time.

"Sam," Erin's voice was small, nonthreatening, "I'm not asking you to do anything you don't want to do." She didn't push and I appreciated the gesture. I could make this decision all on my own. "I was just showing you what we've built and the potential for us to make more."

I continued to stare through the threshold and into the perfectly organized house. It was then I realized how easy Erin made it all seem. I loved doing both the website and reporting to Dawson. It was the best of both worlds—and I couldn't imagine ever having to choose between the two.

"How are you able to afford all this?" I finally had the guts to ask her something I'd always wondered.

Erin swallowed and said, "Okay. You're right. I should have told you when we first met, when we first started this adventure together." She lowered her tailbone on the edge of her desk. "I received a large settlement after the death of my father."

I froze. I didn't know. "I'm sorry."

"Don't be." Erin didn't react, told me it happened shortly before she decided to move to Denver. "It's the only certainty we have in this life."

Erin was right, and now it was all starting to make sense how she was able to do all this without taking pay. She was incredible at what she did, and I couldn't have asked for a better partner, but I didn't have the same opportunity as she did. I had bills stacking up, a teenage son, and now a sister in limbo. Finances were tight, but I couldn't see myself doing anything else.

"I'm in this 100%." Erin looked me directly in the eye as she spoke. "There is nothing I would rather be doing with my time."

Erin wasn't looking for any kind of statement for me to make. She knew where I stood and my actions spoke for themselves. I was committed to both worlds. *But was Dawson?* He made it seem like soon I would be forced to walk the plank or get pushed.

"We better get going," I said when I finally checked the time. "Allison is expecting us to bring breakfast. And Susan would have a fit if we were late."

CHAPTER THIRTY-FOUR

"SHE WANTS TO DO WHAT?"

Erin was dramatic in her delivery—deservingly so—after what I had just shared about Heather. It felt good to get this off my chest, but mostly it felt good to hear someone else's opinion on the subject.

"You heard me right." I nodded and kept driving. "She wants to become a surrogate mother."

The smells of fried chicken, buttered biscuits, and eggs and bacon spilled out of the Chick-fil-A bags we had picked up on our way to St. Joseph's. It was one of Allison's favorite breakfasts. Picking it up was the least we could do to make her feel like she hadn't been cooped up inside a hospital room for the past two nights.

Erin was still in a state of shock when she murmured, "I've never been pregnant, so I don't really know what it's like, but your sister doesn't come across as a fool."

"You don't know her the way I do."

"It sounds like she's put a lot of thought into this."

"I had an easy pregnancy." I flicked my gaze to Erin, the corners of my eyes crinkling with the warm memory of my youth. "That isn't the case for everyone. There's morning sickness. Exhaustion. Aches and pains. Never enough sleep because you can't get comfortable. She thinks she'll have as much energy and drive as she does now to go back to school." I let out a disbelieving laugh.

"Seventy-five grand is a lot of cheese. Maybe Heather thinks it's worth the risk."

"If you didn't receive that settlement, you're saying you would do it?"

"Oh, no honey." Erin laughed like I was crazy. "I didn't say I would do it, but I understand the appeal."

"The money, or being a surrogate?"

"Both." Erin's gaze wandered. "I'd take the money if I had debt to pay."

"And that's what I'm afraid Heather isn't telling me."

"Maybe she really does only want to go to school."

"I hope so."

"Then it's a win-win. She gets the money she needs for school and a couple receives the baby they've always wanted."

My stomach flexed at the idea. I still felt unsettled about it. "It's not as easy as you're making it out to be." I shared my concerns with Erin—the same ones I had shared with my sister—hoping Erin would back me up.

"Those are her decisions to make."

"I know that," I said. This conversation wasn't going anywhere fast.

"What's really bothering you, Sam? There must be something else that has you trying to stop Heather from doing this."

I paused a moment to make sure I got the words right. "Okay. Fine. The real reason I don't want Heather to go through with this is because of the missing women."

Erin's brows pinched.

"All of them were—*are*—pregnant."

"Your sister is attractive, but not eighteen-years-old attractive." Erin had a point—something that differentiated her from the victims we were chasing. "But couldn't you be thinking too much into this?"

Maybe I was. But it was my sister and I wanted only the best for her.

"Sam, I've been thinking about what happened last night." Erin changed the subject like a casual breeze rustling the trees. "Please don't take this the wrong way."

I swallowed and felt my ribs squeeze the air out from deep within my lungs.

"You know how much I love seeing you happy. You and Alex are perfect for each other, but after what I witnessed last night..." Erin paused. I could feel her unease as her hands twisted in her lap.

I regretted the way I approached King for all to see. I should have waited. Should have kept my cool and talked to him outside. Alone. But I didn't, and now I was sure I was going to pay the price for my mistake. "Erin, if you have something to say, just say it."

"I can just see the writing on the wall."

I slowed the car and made the next turn, trying my best not to jump to conclusions.

"Your professions mix like oil and water."

I rolled my eyes and gave her a look of annoyance.

"Am I wrong?"

"It's different with him."

"No doubt. But aren't you afraid that it will eventually come between you?"

"No. I'm not."

"At some point, every story you get ahead on will make his life hell. Everyone he works with will think you're manipulating him for the inside scoop."

As I ground my molars, I thought about Campbell and my

history with the department. I appreciated Erin's concern—it was worth the extra thought—but I refused to get rid of either King or my career. They weren't mutually exclusive. Worst of all, I knew the only reason Lieutenant Baker didn't stop our relationship before it ever took off was because of Gavin's reputation. But even that was fading into oblivion with each year that passed.

"I'm not giving either of them up," I said, and Erin left it at that. We finished the ride in silence.

Parking was a hassle at the hospital. Erin let her concerns go, choosing instead to concentrate on our visit with Allison. We spent ten minutes driving through the garage searching for a space, and by the time we met up with Susan inside, she let us know how late we were.

"But we brought breakfast." I smiled and held up two paper bags. Erin was hanging on to two more—more than enough for just the four of us.

"Anyway, we thought you would be with your *Benjamin*," Erin cooed as she leaned into Susan's shoulder.

"*Benjamin*," Susan mocked, "isn't on the schedule today."

It was all Susan shared, which was strange since she usually couldn't stop bragging about him. I knew they'd gone away for a night and wanted to learn more about the conference. And how she could keep the spark in a relationship that seemed to be moving at the speed of light. Instead, we got nothing. Cold as ice.

We moved through the maze toward Allison's room in silence. Susan led the our pack of three and I shared an arched look with Erin. She was also hoping Susan would have shared more.

Erin shrugged and asked Susan, "How was your night away? Were all your expectations met?"

There was innuendo in her tone and Susan still spit out the bait by only saying, "Hotel was magnificent and the conference spectacular." She said nothing about Benjamin and that had me wondering what might have happened.

Together we took a ride up the elevator to the third floor and we were silent as we entered Allison's room. "I hope you're hungry," I said, holding up the food bags.

Allison's eyes landed on our loot and lit up. Her electric white smile stretched to her ears. "You didn't."

"We did."

"We tried to bring in the ingredients for Bloody Mary's but they were confiscated at the door," Erin joked.

Allison laughed and flicked off the TV.

We passed the bags around, each of us choosing our favorites first. It felt like old times, sitting around a table at a restaurant, as we discussed the merits of fast food and made jokes that only we thought were funny. By the time we were finished eating and the room had fallen silent, our bodies heavy with digestion, I found myself looking into Allison's eyes. "Now that you've got us all here. What's the bad news?"

The mood changed in an instant. It seemed like the bright overhead lights had dimmed even though they hadn't. Susan sat stiff with her arms crossed over her chest and Erin's elbows were perched on her knees as she cast her gaze to the floor.

Allison didn't take her eyes off of mine, but her smile certainly flipped upside down. It was serious—I could see it in her eyes. I wasn't sure I was ready to learn what it was, but I braced myself for impact, nonetheless.

"I have the gene for Huntington's Disease." Allison's small voice was flat, emotionless.

I caught Susan's and then Erin's eye. The blood had drained from each of our faces. What little I knew about Huntington's Disease meant that Allison had just been issued her death sentence.

"Oh, c'mon guys," Allison tried to cheer us up. "I haven't died. I'm still here. I don't even have symptoms."

Erin shared a smile with Susan before turning her gaze to Allison. We all forced smiles. I reached for Allison's hand and gave it a firm squeeze. It was warm and inviting—her usual strength still there. "Yes, you are."

It didn't take long for the flood of questions to begin. We learned that her mother had died of the disease years ago and that it was genetic. Allison had always known that she had a 50% chance of developing Huntington's Disease but kept putting off the genetic test to tell her for sure. Her doctor had suggested the test after reviewing her family history and Allison agreed. Her symptoms that brought her to the hospital had nothing to do with this diagnosis.

Now, with support from a genetic counselor, she was surprisingly upbeat about it all. But before we could get into how the doctors were going to treat Allison, she wanted to know what she had missed.

"It feels like I've been in here for two weeks." Allison laughed. She turned to Susan. "How was your night with Benjamin?"

Susan stood and dragged the soles of her shoes to the opposite wall. "I don't want to talk about it."

I shrugged, now sure something had happened.

"Tell me a story, Sam." Allison's eyes glimmered. "Have you found that woman's daughter yet?"

Through the dizzying array of detail, I caught Allison up to speed. It was more complicated than we'd imagined. We told her about Campbell pushing me away from Kate Wilson's crime scene, and Cameron's mother hiding her alleged affair with Tyler. Allison couldn't get enough, her facial expressions hitting the mark each and every time through the ups and downs of this rollercoaster.

"Three different girls, all of them pregnant." Allison's gaze went distant as she internalized the story we were working.

"Yeah." My shoulders were suddenly heavy with the knot I was attempting to untangle.

We considered who might only want the babies, but nothing we came up with fit the profile of the suspects. Allison wished she could help, and when I told her about wanting the police to triangulate Cameron's cell phone, Allison said, "You know there is an easy way to do that."

"I was hoping you would say that." I smiled. "But I want you to rest and get better so you can get out of here."

"Lucky for you," she raised her chin, "you can do all this without my assistance."

I gave her a questioning look just before Allison told me about a legal way I could purchase the data to Cameron's cell phone and track her last movements.

"Do I even want to know what that would cost?"

"Probably not."

I stood and began collecting our trash. Beneath a Chick-fil-A bag was a pamphlet for CRISPR gene therapy. "What's this?" I asked.

"Just something the doctor wanted me to read."

Allison spoke as if it was no big deal. Susan's expression said otherwise and I was suddenly interested in knowing more. I read over the bullet points when Susan asked Allison, "Are you a candidate for genetic therapy?"

"It may be my only option." Allison grimaced and wagged her head. "Truthfully, it sounds too good to be true."

"No, you should definitely check this out." Susan's delivery was non-argumentative and completely optimistic. "The conference I attended," she looked up at all of us, "that's what it was all about. Biotech gene editing."

Erin stepped forward with a deep crease forming between

her eyebrows. My toes were tingling with anticipation as I listened to Susan.

"And what did you learn?" I asked.

"I've seen this therapy in action. Through video, of course." Susan went on, clearly believing its potential. "It's incredible. I think you should give it some serious thought. It might be the answer to your problems."

CHAPTER THIRTY-FIVE

HIS CHEST ROSE AND FELL AS HE CONCENTRATED ON THE first cut.

It had been years since the Guardian Angel had done this procedure himself. He'd been witness to it a couple dozen times since, and he hoped that his memory and attention to detail would be enough to guide him through the surgery he was about to begin.

The baby was still breech and needed to be extracted. The clock was ticking. He didn't have time to change into traditional scrubs. He'd washed his hands before snapping on a pair of latex gloves. He wore a mask and covered his eyes with protective glasses, but that was it. It was all he could manage—more concerned with saving the only thing that truly mattered to him; the baby.

A line had been drawn horizontal across the lower quadrant of the patient's womb to help guide his incision. The surgical tech had his tools laid out and ready. They shined beneath the bright flood lights, impressive in their arrangement.

The Guardian Angel looked once more at the mother's

vitals before beginning his work. She was under anesthesia and her data was reading normally when suddenly there was a voice calling out to the doctor.

"It's confirmed, Sir. We've traced the number she called."

The Guardian Angel held his hands in the air and turned to face the nurse. "And?"

"It was him." The nurse's bright eyes blinked. "She called the baby's father."

"Very well." The Guardian Angel thanked his assistant then turned to his patient. "You've been a bad girl," he said to her. "But your mistake may very well be just what I needed." He grinned beneath his surgical mask.

Stepping to his right, he adjusted the light and reached for the scalpel. Hot blood coursed through his body, swishing in his ears as he lowered the blade to the woman's stretched skin.

"Are we ready?" His tech nodded. "Then let's deliver this baby."

The skin opened and peeled back like a baked potato as the Guardian Angel made his first cut. The surgical tech dabbed the patient's blood with gauze and placed the clamp inside, keeping access to the womb open.

It didn't take long to cut through the layers of fat, muscle, and tissue before the doctor was setting down his scalpel and reaching inside the mother's womb, working the baby free.

The room exploded with frantic activity as the doctor stepped back, feeling a shortness of breath consume him. The surgical tech's focus turned to the mother as the Guardian Angel seemed to forget about everything else happening around him.

His smile stretched wide with absolute joy as he held his baby girl for the very first time. He stared into the little girl's scrunched face and laughed as he listened to her little cries crack the still air.

"Incredible," he said to himself.

Pinching the umbilical cord between his fingers, he felt it still pulsing with life. The surgical tech worked to free the placenta from the mother's womb and blood was everywhere. It was a miracle. There was nothing like it. And so much better than the way he had to bring little Mystery into this world. Everything was perfect. Her. Him. And the miracle he'd created.

A flood of fast beeps broke his focus just as he cut the umbilical cord and moved little Miracle under the heat lamp.

"Sir, she's hemorrhaging," the surgical tech said to the Guardian Angel as they tried to stop the bleeding.

He rushed to the mother's side, analyzed the data, and put his hand on the surgical tech's arm. "No. Stop."

Confusion flashed behind the tech's protective eye glasses. "We can save her."

The Guardian Angel shook his head. "Leave the room. I'll take it from here."

The tech reluctantly backed away. The Guardian Angel watched as his assistant's eyes bounced between the patient, the doctor, and the baby they had just delivered.

"It's best we keep our work a secret," the Guardian Angel said as the surgical tech left the room. As soon he was alone with the patient, the Guardian Angel spun around and began the IV drip.

"We have what we wanted," he whispered to himself. "Her job here is done."

CHAPTER 36: NOT SO SORRY

DETECTIVE ALEX KING WAS BEHIND HIS DESK AT THE station early that morning. His eyes were bloodshot from having spent the last two hours scouring the internet for any leads to the online ad Tracey may have responded to. He'd searched places like Craigslist and Facebook but kept coming up with nothing.

"It has to be somewhere," he muttered to himself as he entered a new inquiry into the search bar. The paid ads populated and still nothing led him to what he was looking for. Frustration was building. He was beginning to lose hope.

"I can't take it anymore," Alvarez grumbled from his desk. He had been doing the same as King and had finally lost patience himself. "I'm going to talk with the IT guys. Maybe they'll have a better strategy than the one we have."

King blinked and cast his gaze to his fingers curled over the keys. He thought of what to type next when suddenly a woman tapped him on his shoulder.

"The information you requested on Kate Wilson's father." Her voice was light but direct.

King swiveled his chair around and stared at the printed

sheet of paper. He pinched it between his fingers and turned back to his desk, thanking the professionally dressed woman for her assistance. The woman strode away and King immediately picked up the phone to dial the number written next to Matt Wilson's name. After several rings, the line clicked over. "Matt Wilson, please."

"Who the hell is this?"

"My name is Alex King. I'm a homicide detective with DPD."

"Homicide? Is this about Kate?" The man's tone softened.

"I'd like to ask you a few questions about your daughter. Is now a good time to speak with me?"

"I wasn't aware that Kate's death was a homicide."

"At this time, it's still being ruled as an accidental overdose."

"But you have your doubts?"

"When was the last time you had contact with your daughter?" King continued.

"Am I a suspect?"

"No, Mr. Wilson. I'm just trying to piece together Kate's pregnancy."

"What for?"

"Please, Mr. Wilson, just answer my questions. You'd be doing a great service to Kate if you did."

Matt Wilson sighed a heavy breath that King could almost feel drift into his ear. "When she first learned she was pregnant, she came to me for help."

"What kind of help was she looking for?"

"I hadn't heard from or seen my daughter in years. Kate's mother kicked me out of their lives long ago and did everything in her power to keep it that way. So you could imagine my surprise when Kate called me."

"How did you react to the news of her being pregnant?"

"Are you kidding? I was angry and disappointed."

"Did you tell her that?"

"I made myself clear. Kate could have been anything she wanted to be, I just didn't want her to follow in the footsteps of her junky mother. But that's exactly what happened."

King pressed the phone to his ear and scribbled notes as he talked.

"You know, that's who you should really be directing your questions to. Hell, you should pay Kate's mother a visit, too. I'm sure that's where Kate was getting her dope from." A pause. "Just a fair warning if you do, despite what she might say about me, I'm not a man to hold grudges. I wanted Kate to move forward. Take responsibility for her actions. You know, own it."

"And what about her mother? Did she want Kate to take responsibility?"

Mr. Wilson laughed. "God no. Kate's mother wanted her to get an abortion and not tell a soul about it."

"Any idea why that may be?"

"What you don't understand about Kate's mother is she believes a woman can only make her way in this world through sex and appeal. How do you think Kate got in this mess in the first place? She watched her mother whore around and squeeze her sugar daddies to pay her bills."

"Did you offer to help your daughter with any of the expenses?"

"I work hard but I'm not a rich man, Detective. Neither is Kate's mother. Kate didn't have access to healthcare, and her financial future was rather bleak. We did what we could, but what I couldn't offer in financial assistance I offered Kate in other ways."

King perked up and held the point of his pen above the paper. "Such as..."

"Adoption."

"And what did your daughter ultimately decide?"

"Kate wanted to keep the baby."

"You don't sound happy about her decision. I thought you wanted her to own her decision."

"I did, but not the way Kate went about it."

King leaned back and felt his pulse tick hard in his neck. "Mr. Wilson, are you aware of your daughter ever responding to an online ad promising medical and financial assistance to help cover the costs of her pregnancy?"

"If she did, I never heard about it. But what I can tell you is that Kate seemed to have found a doctor she really liked at the Mile High Health Clinic. I believe that was where she was going for regular checkups since they confirmed she was pregnant. If I'm not mistaken, he was also the one Kate said convinced her that adoption wasn't an option."

CHAPTER THIRTY-SEVEN

WE ALL LISTENED CLOSELY TO WHAT SUSAN HAD TO SAY. She was busy explaining everything she'd learned at the biotech conference. She seemed to know more than Allison about the scientific breakthrough in CRISPR gene editing technology that promised to cure a variety of diseases, including Huntington's Disease.

I was blown away by what I was hearing—completely fascinated by everything scientists were capable of achieving. I had heard stories of this kind of science, but hadn't realized it was already playing a role in modern medicine.

"That's what they are saying," Allison agreed with Susan. "Genome editing is the best way to treat my disease."

Allison was a tech person herself, and I thought how perfect a fit this type of treatment was for her. We wanted what was best for her, and we'd do anything to get her back to living her life. But, as enthralling as it all was, I shared my own reservations. The technology was so new, there had to be risks associated with the treatment. And, if so, what were those risks and was it even worth it?

"Give it some time," Susan told Allison. "You don't have to make this decision now."

Despite my hesitations, I could see the hope and optimism swirling in Allison's chestnut eyes. "I knew you attended that conference for a reason," Allison razzed Susan.

"Benjamin isn't fully on board." Susan's shoulders drooped. "In fact, we were almost given the chance to meet the leading scientist, and Benjamin wasn't interested."

My head floated up like a balloon. "That's why you're refusing to tell us about him."

Susan was sitting on the edge of Allison's bed when she twisted around to meet my eye. "We didn't see eye to eye on the merits of what this scientist is doing, and Benjamin refused to speak any more about the technology until after he did some further research himself."

My brows pinched. "What had him hesitating?"

"Something about it being morally wrong to change an embryo's genes without the consent of the person they were doing it to." Susan shrugged and turned back to Allison. "But you, darling, you do have the power to decide."

I caught Erin staring. Something told me we were swimming in the same pool of thought.

"Can you repeat that?" Erin asked Susan.

"Which part?"

"About Benjamin's moral objections."

Susan repeated herself. "It doesn't matter what he believes. The technology is already being applied to real life scenarios." Susan went on to explain how the conference used a couple struggling to conceive as an example of the technology already making a positive contribution. "I mean, who wouldn't elect to erase a potentially cancerous gene in your baby's DNA if you could?"

Erin's eyes were back on mine and I felt my heart knocking harder against my chest. Wiping my sweaty palms on my thigh, the pressure in my head squeezed as my thoughts tumbled as loud as a shoe in a washing machine.

Susan was talking to Allison about this being a miracle drug and how Allison needed to get her name added to the list ASAP. She would have to apply to be in a trial, and there was no time to waste. Without realizing it, I felt my lips flutter with the words, "the missing babies."

No one heard me, and I was thankful. I wasn't sure I was ready to accept what I was thinking could actually be true. But a scientist would need embryos to test his research, and he would also need women to grow those embryos he was testing. This approach was far from legal, of course. And would a doctor go so far as to put women's and babies' lives at risk?

A heat wave rolled up the center of my spine.

I felt dizzy all of a sudden.

Was I trying to fit a round peg in a square hole? Or was I actually onto something?

When I heard Erin calling my name, I snapped out of my head and came back to the room. "Huh? What?"

Erin tapped her wrist. "We don't want to be late for our meeting."

"Yeah. Of course."

No one seemed to notice how out of it I felt. Erin was hugging Allison goodbye when Allison asked her where we were running off to. I floated to the opposite side of Allison's bed and listened to Erin explain the story she was working for her podcast. Allison locked eyes with me and said, "I'm jealous of how busy you two are."

I felt the corners of my eyes crinkle with a smile. "You'll be back to work before you know it." I kissed Ali on the cheek and hugged her goodbye, promising to call later.

"But this wasn't the vacation I dreamed of taking." Allison laughed.

We said our goodbyes and, as soon as we stepped into the hallway, Erin said in a low voice, "Are you thinking what I'm thinking?"

"Not here," I breathed.

My eyes were shifty as they bounced off every face we passed. I had made judgements far too quickly to not notice my own feelings of paranoia. We were surrounded by doctors, researchers, and people of medicine who were suggesting our friend get on the next clinical trial for a technology that may or may not be linked to the women we were actively searching for.

We rode the elevator down to the lobby floor and Erin kept giving me funny glances.

I couldn't believe I was even thinking a doctor could be behind these deaths, but with everything Susan shared about the conference, it was the only thing that answered all of our questions. Someone wanted the babies, but not the mothers. Young women were offered medical care and money during their pregnancy. Once the mothers gave birth, a staged suicide got rid of the evidence.

My stomach turned on itself, threatening to offer a rerun of this morning's breakfast. Who, and where, were these people willing to go to such horrendous lengths? And what were they really testing?

"Sam, did you hear what Susan was saying?" Erin opened her mouth as soon as we were within sight of my car.

I unlocked my door and swung it open. "Remind me again, who are we meeting with?"

Erin stared and sighed. "Tony and Kristi Patterson."

"Ah, right. The couple who thinks their IVF baby might not be theirs."

"Yes." Erin's lips pursed. "So, you *are* thinking what I'm thinking."

I fell behind the wheel and started the car. Erin followed a second after and buckled herself in. I struggled to see how this was relevant and questioned whether it was just a waste of our time when Cameron Dee's life depended on us. But something told me we needed to speak with the Pattersons—and that in doing so, our conversation would somehow lead us to Cameron and Tracey.

"Sam—"

"Yes," I snapped. "I'm thinking what you are." My body was on fire. "That these women we're looking for don't have a chance at seeing tomorrow if we can't track them down."

CHAPTER THIRTY-EIGHT

DETECTIVE KING COULDN'T GET MATT WILSON'S WORDS out of his head. They played on repeat as King sat hunched over his desk tracing the same circle around the name of the clinic Matt thought his daughter visited.

King's pulse was faint as he tried to piece together Kate's death. He had more doubts than he had answers and wasn't sure that labeling her death a homicide was the correct use of department resources. But with the ME making the same conclusion for the Browns' deaths, he made a promise to Lieutenant to look further into both cases.

King turned to his computer and tapped at the keyboard. A second later, the browser populated with the Mile High Health Clinic website. The clinic was a non-profit organization designed to better serve the underprivileged and at-risk community of Denver. King was aware of their existence but a brief familiarization didn't hurt. The clinic provided basic services in health including sex education, birth control, abortion, emergency contraception, as well as healthcare during pregnancy. It all lined up with what Kate's father said.

As King clicked his way through the website, he knew the

clinic provided the perfect solution for someone in Kate's position. Navigating his way to the contact page, King picked up his desk phone and made the call.

"Mile High Health Clinic. This is Lauren. How may I help you?" King identified himself before asking Lauren if she was familiar with the clinic's online marketing strategy. "Most of our patients come to us by word of mouth."

"And what about online? Do you actively run an ad campaign on the internet?"

"Not that I'm aware of. You would have to ask Franky about that. She manages the social media page and website." Detective King took Franky's information before Lauren continued, "Our presence online is well established. A simple internet search will direct inquiries straight to our website. We try to have the least amount of resistance when someone is seeking our help."

King was scratching his scalp, his mind churning. "I searched your website, but maybe you could help answer a question I have about your services."

"I'll do my best."

"Do you offer financial assistance to any of your patients?"

"No. We promise only healthcare. Of course, since we are a non-profit, we cover those costs—as nothing comes for free." Lauren chuckled. "But only for the treatment conducted in our own facility. And, just so we're clear, we never offer personal financial assistance, say, to help a client pay their rent. There are other services that can help with that."

King leaned back in his chair and sighed. "I'm curious, could you confirm if a Tracey Brown visited your clinic at any time during the past nine months?"

Lauren chuckled lightly. "I'm sorry, Detective. I can't legally share that kind of information with you."

"If not a Tracey Brown, perhaps a Cameron Dee?" King

rolled the dice again, hoping he'd have better luck on his second try.

"I'm sorry." Lauren's voice was full of disappointment. "You're asking about private information. What's this all about?"

King debated whether or not to say. "A possible kidnapping and conspiracy to murder."

Lauren gasped—shocked into complete silence. "I'm sorry." She cleared her throat and got her voice back. "I wish I could help. Maybe if you had a warrant we'd be able to release that information but, honestly, you really should be speaking to our attorney at this point."

King ended the call, leaned back, and rubbed his face inside his hands.

It was time he started fresh—moved on from trying to track down the mysterious online ad that didn't seem to exist at all. His focus returned to the victims with fentanyl in their systems when remembering Lieutenant Baker's instruction.

Rolling himself closer to his desk, he opened up the file he had on Keith and Pam Brown.

There was no ransom for Tracey's safe return, nor for either of the other two victims. Though, according to the Browns' file, they had money—lots of it. So, why did Tracey disappear?

King was beginning to doubt her disappearance had any relation to Kate's or Cameron's. Of the three women, Tracey was the anomaly. She wasn't poor. She lived in an upper, middle-class neighborhood with parents who were still married. Tracey was the exact opposite of everything Cameron and Kate were. So how did she fit inside this puzzle? King wasn't sure she did, but he kept coming back to the bottle of prenatal vitamins found in Tracey's abandoned car and the amount of money her parents had.

"I don't know why I wasted my time," Alvarez said as he

passed behind King. "Unless your computer is broken, those guys in IT are useless." Alvarez dropped into his chair like an anchor. "Their suggestions weren't any better than our own ideas." He threaded his fingers behind his head, leaned back his chair, and stared at King. "Anything?"

King told his partner about his conversation with Matt Wilson, his call to the clinic, and how he wanted to restart their entire investigation by revisiting the Browns' case.

"You think we might have missed something?"

King looked his partner in the eye and nodded once. "I think we're missing something big, and her name is Tracey."

CHAPTER THIRTY-NINE

ALEX KING STEERED THEIR SEDAN TOWARD THE FIRST
Bank on 17th Street in the Central Business District where
Keith Brown had been employed. As he drove, the two detectives discussed the Browns' crime scene.

"I've been thinking about their dog," King said.

"What about it?"

"Wouldn't Tracey have picked it up from the shelter
by now?"

Alvarez's eyebrows furrowed as he leaned into the car
door and stared. "And not come to us first to learn what
happened to her parents? Doesn't make sense."

"You heard what their neighbor said about them." King
pulled down the visor to block the sun's glare. "I'm starting to
think he might have been right."

"Are you suggesting Tracey may have killed them?"

It had certainly crossed King's mind. "What I'm saying is
that if it weren't for Tracey to have gone missing that same
night—which does make her seem guilty—we would have
ruled her parents' deaths a suicide without question."

"Except we found her car."

King rolled his neck to Alvarez. "The perfect getaway."

Alvarez turned his head to the window and the car fell still for a moment before King asked, "Do you think Campbell is a good detective?"

"Why do you ask?"

"I can't help but feel like he's dragging his feet on this investigation." King adjusted his grip on the steering wheel. "He doesn't give two shits about Cameron or Kate because no one does. It's the same story of neglect when dealing with crimes stemming from Denver's poor neighborhoods."

"Are you sure this isn't about what he said about Samantha?"

"It has everything to do with Samantha, but am I wrong?"

"No doubt Samantha is beating him to the punch, but let me tell you something." Alvarez pushed himself up in his seat and King watched his partner's face harden into stone. "Campbell doesn't know dick about how great an officer Gavin Bell was. As far as he's concerned, Samantha is just like the rest of the media vultures."

"Samantha's not going to stop."

"I wouldn't expect her to." Alvarez shifted his focus to the road ahead. "But if she makes Campbell look bad, we'll all feel the repercussions."

King curbed the car in front of the bank and, once inside, they badged their way to upper management. The manager on duty was Sandy Faulkner and, by the haunting look on her face, she was still coming to terms with the news of Keith's sudden death.

"I was shocked when I heard the news," she said. "Obviously, I've been thinking a lot about it and my thoughts are with his—and Pam's—family."

King asked Sandy a half-dozen questions and nothing about her answers were suspicious. She spoke highly of Keith and the work he did for the bank. She had only good things to say about both Pam and Tracey as well. She admitted her relationship with Keith was purely professional and their private lives rarely crossed so her knowledge of what he was *actually* like was limited.

"May we see his desk?" King asked.

"Certainly." Sandy began walking. "Just this way."

As they approached Keith's desk, King was quick to spot a framed photograph of Tracey perched near his computer. He took it into his hand and stared.

It was a nice picture—a school picture—perhaps her senior photo. Tracey was bright-eyed and full of teenage spirit. She had obviously taken the time to look perfect for the photo. She looked smarter in this picture than any of the others they had found at the house. He could understand why Keith had wanted to keep it on his desk. It was hard for King to imagine Tracey having anything to do with her parents' deaths, but he'd been surprised before; why not again?

"Take all the time you need," Sandy said, leaving the detectives to freely browse.

Alvarez was busy opening and shutting drawers while King pawed his way through stacks of paperwork that was mostly blank sheets waiting to be completed by clients.

"Are you police officers?" a man's voice asked softly from behind.

King swept his eyes up and stared at the man from beneath his brow. "Detectives."

The sharply dressed man with carefully combed hair glanced around nervously. "Mind if we talk outside?"

King rolled his gaze to Alvarez. They shared a knowing look and said, "Yeah. After you tell us who you are."

His name was Joshua Zinn and he was a commercial lender with the bank. As soon as they stepped outside and rounded the corner of the building, Joshua asked the detectives, "What's this about?"

"You worked with Keith?" King responded.

"He was my colleague, but different areas of expertise." Joshua kept his hands buried inside his pockets as he talked. "We're still feeling his absence in the office. That's why you're here? To investigate his death?"

Alvarez stared and King nodded. "How did you learn that he died?"

"Sandy told me." Joshua paused, acting like he had something he wanted to get off his chest.

"Whatever you have to say, you can tell us," Alvarez gently pushed.

Joshua bounced his gaze between the two detectives. "I can't say I was surprised to hear Keith died."

King's eyes narrowed, wondering why Joshua said *died* and not *took his life*. "And why is that?"

"Keith didn't seem himself lately." Joshua licked his lips, and when King asked what he meant by it, Joshua said, "It's none of my business but I know it devastated him."

"What did, Joshua?"

"His daughter, Tracey, was pregnant."

King shared a knowing glance with Alvarez. Joshua's story was lining up with Beth's from Olive Garden.

"It wasn't just that Tracey was pregnant that destroyed Keith, but it was the fact that it was out of wedlock when it happened." Joshua's right hand was now pointing at the ground as he locked his eyes with King's. "That's when I saw Keith go downhill."

"Did you know that his daughter is missing?"

"Oh, geeze." He wiped a hand over his face. "I hadn't heard."

"Any idea where we might be able to find her?"

Joshua shook his head.

"She wouldn't think of stopping in the bank to collect her father's things, would she?"

"Tracey hasn't been around for close to a year. Look, I felt like Keith had lost all sense of direction. He was venturing into murky waters and doing things I had never known him to do before."

Alvarez shifted his weight to his opposite leg. "Like what? Can you give us an example?"

"I wanted to come out sooner and give a statement, but when I heard that their deaths had been ruled a suicide," Joshua lifted his shoulders to hide his neck, "I didn't think anyone would care."

"What kind of clients did Keith work with?" King attempted to bring Joshua back on track.

"Wait, are you investigating his death as a homicide?"

King lowered his voice and said, "We're not ruling anything out at this point."

"Christ."

"Know anyone who might have wanted him dead?"

Joshua's gaze was distant, his face a pale green. Slowly, his head began to nod. "The Browns were involved in some lawsuit against a doctor." He lifted his gaze and looked the detectives in the eyes as he spoke. "I didn't ask too much about it—wasn't really my business—but the few times I heard Keith griping about the stress it was causing him, I thought maybe it had something to do with his daughter's pregnancy."

"Do you still believe that was what this lawsuit was about?"

Joshua shook his head and told the detectives about a conversation he had overheard one afternoon while Keith was on the phone. "I only caught bits and pieces of it, but it sounded like some kind of investment gone bad."

King's eyebrows lifted. His stomach hardened with thoughts of motives to kill someone running through his head. "And the lawsuit was with a doctor?"

"I think so."

"Do you have a name for the doctor?"

Joshua shook his head. "I assumed it was for a boat-load of money. With Keith, it was always about money. He was ruthless in his pursuit of riches and the greediest SOB I've ever known." Joshua cracked a smile. "But here is where it gets really scary." Joshua tipped his body forward and King watched his eyes go wide. "The trial was supposed to begin yesterday, the day after they died."

CHAPTER FORTY

WE ARRIVED AT A MODEST HOUSE IN THE DENVER SUBURB of Wheat Ridge. I didn't say much on our drive from the hospital and it was for the better. I needed to cool my frustration, gather my wits, and decide if what I was thinking could actually be possible.

Erin took the lead and knocked on the Pattersons' door without asking if I was ready. It didn't matter. This was her story. All I wanted was to get back to figuring out where Cameron and Tracey may have sought medical treatment and if Cameron responded to the same online advertisement Tracey had to get her through the doors.

A moment passed before a woman, who I assumed was Kristi Patterson, opened the door and smiled. "Now, which one of you is Erin?"

"That's me." Erin extended her hand for Kristi to shake. "Thanks for inviting us here. This is my colleague, Samantha Bell."

Kristi's eyes found their way to me and she smiled. "I'm a huge fan of your work."

"Thank you," I said just as a three-year-old boy came out

of nowhere and wrapped my leg up in the biggest hug he could give.

"That's our boy, Tommy." Kristi's eyes swelled with pride. "He's the reason I called you here." Kristi's eyes drooped slightly. "Please, come inside."

Tommy reminded me of Mason at that age. The roller-coaster ride of emotions and boundless energy before the inevitable crash. He made me smile and laugh and, without realizing it, he was the reason for my lessened anxieties.

"I'm sorry, my husband Tony is working." Kristi was in khakis and a fleece vest, casually dressed, which made me think she was a stay at home parent.

"That's quite all right," Erin said.

"Can I offer anybody anything to drink?" Tommy clawed at his mother's legs, begging for her to play with him, and Kristi scooped him up and set him on her side.

"No. I'm fine. Thank you," I said.

Erin declined as well and, when Tommy wouldn't settle down, Kristi told us she was going to try putting him down for a nap. He'd had an interrupted night of sleep with an unrelenting cold keeping him up.

While we waited for Kristi to return, I took the liberty of browsing the framed family photographs on the dining room hutch and shelves. Their house was comfortable. Lots a plants, full of bright colors, and toys scattered over the floor.

"Cute family," Erin said.

I was bent at the waist staring at one photograph in particular. "There is no doubt Tommy has his mother's eyes, but can you see any relation to his father?"

Erin took a closer look. "Maybe that's where her story begins."

Kristi came back to the front without her son and seemed noticeably lighter in spirit. We could hear him fussing in the back but like the seasoned pro Kristi was, it didn't faze her.

"I'm sorry, I forget," she held one hand up, "did you say you wanted something to drink? Coffee? Tea?"

"We really can't stay long, Mrs. Patterson," Erin said, shaking her head.

"Please, call me Kristi." She smiled and guided us to the living room. She perched herself in the corner of the couch, Erin opposite her, and I made myself comfortable in an armchair.

"The reason I called was because of your podcast," Kristi reminded Erin. "While not the same as my story, it was eerily familiar for both Tony and me. We thought that our story would also be of interest to you."

"I'd like to hear it," Erin turned to me, "from the beginning so that Samantha could hear what you said to me last night on the phone."

Kristi licked her lips and was sitting up with her hands clasped between her knees. It was clear she was nervous, and perhaps a bit insecure, when she began telling us her difficult journey to conceive.

"Tony and I knew from the beginning that we wanted to be parents. He talked about having four children; I wanted two." Her smile reached her eyes when she took the trip down memory lane. "Anyway, soon the excitement waned as nothing happened. No matter what we did, our efforts kept failing us. Tony remained supportive in the beginning, but I took it personally—like there was something wrong with me. We kept trying to conceive, and it nearly destroyed our marriage."

"But you now have Tommy." I smiled.

"Yes." Kristi lowered her chin and mirrored my smile with one of her own. "We have Tommy."

"Tell us how that happened."

"One day I was having lunch with my mother—she lives not far from here—and mentioned I should consider IVF.

When I got home, I looked into it. I had sticker shock. The cost was astronomical and the results weren't guaranteed. I let a couple of days pass before bringing it up with Tony. He wanted to take the risk—even if it would have drained our savings—and it worked. The embryo held."

"And that was how you got Tommy," Erin confirmed.

Kristi's eyes watered with joy as she nodded. "My pregnancy with Tommy was *horrendous*. I never felt as awful as I did during those months I was pregnant." She paused and set her eyes on Erin. "Are you a mother?"

Erin shook her head. "Samantha has a boy."

"Teenager," I said, raising a single eyebrow.

Kristi shared a knowing look before continuing. "I didn't feel myself. I was moody and Tony received the blunt of my emotions. Then, toward the end of the pregnancy, I was put on bedrest. And, just when I thought it couldn't get any worse, it did." Kristi laughed, her eyes popping with disbelief. "I was in labor for fifty grueling hours before Tommy finally decided he wanted to come out."

My eyebrows raised and I felt sorry for her.

Kristi rolled her neck and let her gaze travel to the back of the house where Tommy was now quietly sleeping. "But we have him."

"At what point did you start to think that Tommy wasn't yours?" Erin asked.

Kristi turned her attention back to the room, her lips curling into a frown. "After Tommy's first birthday Tony began asking questions."

I gripped my knee cap and asked, "Was he blaming you for having an affair?"

"No." Kristi's chin trembled. "Nothing like that. At first, I couldn't admit that his concerns were valid. I never told Tony, but I began seeing it from his perspective and realized there was just...something...about Tommy. I mean, he was fine physically—a healthy little boy—but he didn't seem completely ours. My husband kept at it and I told him to let it go."

"Did he?"

"I tried to make up excuses for Tony. I told him it was stress from work that was making him think Tommy wasn't ours, that he was exhausted from being a first-time father. But no matter what I said, Tony just couldn't convince himself that Tommy was his."

"I can imagine that was hard on your marriage." Erin was direct in her delivery.

"Extremely." Kristi pressed her hand over her heart. "But I knew Tommy was mine." She paused and let her gaze lock on a family photo across the room. "I thought this was Tony's way of pushing me and Tommy out of his life. I knew our journey to becoming parents wasn't how Tony imagined it would be. So, one day, he surprised me and demanded we request Tommy's charts from the clinic. You know, to see if he was ours."

"And did you get them?"

"I would do anything for my husband to keep my family together. Yes, I agreed to go along with Tony's plan and finally see the proof of Tommy's genetics. I just needed to move on with our lives. By now, I didn't care if Tommy didn't share our genes because he was still ours no matter what. But when we requested the chart from the clinic, the doctor refused to hand it over."

My brows pinched as I shared a look with Erin. Her spine was ramrod straight and I felt myself scoot my bottom to the edge of the chair with sudden interest. "What did you do?"

"Well, now I was convinced Tony had been right all along." Her lips pinched. "We threatened legal action if the clinic didn't give us Tommy's records."

"And did they comply?"

"Eventually our request was met."

"Was the information you were looking for included in what the clinic provided?"

Kristi gave a hesitant nod. "Yes. But the information seemed forged."

"What do you mean?"

"Like it had been doctored to say what we wanted to hear." Kristi swallowed. "Now I was convinced Tony was right. So we did our own maternity and paternity tests." Her eyes hardened. "Tony had been right all along. Tommy doesn't share Tony's DNA. Only mine."

I tucked a loose strand of hair behind my ear and sighed. Erin was still openly staring, trying to make sense of the story we had just been told.

"If it wasn't your husband's sperm," Erin's brows were knitted, "then whose was it?"

"We suspect it was the doctor's, but we could never prove it. We put our life savings into the IVF treatment and have nothing left. I'm sure the doctor knew that from the beginning. Without a lawyer to sue, or the money to hire a private investigator, we had no other options but to keep living our lives. Then I heard your podcast," Kristi turned to Erin, "and I called you." Kristi nodded to Erin and pleaded with her eyes. "I can only imagine how busy your schedules must be, but maybe you could use your platform to tell our story as well?"

Erin didn't budge. Her body was frozen as she stared into the eyes of a desperate mother looking for answers.

"Will you investigate this clinic for me? For my family?"

Erin flicked her gaze to me and, without speaking, I let her know it was her call. I'd have her back no matter what she decided. It was certainly an interesting story.

Erin turned her attention back to Kristi. "May I see the files?"

Kristi's eyes watered with relief as she left for the kitchen. "Everything is inside," she said as she came back to the room. "The details of my pregnancy and the data we believed to be forged are highlighted in green." She spread the papers down on the coffee table. "All my notes are attached." She pointed to the name at the top of the page. "This is the fertility clinic."

Kristi lifted the paper and handed it to Erin. I could see it all the way from where I was sitting. The familiar logo and the emotions that came attached with it. My heart beat itself up against my ribcage as I felt my blood boil once again with sudden feelings of anger.

"That's where you had your IVF?" I asked, trying not to sound as tense as I felt.

Kristi turned to me with a questioning look lining her brow. "Yeah. You know it?"

North Denver Reproductive Medicine, the same clinic whose packet my sister brought home with promises of riches. "Yeah, I know it." My eyes hooded with regret and my voice sounded rough like gravel. "But I wish I didn't."

CHAPTER FORTY-ONE

TRACEY BROWN FELT HER BABY KICK FOR THE VERY FIRST time. She sat up in bed and placed one hand on her belly where she'd felt the tiny movement, like a butterfly's wings opening. She closed her eyes and felt her lips curl into a closed-lip smile. Her body tingled with a sense of euphoria she had never felt before.

It didn't matter if her eyes were open or closed because the room was dark. To her, it was all the same. Not even a sliver of light worked its way beneath the door.

Tracey only assumed it was night once the lights had been shut off. Either way, it didn't matter. With each hour that slipped by, Tracey's sense of time lost all meaning.

Tracey lowered herself back down onto the bed, hoping to feel another flutter of life inside her. She stared into the dark abyss, thinking about her parents. She missed them dearly, regretted the last argument she'd had with her father. Her life had changed so quickly these last few months and everything seemed to have twisted out of control before Tracey had time to process her future—the future she knew her father wanted her to imagine.

I'm sorry, Daddy. Tracey's soft voice whispered past her lips. *I hope you will forgive me.*

Tracey reasoned that it was because of their last argument that her parents still hadn't bothered to visit. Her mom was siding with her dad, and her dad was a stubborn old mule. Regardless, she missed them. She wanted to call them but Dr. Cherub told her that he had done it for her—Tracey needed the rest to keep the baby healthy.

Rolling to her side, Tracey curled herself into a ball and hugged her knees to her chest. She felt sick and wasn't sure if it was because of her hormones from the pregnancy, something she ate, or the stress of isolation taking its toll.

She didn't want to be here anymore. She wanted to go home. This place wasn't what she thought it was. It was darker, more depressing, and not a friendly place anyone would want to stay. Her fear had increased when she was abruptly woken by more screams from another room.

Tracey was certain that was what woke her baby as well. The woman's piercing wails sounded like torture. Tracey could feel the pain in her cries that came through the walls.

Tracey didn't know the woman—didn't know how many were here in the facility with her—so could only assume that she was another pregnant woman the clinic had picked up.

Then, the strangest thing happened. Everything stopped. The building went still. One second, screams of bloody murder shook the walls. Then, the next, dead silent.

Tracey's heart beat steadily inside her chest. Her eyes were wide and alert. Her breaths were shallow and she remained hidden beneath her bed sheets, afraid to come out.

Now, as Tracey lay there without the lights, she wondered if she would ever make it out of this place alive. Her mind wandered to the deepest and darkest parts of her imagination. Her skin was taut with goosebumps. No matter how hard she tried, she couldn't escape her mind's torment of what happened to make the woman stop screaming. It had been so sudden, Tracey couldn't help but consider two options—a baby had been born, or the mother had died.

Suddenly, the door opened and her heart stopped.

Tracey lifted her head off the pillow and stared into the bright white light.

A dark silhouette stood in the threshold and Tracey was certain that whatever happened to the woman next door would also be her destiny.

CHAPTER FORTY-TWO

We thanked Kristi Patterson for sharing her story with us and stepped out under the afternoon sun, leaving her house with our heads swimming in questions.

The walk to my car was quiet. Kristi had rendered us speechless.

Mrs. Patterson's delivery left little doubt that what she said could be true. I sympathized with her. Their journey to conceive was one of the most difficult—physically and emotionally—I had ever heard. As if that wasn't exhausting enough, they had to now deal with immense doubt. Unbelievable.

Feeling the pinch, I checked the time and knew we had to get moving to our next line item for the day. Swinging my car door opened, Erin asked, "Could you imagine?"

I shook my head, dropped into my seat, and set the wheels in motion as soon as Erin shut her door.

"What if Kristi's theories are true," Erin was looking through the paperwork Kristi provided us, "and Tommy's biological father is the doctor who administered her IVF?"

The thought sickened me. It also had me concerned with

how many others were out there with the same story but didn't know it. Or maybe they had their own doubts but couldn't find the courage to speak up. Either way, the whole story left me feeling queasy.

I accelerated through a yellow light, zipped up the onramp, and merged onto the highway, pointing my car east.

"Sam, are you all right?"

The concerned look Erin was giving me had me wondering just how bad I looked. I angled the rearview mirror on my face and took a look myself. I was pale.

"You've barely said a word since we arrived at the Pattersons'." Her brow folded like an accordion. "You're not still thinking about what Susan said, are you? About genetically modified babies?"

I flicked my gaze in her direction. "Aren't you?"

"Of course I am."

"After everything I've heard in the last twenty-four hours, anybody even remotely interested in working with embryos or pregnant women or women who want to conceive has jumped to the top of my list of possible suspects."

"Okay, I'm with you on that. But this seems personal."

I lowered my brow. "Because it is." I turned and locked eyes with Erin. "North Denver Reproductive Medicine was the clinic my sister visited about surrogacy."

Erin held my gaze for a moment before turning away. "Wow."

"Full circle." I couldn't believe it myself.

Erin tipped her body toward me and glanced to the speedometer. Without realizing it, I was clocking 80MPH with ease. I didn't let up. My adrenaline was spiking and I was afraid of missing our chance to speak with Ms. Dee.

"You never did say how your sister was recruited," Erin said.

"I'm not sure she was, but I know she found them online. At least, that's all she told me."

"Could it be the same doctor posting the online ad Tracey responded to? Cameron and Kate could have, too."

My stomach dropped. It wasn't something I wanted to consider, but Erin had a point.

"Sorry, Sam. I didn't mean to frighten you like that."

"It's okay." I watched my knuckles go white on the wheel. "Now we know where to go next."

"You still want to speak with Ms. Dee?"

"Where do you think we're going now?"

"It's probably safe for us to cross Tyler's name off our list."

Dr. Benjamin Firestone kept coming to mind. I tried to think what his hesitation might have been to CRISPR technology. I tried to see it from a doctor's point of view but I didn't know where I was even supposed to be looking. As far as I was concerned, CRISPR gene editing was the same miracle cure that was supposed to help free Allison from her disease. *What was I missing?*

"I want to see Ms. Dee's eyes when we confront her with the video of her and Tyler. But, more importantly, I want to know if Cameron responded to an ad similar to the one King said Tracey did."

CHAPTER FORTY-THREE

"Now what did that scumbag accuse me of doing this time?"

Ms. Dee seemed particularly feisty today. We surprised her at work. She was busy unpacking boxes of bananas in the produce section of the downtown Safeway when we arrived. I watched her hands delve deep and they moved fast, not once pausing for even a moment.

"Why do you assume we're here to speak to you about Tyler?"

Finally, she stopped moving and looked me directly in the eye. "Well, aren't you?"

I reached into my back pocket and pulled out my phone. Unlocking the screen, I brushed shoulders with Ms. Dee as I threatened to press the play button with my thumb. Ms. Dee's eyes dropped to the screen and I waited for her to beg me to not let the video roll. Instead, she played dumb—something I would soon make sure she would regret.

"What's that?" she said.

Cocking my jaw, I tapped the screen. The video of her and Tyler came to life. "Care to tell us about this night?"

Ms. Dee's chest expanded before she breathed a deep exhale. "Stop it." Her hand blanketed the screen as she nervously glanced around to see if anyone saw who shouldn't have. "If anyone sees this I'll be fired."

"This is public. Anyone can find this if they go looking."

Ms. Dee's eyebrows drew together as the cords in her neck strained.

"You thought I wouldn't find out about this?" The insulting jab at my intelligence twisted my side, reminding me to tread lightly with Ms. Dee. I remained calmed despite the heat spinning in my chest. This wasn't about Ms. Dee. This was about Cameron.

Ms. Dee's watery gaze was unwavering. I could only assume she was trying to decide how best to move on and refocus our investigation to the original reason she'd sought our help in the first place.

"Because now I'm beginning to believe that you did use your daughter to get closer to Tyler," I said, holding her eyes inside of mine.

"Let's get out of here." Erin took one step back. "She's clearly not interested in finding her daughter."

"Wait," Ms. Dee answered quickly, her eyes bouncing between Erin and me. "I'll tell you the truth, but not here."

We agreed to meet outside. As Ms. Dee left for the break-room in the back to clock out, Erin and I headed for the exit.

"Nice work," I told her.

"I knew she would cave." Erin playfully nudged her shoulder into mine. "Maybe she really does love her daughter."

Not long after, Ms. Dee was leading us to an empty picnic table on the far outside corner of the grocery store. Cars lazily passed by and the rattle of shopping carts being pushed kept our conversation hidden.

"Detective Campbell said that Cameron was missing

because I wasn't being cooperative, and he might not be wrong." Ms. Dee spoke without any prompting on our part. "But I couldn't tell him about *that*." She jutted her chin to my phone's screen. It lay on top of the table in front of me.

"Tyler told us about the affair," I said. "You think he would keep something like that a secret?" It was clear to us Ms. Dee knew more than she had told anyone—including Detective Campbell—so I did my best not to push her too hard with hopes of finally hearing the complete truth.

"It was a mistake."

"You think?" Erin's mouth slackened.

I shot her a look to keep her mouth shut. Now was not the time to be judgmental.

Ms. Dee squinted off into the distance when she began speaking. "Things moved quickly and I lost track of my role as a mother—how a woman my age is supposed to act." She flicked her gaze over to me. "Tyler has that effect on women of all ages, and I fell for it."

"Tell us what happened. Where was Cameron when all this was happening?"

Ms. Dee's hands shook as she wrapped her lips around a smoke and lit up. "I didn't want Cameron to be like me." She pulled a deep inhale into her lungs—the end glowing a cherry red—and exhaled a big plume of smoke.

"What do you mean, you didn't want her to be like you?"

"To become a teen mother." Ms. Dee's face hardened, the look of a lifetime worth of mistakes and hard knocks. "But that is exactly what happened and Tyler was never going to admit that the baby was his."

"But you knew it was."

"Cameron knew it, too." Ms. Dee tapped the ash off the end of her cigarette. "My baby was scared, but not as frightened as I was. Of course, I could never admit that to my daughter. I was already struggling to survive, and the thought of having to do it all over again—for the next eighteen years..." Ms. Dee shook her head. "I just couldn't do it."

Erin brought her elbows to the table and asked, "What are you saying?"

Ms. Dee's expression pinched. "What I'm saying is that I thought if I could win Tyler over, he'd offer to help with the expenses."

I watched Erin's shoulders relax before turning back to Ms. Dee. "When did your affair with him begin?"

"I wouldn't call it an affair. It was only one night; the night of that video." She stamped out her cigarette and muttered, "I can't believe it's posted online."

"Did Cameron ever find out?"

Ms. Dee stared into the grains of the picnic table wood as she nodded. "You can imagine how awkward it was for her. I've never seen her so angry."

"Did you try to extort him for money?"

Ms. Dee's mouth twisted with a sour expression. "Tyler was generous with his money, fun, and liked to party. We don't have much. So, when someone like Tyler came around, it was easy to get sucked into the glamorous life he lives. To this day, Tyler has never owned up to being the father of my grandbaby, nor has he offered to help with the expenses. The party stopped for him and Cameron the moment shit got real."

"Ms. Dee, how is Cameron paying for her healthcare?"

Ms. Dee's gaze went distant as she shook her head. "When Tyler pushed both of us out of his life, I knew I had to do something to help Cameron. There were only so many hours I could pick up here, so when I came across a website promising first-time mothers financial assistance," she rolled her neck and looked me straight in the eye, "it was like God had finally answered my prayers."

CHAPTER FORTY-FOUR

JONNY MONTOYA HAD HAD THE NIGHT OF HIS LIFE, letting it continue through most of the morning. He was still floating on cloud nine when he arrived home safely, well into the next day. His breath smelled of alcohol and he felt the effects of micro-dosing designer drugs while partying it up at a local nightclub where his roommate was host to a party.

"Let me inside," the woman to his left mewed as she clawed at his belt.

"Patience baby." Johnny pecked at the soft spot behind her ear.

Jonny tripped over the curb, and the woman to his right giggled. Then the other woman joined in on the laughter. Soon, they were all laughing over the lawn when Jonny spotted Tyler's black Range Rover parked at the neighbor's. The wheels were half on the sidewalk, half on the lawn.

"Son of a bitch got home before me," Johnny muttered to himself.

Tyler was as crunk as Jonny, but Jonny couldn't recall when Tyler left the party, just that he seemed to have disappeared earlier than usual.

"Is that Tyler's car?" one of the women asked.

Jonny told her to shut up and remember who brought her home—him.

"That is Tyler's car," the other woman responded. "Maybe he'll show you how to treat women right." The women shared a giggle as they teased Jonny.

Jonny slapped her butt and told her to behave.

"And if I don't?" she tempted him.

"Wait to find out." Jonny pinched the woman's mouth and shoved his tongue deep into her throat.

The two of them were busy making out on the front lawn when the other woman said, "What is that?"

Jonny slowly peeled himself away, turned, and looked at what the woman was pointing at on the ground. A dark stain colored the grass. Jonny wasn't sure what it was, but he thought it looked like oil. "It's nothing. Let's get our asses inside so I can finally do something about this hard-on."

The three of them stomped over another splotch on the ground before marching up to the front door. Jonny kept taking turns nuzzling his face in the crooks of their necks, making them squirm and beg for more.

He reached for the door handle and felt his heart drop to his stomach. It was cracked open, something that neither Jonny nor Tyler would do. Tyler owned too many valuable electronics and had thousands of dollars' worth of jewelry and clothes inside to be so careless to have allowed this to happen. Something was up.

With his brows pinched, Jonny stepped forward and nudged the door open with his foot.

The girls covered their noses. "Oh, my God. What is that smell?"

Jonny smelled it, too, but didn't react. His pulse was ticking hard and fast now, only getting worse when he noticed the blood everywhere on the floor. It looked like a deer had been dragged from the woods and had somehow found its way inside his house.

Reaching for the window, Jonny peeled the curtain back and both women screamed in horror at the same time.

"Get out of here!" Jonny yelled at them.

They took off running. Jonny didn't care where they went, just that they got the hell away from his house. He turned back around and stared at the back of Tyler's head. His roommate kneeled over the body of a woman, a bloody kitchen knife by his side.

"Tyler?"

Jonny's roommate glanced over his shoulder. Tyler's eyes were bloodshot, his face ghost-white. It was the first time Jonny had ever seen Tyler actually look scared.

"Get out of here, Jonny."

"Fuck, Tyler. What did you do?" Who was the woman who had her guts spilling out of her?

CHAPTER 45: HURTS SO BAD

WHEN WORD CAME THROUGH THE RADIO, BOTH KING AND Alvarez knew it had to be one of the missing girls. Already in the car and leaving the bank, King flicked on the lights and turned on the siren as they raced through LoDo toward the Chaffee Park neighborhood.

King weaved through traffic with a flexed stomach.

The description of the crime sounded horrendous, and King prepared himself to deal with another visual that would be permanently engrained in his memory forever.

Several patrol cars were already on scene when they arrived. King curbed the sedan off to the side and flicked his gaze to the EMS wagon. A couple paramedics loaded up the gurney into the back when King kicked his door opened. He ran as fast as he could to get a visual on the victim but, by the time he arrived, the doors were slammed shut in his face.

Pounding his fist on the back of the van, he demanded they open up. Instead, he swallowed a thick puff of exhaust as it turned on its lights and sped away.

"Did you see who it was?" Alvarez's face was red as he struggled to breathe after chasing after King.

"No." King cursed.

Heading for the house, King badged his way to the front. A young officer stood guard at the front door. "Were you first on scene?"

The rookie nodded.

The rookie's blank stare and pale face told him the young officer had never seen anything like it. The rotten smell of infection and death drifted over King's shoulder and circled back around into his nose. His insides curdled. There was blood everywhere.

"Jesus Christ." Alvarez pinched his nose before peering inside the house.

They could see everything they needed from the front step. Lab techs and forensics were inside, moving across the floor in their plastics, scouring for evidence.

"Anybody know what happened?" Alvarez asked the rookie.

"The woman's womb had been cut open."

Alvarez's eyes went wide. "Someone *ripped* the baby from the womb?"

The rookie nodded. He looked like he was about to hurl his lunch any second.

King's insides froze. He couldn't believe what he was hearing. The scene playing out inside his head was the stuff that made horror movies. He looked around the room once more.

"Who called it in?" King heard Alvarez ask the rookie.

"Her." The rookie pointed to the young brunette whose wrists and clothes were bright with florescent colors. She looked like she had just come from a concert.

King followed his finger and felt his ribs squeeze when he met eyes with Detective Campbell. He had missed seeing Campbell on his way in, but of course he wasn't surprised he was here.

Campbell told the woman to take a seat in the front of his cruiser when he saw King approach.

"Nikki, over there," Campbell flicked his eyes to his car, "called it in."

"Does she live here?"

"No. But the man she came home with does. He's over there." Campbell nodded to a police cruiser. "That is Jonny Montoya, the man who thought he was going to be getting lucky with Nikki. Apparently, they met at a club on South Federal and were coming here when they discovered the victim inside."

"Is he talking?" King asked, referring to Jonny.

Campbell nodded. "Their statements line up. But Jonny also happens to be on probation and had one too many drinks, hence the cuffs."

King watched the spooked young man blankly staring through the cruiser window. The petite woman shook, a ghostly look stamped on her impressionable face.

"Has the victim been IDed?" King asked.

"Name is Cameron Dee. It would be a miracle if she makes it."

King didn't react to the news. This was Campbell's case. If he had only taken it seriously from the start, then maybe he could have saved at least one life.

King remained calm. "But there is a chance?"

Campbell nodded once. "Sounds like Jonny Montoya came home to find his roommate, Tyler Lopez, hovering over the body. The techs found a kitchen knife near where the victim was unconscious. Forensics will confirm if it was the one used on the victim's body, but first impression paints an easy picture to assume it was."

King looked for the second suspect.

As if reading his thoughts, Campbell said, "Tyler Lopez fled the scene. Last I heard, he's still on the loose."

"With or without the baby?"

"No one ever saw a baby. At this time, internally, we're saying without."

"And publicly?"

"Nothing is being ruled out."

King stepped away, wanting to speak with Jonny. He opened the door and introduced himself. "I know you're not going to want to repeat what you've already told the other detective, but I want to hear what you saw."

Jonny didn't fight. He spoke in a whispery monotone, telling the same story King just heard from Campbell. Then, suddenly, he went off script. "This is all my fault."

King tilted his head to the side. "Tell me, Jonny, how is what happened here your fault?"

Jonny lifted his sunken eyes up to King and said, "If only I would have told the truth yesterday, maybe then I could have saved her life. But I never thought Tyler would actually kill her." Jonny's head hung. "This is so fucked up."

CHAPTER FORTY-SIX

Ms. Dee couldn't recall the name of the organization Cameron responded to, but now I knew we were getting close. The ad—a website—existed. Now we only had to find out who posted it, and where. No easy feat.

"Was it North Denver Reproductive Medicine?" I asked, hoping to spark Ms. Dee's memory.

Ms. Dee thought about it for a moment before shaking her head. "That doesn't sound right. I would have to do some searching." Her brows knitted. "Why are you asking?"

I shared that the police were actively searching for another woman who'd gone missing around the same time as Cameron.

"Oh my god." Ms. Dee gasped.

I didn't mention Tracey's name, or tell Ms. Dee of Kate's death, but Ms. Dee needed to know there were others. "That's why it's essential you're telling us everything you know."

Ms. Dee shared a look of confidence when her cell phone lit up.

Without a thought, she picked it up and answered.

Erin stood from the table and stretched her arms over her head when I noticed Ms. Dee stop breathing. *What did she just learn?*

She stared into my eyes but I knew she wasn't looking at me. Her distant gaze and flaring nostrils had me thinking something was wrong. I felt the hairs on the back of my neck stand, and a shiver worked its way up my spine.

I angled my head and listened intently, trying to hear as much of the conversation as I could. Then I felt my stomach drop and I knew that Ms. Dee was getting bad news.

Tears filled her eyes and suddenly Ms. Dee's fingers snapped open as quickly as a mouse trap. The phone dropped to the concrete, its case shattering upon impact. It all happened in slow motion and I wasn't fast enough to react.

Ms. Dee flung her head back on her shoulders and released a ripping wail into the air that was powerful enough to shatter glass. Twirling to the side, I watched Ms. Dee collapse to the cold concrete.

I immediately reached for her but I was too late to keep her from smacking her knees hard on the ground.

Erin spun around to see what was happening.

I had my arms draped over Ms. Dee's shoulders in an attempt to comfort her. Her body was tense and coiled; nothing I did could release the tension I felt radiating in the tips of my fingers.

"It's Cameron," I said softly to Erin. Then my heart said a quick prayer for the girl, hoping it wasn't as bad as it seemed.

"My baby. They hurt my baby," Ms. Dee cried.

"Who called?"

Ms. Dee continued to cry, slapping her palms down on the concrete. "How could they?"

I let her do what she needed to do before helping her to

her feet. She clung to me for support and I brushed off the dirt from her knees. A flood of tears pooled in her eyes when she locked her gaze with mine.

"What happened?" I asked.

"They found my baby but she's badly injured and on the way to the hospital now."

I didn't know what to say, so I hugged Ms. Dee and she accepted my embrace. She whispered more of what she'd learned into my ear. We didn't know the details but we both assumed the worst.

"Let us take you." I pulled back and looked her in her eyes. "We have a car. It will be quicker."

Ms. Dee swallowed back the tears and agreed, telling us Cameron was taken to Presbyterian St. Luke's Medical Center.

We left the picnic table without telling her boss she was leaving. It didn't matter. Not with her daughter having been found. Everything else seemed so small.

The drive across town was silent and felt like it took forever. My thoughts were scattered, churning with possibility as I tried to hang on to hope. I thought about how Kate was found, how Tracey was still missing, and kept circling back to questioning what happened to Cameron.

Ms. Dee sat in the backseat and I kept stealing quick, unassuming glances.

She quietly stared out the window—her tears now dry—busy flicking an unlit cigarette between her fingers. Ms. Dee respected my request to not light up in the car. She didn't even bother once we arrived to the hospital.

I pulled up to the entrance with Erin sliding behind the wheel as I led Ms. Dee through the front doors. We tracked down her daughter to surgery, and immediately began fighting with the staff to learn what happened.

All anybody could say was that Cameron had been found unconscious and was badly hurt.

Erin soon met us in the waiting room, taking turns holding Ms. Dee's trembling hands. We offered food and drink, but Ms. Dee was too anxious to accept any kind of offering.

My thoughts went to Mason and I gave him a call. When he picked up, I could breathe again.

Our conversation was short, and Mason thought it was ridiculous for me to call just to say I loved him, but that's what I did—all I needed to say. Then I called King while I had the chance.

King answered after the second ring. I told him I had been thinking about him and after we exchanged pleasantries, I asked, "Did you hear about Cameron Dee?"

"I'm at the scene now."

King shared the location and I knew immediately it was Tyler's place. "Does Tyler have anything to do with this?"

"Why would you ask that?"

"Because Erin and I were there yesterday speaking to Tyler's roommate about Cameron."

"Jesus." King's gravel voice was the rockiest I'd ever heard. "Where are you?"

I told him I was with Ms. Dee at the hospital, waiting for the doctors to give us an update.

"She's alive?"

I glanced over my shoulder to Ms. Dee's ghostly figure.

"For now."

King filled me in on what happened as much as he was allowed, pausing between words as if needing to gather his emotions about to crack through the surface. "It was horrific; her baby was ripped from her womb, Sam."

I couldn't believe Tyler did this. What else did we have

wrong? It now felt like Tracey's disappearance had nothing to do with Cameron or Kate.

"There's a press conference scheduled one hour from now," King said. "I suggest you attend."

CHAPTER FORTY-SEVEN

By the time I arrived, everyone was there. Word spread like a brush fire and anticipation was high. News vans from all the local stations were set up and waiting to hear what had happened. I didn't waste any time in pushing my way to the front.

Erin elected to stay with Ms. Dee so that I could fulfill my assigned duties to the *Times*. I relayed what I knew before I left, and Erin promised to find a way to watch the press conference so we stayed on the same page.

Colleagues greeted me as I passed, but even I was feeling a little caught off guard with this one.

Tyler's black Range Rover was still parked like he had been driving while a sleep at the wheel. The house, now cordoned off, was marked by several evidence tags dotting the lawn—the same yard I had walked only yesterday. *What did that scumbag do? And where had Cameron been hiding all this time?*

There was movement in the corner of my eye and I spotted Chief Gordon Watts of DPD and his team of PR personnel moving toward the podium like a flock of geese with Mayor Noah Goldberg leading the way.

Every single one of us was dancing on our toes, unable to keep our minds from guessing what, and how much, they were going to make public. Even though I assumed I knew more than most other reporters, the suspense was buzzing in my ears.

My cell phone rang. I answered. "Dawson, I'm at the press conference."

"Good. That's what I was hoping you'd say."

"Any idea what they are going to reveal?"

"I have my guesses, but honestly, this seems to be much bigger than anything I could have imagined."

Dawson had heard about Cameron and I summed up my day—making sure he knew I'd been at the hospital with Ms. Dee. "I want this to be tomorrow's headline, understand?"

A flash of heat rushed through my body. "These aren't sex workers, Dawson. They're young women who found themselves in impossible situations with tough decisions to make." I knew at least that much to be true.

"All the same, Sam."

It wasn't. I was willing to cover what was about to be said, but I wasn't about to fall into the trap of glorifying what had happened to Kate or Cameron until I knew I had their story honest and true.

Chief Watts stepped up to the podium. The tentacles of microphones raised and lowered in front of his face. Cameras raised and everyone held their breath to listen.

"I gotta go. I'll call you later," I said to Dawson.

As soon as I was off the phone with my editor, I set up my voice recorder app and pointed it toward the chief of police just as he began speaking.

"What happened here today is *not* an isolated case." The air went still and, when the chief recognized his opportunity, he shared Cameron's name and that she was currently in critical condition. Everyone gasped with disbelief when Watts mentioned what happened to her baby. "We believe that our suspect, Tyler Lopez, may also be responsible for the death of Kate Wilson," he paused and turned to look at a tall slender man I assumed was Kate's father, "as well as the disappearance of Tracey Brown."

I bit the edge of my lips and shuffled my feet, feeling the crease between my brows deepen.

"Tracey Brown is still missing and she is our top priority. We don't know if our suspect is with Tracey now, but we're treating it as if he is." Chief raised his gaze and looked out into the sea of reporters. "Again, just to reiterate, Tyler Lopez is considered armed and dangerous."

This wasn't right. I shook my head. Kate's and Cameron's crime scenes were too different. Tyler wasn't responsible for both women. As far as I could tell, he had nothing to do with Kate. *Why were the police doing this? What was their end goal?* I needed to talk with King.

As I stood there feeling the blood leave my face, I felt a pair of eyes boring a hole into the side of my head. When I turned to look, my breath hitched.

Detective Campbell had an evil smirk stamped on his ugly mug as his beady little eyes stared me down.

I stared back, refusing to be intimated by him.

Campbell brushed shoulders with Mayor Goldberg and now my head was really spinning. Why did it seem like they were trying to make this case far simpler than it actually was? Tyler may have been a piece to the puzzle, but he certainly wasn't the complete board.

Suddenly, a roar of questions exploded around me.

Early reports said Cameron was pregnant. Can you confirm? And, if so, is Tyler the father?

What are the police doing to find Tracey?

Is Tyler also responsible for Tracey's parents' deaths?

Does Tyler have a list of priors?

Was a ransom ever demanded for any of these women?

I thought about my meeting with Tyler and his arrogance, but as I retreated into the open fields behind me, all I could think about was Ms. Dee and how it wouldn't be long before the media found that video of her and Tyler.

A hand clamped around my arm and dragged me behind a large police van. *King.*

I wanted to kiss him, have him hold me and tell me that they had it all wrong. Instead, all I could say was, "This isn't right."

A knowing glimmer caught his eye.

"I was just with Ms. Dee," I pleaded. "She's at the hospital waiting for Cameron to come out of surgery. Tyler can't be connected to all the crimes they're claiming he committed."

"You're right."

"I'm right?"

"It wasn't my call."

"Then who's was it?"

"Goldberg's." King anticipated my next question and answered it before I even asked. "He's trying to close this case ASAP before it takes on a life of its own."

I pressed my fist to my mouth and felt my head pound harder as King briefed me on the meeting Chief Watts had with the teams working the case.

"The mayor is afraid of what the public thinks is happening with these women and he's applying pressure for Chief Watts to solve this thing," King went on.

"You mean he's afraid of bad publicity."

King nodded.

I shook my head and cursed the newly elected mayor for his cowardly decision. "And what does he think will happen when this backfires?"

King shrugged. "Tyler presented Campbell with an easy opportunity when he decided to flee the scene. If Campbell can pull this off, he'll be a hero in the eyes of the chief and mayor."

"A hero?"

"It's all perception sometimes, Sam." King set his hands on his hips and sighed. "But Tyler also gave the public a face, which is far better than the alternative."

"You mean, having the police look incompetent?"

King's expression pinched.

I kept shaking my head. My arms were crossed, my muscles stiff. I knew we didn't have much time before we risked being seen, but Mayor Goldberg's decision was just plain wrong.

"Ms. Dee said Cameron responded to an online ad like you said Tracey did." King's mouth snapped shut. "It's a doctor doing this; I'm sure of it."

"Did you get a name of who was behind the advertisement?"

I shook my head. "But I have my eye on North Denver Reproductive Medicine."

King tilted his head and gave me a funny look. "Why that clinic?"

"You have a different health center in mind?"

King's head bobbed up and down. "I spoke with Kate's father over the phone and he believed it was Mile High Health Clinic who Kate went to for her prenatal care."

"Then we check both clinics out and keep looking for the ad we believe lured the women in. We're only one step away from discovering what is happening here, and Tyler isn't it."

Suddenly my phone rang. I took Erin's call. "Cameron just came out of surgery," she said.

"How is she?" I looked directly into King's eyes.

"Lucky to be alive. The doctor is speaking with Ms. Dee now but, Sam, there is something you need to hear."

"What is it?" I plugged my opposite ear with my finger to drown out the noise.

"Cameron's wounds indicate a C-section." Erin paused. "And the doctor is certain that a kitchen knife couldn't have made the cut they sewed up. Whoever did this to her was a professional and knew what they were doing."

CHAPTER FORTY-EIGHT

BABY MIRACLE FUSSED BENEATH THE INCUBATOR LIGHTS. Her face stretched with her little cries and the Guardian Angel thought it was the most adorable thing in the world. She was hungry. It was feeding time for the little girl.

The Guardian Angel approached with a proud father's smile reaching up to his eyes. He delved his hands into the clear plastic tub and opened Miracle's swaddle. She needed a diaper change.

After a quick change, the Guardian Angel picked his beautiful creation up and examined her growing strength. Supporting her weak neck, he ironed his hand down her back, measured her length, and recorded her weight. She was perfect, just as he had known she would be.

"See, there is nothing to fear." The Guardian Angel peered into the baby face that resembled a little of his own. "Look at you. You are beautiful. Healthy. Everything just as it should have been if you were conceived naturally—only better."

He swaddled the baby once again and moved to the rocking chair near the window. The curtains were drawn as he sat, giving her a bottle. The baby latched on to the nipple and settled into his arms.

Rocking back and forth, he reflected on how far his technology had come and said a quick prayer for Mystery. The two girls were his—from the moment he'd created them—and he would do anything to ensure their future was bright and full of opportunity as any father would.

With the bottle empty, he put baby Miracle back to bed, telling the little girl, "Now let's go see about your brother."

Knowing the girl was warm and on her way back to sleep, he exited her room and moved down the empty hall. The clinic was noticeably silent—a stillness in the air that relaxed the doctor. It felt more like a nursery in his home than his place of work. He liked that and could see himself sleeping here.

Once at the patient's room, he stopped just shy of the door, held his ear close and listened. A fan hummed as it swirled the stale air around the room. All was quiet minus the light drumming of his heart.

Opening the room, he flicked on the light.

The young woman lifted her head and blinked the sleep out of her eyes. He moved closer, feeling the heat of arousal spin in his lower spine. She was gorgeous, alone, vulnerable, and scared. All the ingredients needed to take advantage and manipulate her into feeling like he was the only one who could save her.

He lowered himself down on the edge of her bed, the mattress sinking beneath his weight. Her brown doe eyes glistened beneath the bright lights as she stared and waited for him to speak.

The Guardian Angel glanced to the plate of food on the table next to her. It had barely been touched. The vitamins he had given her were still lying next to the juice box.

He frowned with disappointment and audibly sighed.

With a furrowed brow, he worried that his last remaining patient might have heard too much of what happened in the room next door.

"Is everything all right?" she asked him.

He chuckled and rolled his neck to face her. "Funny, I was going to ask you the same."

His gaze softened, along with his voice. He watched her respond with an empathetic grin before casting her gaze to her hands. "I was just..." Her words trailed off and tumbled over the edge into oblivion.

He knew she was going to say *scared*. What she heard earlier couldn't be suppressed. He did what he could to manage the situation but there was only so much he could do before the loud wails seeped through the thick walls. Lucky for him, there was only one patient left—*her*—and now she would receive his complete, undivided attention to ensure his baby boy was born healthy and strong.

"Scared?" he asked.

The woman raised her eyes and nodded once.

"I apologize for not coming to check on you sooner, but there was an issue with the breaker box that needed my immediate attention," he lied.

After a moment of silence, she lifted her head and asked, "Have you heard from my parents? It isn't like them to not respond to my calls."

"I'm sorry, but I haven't."

She tucked her hair behind her ear, turned her head, and visibly tensed as she stared across the room with a wrinkled brow.

"I'll keep trying," the Guardian Angel said.

"I tried watching the news but there were only movie channels available."

He stared into her beautiful eyes, getting lost in the

sparkle of fear exploding with each new admission to her feelings of terror. "It's the package the clinic purchased."

"And where is my phone? Do you really expect me to stay cooped up here inside this small room for the next two months without it?"

The Guardian Angel slid his hand beneath her gown and reached for her bare thigh. She shivered against his invasive touch. Gripping her leg tightly between his fingertips, a radiant heat zipped up his arm and hitched his breath. He stroked her soft tissue with his thumb, feeling his swelling arousal grow. "Don't worry, sweetheart, as long as you're with me, you're in good hands."

CHAPTER FORTY-NINE

ALLISON WAS BORED OUT OF HER MIND. PATTY WAS DOING a perfect job keeping the business going while Allison was cooped up, but she was ready to take the helm and get back to doing what she loved.

Allison ate what she was given, if only to pass the time. The food tasted like cardboard and she was tired of walking the halls that didn't sleep, traveling in an endless circle until her ankles swelled. She was more than ready to pack up her bags and hitch a ride home when she suddenly stopped surfing the channels.

Her lips parted as she turned up the volume.

She listened to Chief Watts's speech, taking note of the names and the incident he described. It was the same man Allison knew Samantha had on her list of suspects when going after the missing women, but she felt her heart stall in her chest when she heard the name Cameron Dee and what the police were accusing her boyfriend, Tyler Lopez, of doing to her baby.

Allison covered her mouth to stifle her gasp when learning what happened to Cameron.

Was Samantha right about Cameron's mother having an affair with Tyler Lopez? Could it be this simple? What about the other women and their babies?

A shiver worked its way out from her core. Allison was sickened by the thought of a baby being cut from a mother's womb. She closed her eyes and shook the image out of her head.

Feeling completely helpless, Allison was antsier than ever. She wanted to do something—wanted to help Samantha with her investigation—when suddenly she received a call from her friend.

"I was just thinking about you," Allison answered.

"Ali, I need your help," Samantha said.

"Anything. But please tell me you're going to bring me dinner now that the police have labeled a suspect in your case?"

"Don't believe what Chief Watts said," Sam shot back. Allison's eyes widened. "It's all for show, Ali, and I'm certain the police have this investigation all wrong."

Allison's mind raced to keep up with Samantha's fast talk. "You mean Tyler Lopez didn't do it?"

"Exactly. Look, I don't have time to explain. I'm here outside the press conference and reporters are chomping at the bit to be the first to break something big."

"Whatever you need, I'm ready."

"I was hoping you would say that." Samantha's tone lightened.

Allison felt her closed lips tug to her ears, happy to accept a new project to take her mind off of being cooped up like a chicken inside a cage she couldn't get out of.

"I need to know how to erase a video from an Instagram account, and fast." Samantha told her whose account it was and the importance of getting rid of the video on Tyler's account. "You can hack it, right?"

"Sam, everyone in the state of Colorado is looking for Tyler." Allison glanced to the closed door and dropped her voice down to a whisper. "I'm not about to hack into an account everyone is already searching."

"Ali, I need this."

Allison sucked back a deep breath of air. "Tell me about the video."

Allison already knew about the alleged affair between Ms. Dee and Tyler, but she didn't know about the video confirming it. Samantha described it with enough detail for Allison to be sure Ms. Dee would suffer immense public shame if it got out. "I don't care about Tyler. But if the media learns that Ms. Dee is on that video with him, they'll slaughter her before the world has a chance to learn about Cameron and her missing baby."

Allison debated her response. She understood Samantha's angle and, when she began to think that Cameron's baby might still be alive, she said, "I have an idea."

"Thank you," Samantha breathed. "I owe you one."

Ending the call, Allison set her phone down by her side and reached for her laptop. Her fingers went to work and soon she was on Tyler's Instagram feed. Allison found the video and watched it to make sure it was the post Samantha requested be taken down. Then she reported the content as inappropriate, knowing the exact language to use to gain the attention of the company's moderators. After her response was written, she pressed 'send' and crossed her fingers, hoping her plan would work.

Suddenly, a knock on her door brought her back to the present.

Dr. Pico stepped inside Allison's room and frowned when seeing her behind her computer, working. "You really should be resting," he said.

"I would really like to go home." Allison closed her computer.

"And you will. Soon. Have you given any more thought to the clinical trial we discussed?"

Allison thought about what Susan said, the miracle she witnessed at the conference, but also thought about why she wasn't talking to Benjamin. "I have."

"And?"

"I'm not sure I'm ready yet."

"It's perfectly natural to have your doubts. And you have time. You haven't shown any symptoms yet."

"Be honest with me, Doctor, what are the risks associated with this type of therapy?"

"There is always the chance your body will reject the therapy and it won't work."

"And if it does work? Besides never having Huntington's Disease, I mean?"

"We don't know how it would affect any offspring."

Allison burst out laughing. "That would mean actually having a love life," she joked.

"Perhaps I'm not the most qualified candidate to be explaining this to you. I'd like for you to speak with a fertility doctor—"

"Whoa." Allison's hand shot up from her side. "No need. I'm already 40. I don't see myself becoming a mother in the near future, if ever. I guess I can at least go ahead and put my name on the trial list."

"That's great." The doctor smiled. "But I'd still like you to know the complete risks even if you're adamant about not having children. It's worth speaking with a specialist, and I think you'll find what he has to say very interesting."

"Fine," Allison conceded. "You connect me with the fertility doctor and, in the meantime, let's organize my release papers so I can finally go home."

"Very well." The doctor's eyes glimmered. "His name is Dr. Glenn Wu, and he's the best that there is on the subject of CRISPR gene therapy. I'll put a call in to him now and see if he's available to speak with you first thing tomorrow morning."

CHAPTER FIFTY

AN HOUR LATER, I WAS BACK AT PRESBYTERIAN ST. LUKE'S Medical Center and stepping into the visitor's lounge when I spotted Erin's blonde hair glowing in a dark corner. She was sitting cross-legged and alone, swiping her thumbs over the screen of her phone. I wondered where Ms. Dee was and how she was handling the tornado of the last couple of hours.

"How is Cameron?" I asked as I fell into the seat next to Erin.

Erin turned her head and looked me in the eye. "Considering what she's lived through? Really great."

"Are we allowed to see her?"

Erin nodded and stood. "Follow me."

We didn't have much time. I knew a team of detectives would be arriving soon to begin questioning Cameron, and I needed to get a statement from her before we were cut off for good, left to pick up only crumbs.

"Sam," Erin leaned into my shoulder as we strode down the hall, "I don't feel right about how the police are going about this."

I didn't either.

"Someone knew that we spoke to Tyler," Erin whispered softly into my ear, not wanting our conversation to be overhead.

"Detective Campbell saw us there."

"Did you see him at the press conference?"

"How could I not?" I said, thinking about how he prominently placed himself next to the mayor—perfectly framed to get his mug on TV. "King said Mayor Goldberg wants this story to end now, and that the chief called a meeting to tell everyone working the case to do what they had to do to make an arrest."

"So it's not even about the facts."

I frowned and shook my head. "Apparently not, but Tyler did give them a way out when he decided to flee."

Erin stared at the floor as we walked. She was quiet for a moment as she gathered her thoughts. "Campbell saw us at Tyler's house, and then Cameron is placed there to make it look like he had something to do with her attack."

I knew what Erin was thinking, but I wasn't convinced Campbell was involved in these crimes. His angle was only to give himself and the mayor a win. "Is that what Cameron is saying happened?"

Erin shook her head.

"I don't take Campbell to be a dirty cop—"

"Just an asshole."

I smiled. "But someone knew about Tyler and Cameron's relationship; how else would they have known to place her inside his house?"

Erin hit the brakes and locked her gaze on mine. "We can't let Tyler go down for this if it wasn't him."

"I know. But why did he run?" I still had my doubts. Even if I didn't believe Tyler was responsible for what happened to Cameron, he knew too much to be completely innocent.

Erin stopped at the desk and logged both of us in. The security door opened and we were escorted to Cameron's room. As soon as we arrived, Ms. Dee stood from her chair and approached us with arms folded across her chest.

As I gauged Ms. Dee's body language, I thought about Allison and the video of Ms. Dee and Tyler. It wasn't worth warning Ms. Dee what I feared might happen if it was discovered. Journalists dug into everything when trying to piece together a story. I was guilty of turning over stones as much as anybody else. The only difference was that some of us reporters had integrity while others did not. It was those few bad apples I most feared because they were often also the reporters who had nothing to lose and everything to gain.

Before we got too far, Ms. Dee warned us about Cameron feeling especially vulnerable after what had happened to her. And who could blame her? We needed to establish trust and get her talking quick. Not easy to do.

"She's terrified her baby might be dead," Ms. Dee whispered to us.

"Does she recall what happened?" I asked.

Ms. Dee shook her head. "Her memory seems a bit fuzzy."

"She's been through a lot. It's going to take some time."

Ms. Dee turned to her daughter and stepped back into the room. "Cameron, honey. Some friends of mine are here to ask you some questions."

We approached, taking small hesitant steps as Ms. Dee explained that she recruited us to help find her when she went missing. I introduced myself and told her who we were. Cameron looked like a mother who had just given birth and then was immediately hit by a bus. But beneath the droopy eyes and purple bruises, it was easy to see her natural beauty.

"Where is my baby?" Cameron flicked her watery eyes between Erin and me.

Her pleas chipped away at my heart as I stood there with my legs rooting themselves into the floor. No one expected her to live. She'd been left to die, just like Kate. Yet she lived to tell the tale. As Cameron kept calling out for her baby, I couldn't decide if that was a good thing or not.

"Do you know where my baby is?" Cameron asked me.

Ms. Dee fought back her own tears as she gripped her daughter's hand and asked her listen to what we'd come to say.

"Someone took my baby," Cameron sobbed into her mother's shoulder.

Tightening my armor, I steeled myself against feeling too deeply about what happened to Cameron and the other young women. Finding Cameron alive was the break in the case we had all been hoping for and I wasn't about to let it go to waste.

"We'd like to ask you some questions to piece together the last four days," I said. "Can you do that for us?"

Cameron wiped her cheeks and nodded.

"Let's work backwards. They found you at Tyler Lopez's house unconscious," I reminded her.

"That's what everyone keeps saying."

"But you don't remember?"

Cameron shook her head and I believed her. She reached for her womb as if forgetting her baby was no longer there. Her brow furrowed and the air around us went still.

I felt bad for her. All she had left was a scar to remind her of the trauma she'd endured and the continuing worry of not knowing whether her baby was dead or alive.

"But you do know who Tyler Lopez is, right?" Erin lifted her pen off her small notepad.

Cameron nodded and shared a knowing glance with her mother.

"May I see?" I asked, pointing to her stomach.

Cameron rolled up her hospital gown and revealed the suture. The line ran parallel to her pelvic bone and was a cesarean just like Erin said the doctor stated. Cameron got lucky—even if whoever did this to her wanted her to die.

"Is it okay if I take a couple photos?"

Cameron gave me the go-ahead and I snapped a quick collage for the story I wanted to publish on my website—knowing Dawson would never approve this for the paper, even if he wanted me to write tomorrow's headline.

"Let's back up," I said, watching Cameron unroll her gown and cover herself back up. "Tell us what you do remember. Like when you first learned you were pregnant."

Cameron's story unfolded like any first-time mother-to-be —the rollercoaster of emotion of thinking you were pregnant; the fear of not knowing how you were going to afford to give this child a life they deserved. I knew those feelings well. But where Cameron's story diverged from my own was when she told me it started with her wanting to get an abortion.

"You knew you were pregnant?"

Cameron picked at her nails without looking up. "I was trying to prevent it."

"By having an abortion?"

"I had unprotected sex and wasn't on birth control." Her eyes swept up to her mother. An apologetic look that said *I know, it was stupid*. "So I went to see about getting a morning after pill."

"And where did you seek emergency contraception?"

"Mile High Health Clinic."

I shared a quick glance with Erin as Cameron went on to explain how she got what she needed and was told to come back for follow-up. She was initially relieved when it seemed her cycle came. But it was too light to be normal. She hoped it was just from the morning after pill. But when she went back for her follow-up appointment for bloodwork and an ultrasound, her excitement was shattered by the devastating news she received.

"They confirmed what a part of me already knew." Cameron's eyes were back on her fidgeting hands.

"You were pregnant?"

"Yes." Cameron's face twisted as she began to cry.

"And Tyler was the father?" I asked, watching Ms. Dee's expression harden.

Cameron picked at her bed sheets. "He's the only one it could have been."

"Why did you choose Mile High Health Clinic?" I asked.

"Their services are free."

I stood there thinking about everything her mother had shared when we were still looking for Cameron. The financial burden, the fear of having to give up the life she knew. It was all lining up but I was stuck on the timing of when she got pregnant.

"Your mom said you responded to an ad online. Can you tell us about that?"

Cameron shook her head. "It wasn't an ad."

I felt my eyebrows knit.

"It was a referral given to me by the physician's assistant at Mile High Health Clinic."

Erin stepped forward. "What exactly was the referral?"

Cameron flicked her eyes to Erin. "I was just told to visit the website and put in my application for financial assistance and medical services. The PA said that he would put a good word in for me and he knew that I needed help."

Ms. Dee tilted her chin down and frowned. She was clearly disappointed that her daughter refused her help throughout this journey.

"After you applied, how long did it take for you to hear back?"

"Not long. A week or two."

"And where did it take you?"

Cameron bit the edge of her lip as she thought about it. "I wish I had my purse with me. The card I was given is inside. But I think the organization was called the Guardian Angel." She rolled her eyes up to mine and shrugged. "Something like that."

Cameron gave us the location of the clinic and Erin jotted it down. We locked eyes and I knew she was also thinking we had struck gold. "Do you remember the physician's name you saw?"

"That was the surprise." Cameron tipped her head back and stared. "I do remember his name because it was the same name of the PA at MHHC."

I tilted my head to one shoulder and felt my body freeze.

"His name was Dr. Cherub, and he's the one who called me the other day requesting I come to the clinic."

"He called you? Why?"

Cameron inhaled a deep breath of air. She stared at her thighs, looking as if her complete memory was coming back to her. "He said he had found something in my charts that needed immediate attention."

"Did you ask if he could tell you over the phone?"

Cameron shook her head. "I was in the area. I didn't think it was a big deal. But when I arrived, he made me stay for observation. I was so scared something was wrong with my baby."

"Did you tell anyone you were there?"

"No," Cameron said in a whispery tone.

"What did Dr. Cherub tell you was wrong?"

Cameron shook her head. "I couldn't repeat his exact

words. But I only saw him occasionally. It was his assistant who made sure that I had everything I needed."

"What was his name?"

"I can't remember."

"And did you have everything you needed?"

"No." Tears pooled in Cameron's eyes. "They took everything from me. My phone, my clothes, and wouldn't let me leave even after I asked to go."

The hair on the back of my neck stood. My mind was churning with possibilities to why these doctors were abusing their powers and why they targeted Cameron. Women were getting kidnapped and killed, but for what? "Did these men deliver your baby?"

"I don't know." Her chin quivered. "My water broke just after I made a phone call to Tyler."

"You called Tyler?" My voice shot to the ceiling with surprise. "From whose phone?"

"I was scared and alone. I wanted someone to know where I was but they wouldn't let me. One day I was able to steal the nurse's phone when she wasn't looking."

"And did Tyler answer?"

Cameron lowered her gaze and shook her head.

I was afraid all this had happened when we were sitting Tyler down to talk. A sharp pang of guilt twisted my side when I asked if there was anyone else at the clinic with her.

"I never saw anyone, but I always had a feeling that I wasn't alone."

"What made you think that?"

"It was the way the staff worked, what I heard them say. Patient in Room 1. Room 2. You get the idea."

I brought my phone from my pocket and was about to bring up photos of Kate Wilson and Tracey Brown with hopes of Cameron identifying them as being at the clinic when suddenly a heavy knock pounded on the door behind us.

I turned my head and knew immediately that we were finished. Our time was up.

"That's enough, you two," Detective Campbell said in an authoritative voice. "Cameron Dee is officially a material witness. Any further questions directed toward her and I'll arrest you for witness tampering."

CHAPTER FIFTY-ONE

"That's fine, I'll wait." King leaned back in his chair after being put on hold.

He was waiting to receive word from Sam on Cameron's status. Checking his cell phone, there was still no message. He knew she had a short window of opportunity to crack Cameron before Detective Campbell put a stop to her questioning. King had messaged her as soon as he knew Campbell was on his way, but he never got a message back.

The music played loudly in his ear and his knee bounced with impatience.

King feared that Samantha had been right in saying the press conference would have the opposite effect of what Mayor Goldberg and Chief Watts had hoped. Instead of easing the public's anxiety, it had only heightened their fears. A monster was not only loose and hiding in the community they called home, but now everyone had a face to go along with their nightmares.

Next to King, Alvarez kept taking calls of sightings of Tyler Lopez. It was a witch hunt. Though experience told them most calls would lead to nowhere, they had to take each one seriously and treat them all as if it was the needle in the haystack they were looking for.

After several minutes of waiting, the line finally clicked over. "Detective King, I'm afraid there is no record of your request."

King tipped forward, bringing his elbows to his desktop. "Are you sure about that?"

"I've doubled checked everything you mentioned. The case files are either not here or have been suppressed by the judge."

King stared at nothing in particular as he tried to make sense of what he was being told. He was busy trying to locate both the judge and the docket of the court filing Joshua Zinn shared about the Browns going to trial, the hearing that was supposed to have begun yesterday.

"Suppressed by the judge?" King asked.

"It's the only conclusion I can think of, besides it not existing at all."

King thanked the county clerk and set the phone back in its cradle before shoving his hand through his thick head of hair. This threw him for a loop. Either Mr. Zinn had been mistaken, or the clerk was right about the case being suppressed. But if it was, why?

King drummed his fingers on top of his desk.

There was only one course of action to take, and he and Alvarez could do it tonight. King knew just what to do.

He rolled his chair back and turned to his partner. "Want to take a ride?"

Alvarez reeled his hand away from the phone and tucked it back against his side. "Anything to quit working these phones. What did you have in mind?"

King wagged his head toward the exit and stood. Alvarez took his sport jacket from the back of his chair and followed. On the way to the car, King explained what the county clerk said about there being no record of the Browns' civil trial being scheduled for yesterday.

"It doesn't make sense. Why would Joshua lie about that?"

"I don't think he did," King said.

"Did you mention you were investigating a homicide?"

"Only a judge can open up those files. It doesn't matter what we're investigating."

"So, what, you think that Keith Brown has something about the trial in his home office?"

King stopped at his car door and gave Alvarez a knowing look. "It's worth a look." Alvarez paused. King recognized that face. "What?" he asked.

"Unless whoever murdered him already got to it."

The thought had already crossed King's mind, and now he was thankful the ME had ruled their death a homicide. If she hadn't, they might never have learned about the trial in the first place.

Not more than fifteen minutes passed before King curbed their unmarked sedan in front of the Browns' house in the Congress Park neighborhood. There was no barking dog, no neighbors standing on their front porches. It was quiet. And King preferred their visit to remain so.

At the door, the detectives logged in and gained access to the house still marked off with crime scene tape. Marching straight to the home office, they scoured the bookshelves and pulled open the desk drawers. It didn't take long for King to find a name that drew his interest.

"Look," he said.

Alvarez lifted his gaze and stared.

"Notes from Keith's lawyer."

Alvarez stepped to the desk and cast his gaze to where King was pointing. "Looks like Keith was taking this trial seriously. But is there a complaint?"

King went back to searching Keith's desk. "Not that I see. But the name Dr. Glenn Wu is mentioned heavily."

"Joshua said Keith was suing a doctor."

King scoured the notes, flipping the pages as he read. "Here. Phanes Biotechnology."

"Doesn't ring a bell."

"It's Dr. Wu's company," King explained, never once taking his eyes off the paper he was holding, "and this trial was over an apparent breach of contract."

Alvarez rested his tailbone on the edge of the desk and took the paper from King's grip. Together they dove into the finer details of the many pages of notes they had found. The room fell silent as anticipation grew.

"Here it is," King said, explaining that, according to the paper, Keith was an early investor in Dr. Wu's gene technology.

"Gene technology?"

King nodded once, explained as best he could, and continued reading. "Then, at some point, Wu backed out of their contract stating moral reasons for his departure. Feeling cheated, Keith knew that without Wu, he would eventually lose big on his investment."

"Okay, so Brown sued Dr. Wu over a contract because he didn't receive the riches he thought he was promised."

King raised his eyebrows.

"Then who is Dr. Wu?"

"More importantly, was this a dispute worth kidnapping Keith and Pam or killing Tracey for?" King certainly thought so.

Alvarez scrubbed a hand over his face and murmured, "I suppose we'll just have to ask him and see where he was the night the Browns were killed."

CHAPTER FIFTY-TWO

THE NEWSROOM WAS QUIET—ONLY THOSE WORKING WITH tight deadlines remaining—as I kept trying to get the search engines to dig up the Guardian Angel's clinic website when King asked me to join him for dinner.

I wasn't sure dinner was the best use of our time, but I was starving. And, besides, King said he had found something I needed to hear.

As I walked to my car, I couldn't stop hearing the grave tone in his voice. It told me everything I needed to know— whatever he'd found was big. My entire body was wound tight as if sensing the danger waiting for me around the next turn, and King's call only pulled the knot tighter.

He met me at a little hole in the wall Thai restaurant near Sloan's Lake that served the most authentic Thai in the greater Denver area. It was my request, but King didn't put up a fight.

I still hadn't pinned down what angle I was going to give to the story Dawson needed. There were a couple different angles I could take, neither of which I liked. As soon as I stepped inside from the cold, the spices floating in the air heated me right up and I left my work worries at the door.

King was sipping off a Tiger beer when I joined him at a table pushed against the back wall.

"Did you get your questions in before Campbell arrived?" King asked me as I shed my coat.

I grabbed his hand and leaned my body across the table to plant a kiss on him. "Good to see you, too."

"I'm sorry. You're right." He pressed his lips against mine. "I should have saved the shop talk for later."

I ordered a beer—the same as King's—and an appetizer to go along with it. We took our minds away from work, flirted, laughed, and talked about Allison's difficult future if the gene therapy didn't work as we casually sipped down our beers. I spoke about Mason and King's planned trip to the mountains. We ate a spicy—yet delicious—meal that left me feeling like I got more than my money's worth. The ambience of the place wasn't spectacular, and the room was small and noisy, but it was my kind of place—an eatery where we could blend in and feel like we'd left the country if only for a couple of hours. Then the inevitable came and it was back to discussing the case.

King swiped through the photos of Cameron's wounds. "Jesus," he said deadpan.

"Her doctor said there was no way a kitchen knife—like the one found in Tyler's house—could have made this cut. It was done by a professional."

King lowered the phone and swept his heavy gaze to me. "She was left for dead."

"But Tyler found her." I stared, hoping King would give me clues into what the department knew that I didn't. He only stared back so I said, "Campbell threatened to arrest me for witness tampering if I spoke to Cameron again."

"He's only trying to intimidate you."

"Why can't he see that I'm trying to help?"

"Campbell is dense. He wants what you have."

I turned my head and stared out the window for a minute, not wanting to make tonight about Campbell. *What did I have that he didn't?*

Rolling my neck back to King, I said, "Cameron didn't respond to an online ad like her mother thought."

King quirked an eyebrow.

"It was a referral to a website from a physician's assistant at Mile High Health Clinic."

King slid forward on his elbows. His brow furrowed as he squinted his intelligent eyes at me. "Promising money and medical services?"

I nodded. "Cameron couldn't remember exactly what the URL was, but thought the clinic was called something along the lines of Guardian Angels."

King shook his head and said he'd never heard of it. "Kate's father thought his daughter found a doctor at MHHC she really liked and was certain it was there she was convinced not to have an abortion."

My eyes shot to King's face. Blood rushed through my pounding heart and I couldn't dampen the jolt of excitement for finally having facts to work with. We were getting close—closing in on who was taking the missing women. It felt good to finally be making progress.

I shared what little I knew from my own research that both Erin and I had gathered from our phones. "Cameron mentioned a Dr. Cherub, cherub being another word for—"

"Angel."

"Yes," I whispered not at all surprised by King's quickness. "Coincidence?"

"You think it's a made-up name?"

"Seems likely." Neither of us knew if Dr. Cherub was the one Kate saw, but that, too, also seemed likely.

"Were you able to find the clinic's website?"

My spine curled as I slumped in my chair. "No, and not because I don't think it exists, because I do. I just think it hasn't been indexed in the search engine results pages."

"Strange, considering it's being sold as a service to assist the community."

"I thought so, too. But wouldn't you want to hide your tracks if you're only recruiting certain women?"

"So whoever is doing this is smart enough to make their operation seem like it's open to all, but clever enough to only provide the information they want to share to a select few."

King was breaking down my thoughts exactly. "Precisely. From what we know about these women, they would never refuse to accept an offer promising so much when each of them had so little to begin with."

"Except Tracey." King's deep voice floated across the table. "She had access to resources Kate and Cameron didn't have."

"But here is where it gets even more interesting," I said, telling him about Kristi Patterson's story and how she believed someone at North Denver Reproductive Medicine had messed with her embryo.

King lifted his bottle of beer but it was empty. He set it down, and I could tell he was lost in thought. Something was on his mind. I asked myself if he could be holding something back.

"I haven't had time to visit that clinic, if that's what you're thinking," I said, remembering the conversation we'd had immediately after the press conference.

King gave me a hesitant look before dropping his voice down to a whisper. "What I'm about to tell you, you can't tell anybody else. Understand?"

I nodded my head in agreement, asking myself if he

meant Erin, too. I assumed he didn't, but I'd rather ask for forgiveness than for permission.

His eyes swayed along with mine. "And it has to be completely off record."

"I promise," I said, feeling my arm muscles flex as I leaned in closer.

King told me about his visit to First Bank and that it was there he talked to Keith Brown's colleague about a civil case the Browns were involved in. I felt my jaw unhinge when learning their deaths happened the day before their trial was supposed to have begun.

"They *were* murdered," I said under my breath.

"Made to look like a suicide." King wet his lips and glanced around the room, making sure no one was eavesdropping. "But there was no record the trial ever existed. Even the county clerk couldn't find anything about it when I called."

My stomach sank, and suddenly it all came back to me. The suppressed court case I'd missed yesterday and the other trials crossed out in secrecy. King had been right about treating the Browns' death as a homicide, but the examiner got it wrong in thinking it had been something as simple as a drug overdose. This was no longer about going after a street drug dealer to please the upper brass, but something much bigger.

"So, Alvarez and I went back to the Browns' house and found evidence to prove that the trial did in fact exist. Whoever killed them must not have known about the papers Keith's lawyer supplied to get him ready for trial. I can't imagine this is about anything other than what was going to be revealed during the hearing."

"Who was the complaint against?" I asked, thinking about the whereabouts of Tracey.

"The founder of Phanes Biotechnologies, Dr. Glenn Wu."

King briefed me on what the company did and how Wu was a fertility doctor. "Apparently, it was over a breach of contract."

I had about a dozen questions ready to fly off the tip of my tongue when King told me more about the details of the case. When he was finished, I asked, "When did the Browns and Wu part ways?"

King's shoulders hit the back of his chair. "According to the records we found, four years ago."

"Tommy Patterson," I murmured. And when I saw the look of confusion on King's face I said, "That was about the time he would have been conceived at North Denver Reproductive Medicine."

"You think Dr. Wu is Tommy's biological father?"

"Does he work there?"

King nodded. "I thought you knew."

I shook my head and cast my gaze to the table with the pressure in my head pounding. This trial provided motive to kidnap Tracey and murder the Browns, but it didn't explain how Kate and Cameron fit into the puzzle. Either way, I kept coming back to the same conclusion—Dr. Glenn Wu was guilty of something.

"It's not that easy, Sam."

"C'mon King." I pressed my palms flat into the table when leaning forward. "I know you see it, too. You said it yourself—Wu stopped his research claiming moral reasons right about the time Tommy was conceived. Everything we know is pointing at him. We *have* to question him."

"And we will. Planning to do it first thing in the morning. But it's too late to do anything tonight."

I checked the time. My adrenaline spiked. King was right. It was too late to knock on doors without an arrest warrant. We didn't know if Dr. Wu was guilty, but it was the closest thing we had to identifying a suspect we could work with.

"He does business here." King turned his palms up and reached for my hands. "He's not going anywhere."

I settled my hands inside of his and his embrace was warm and inviting but I couldn't stop thinking about Tracey. Imagining her all alone and scared left me feeling cold. She was still out there somewhere—dead or alive—and I was determined to know what happened to her before she met the same fate as Cameron.

King squeezed my hand and, by the look he was giving me, I knew he wanted me to go home with him. But I couldn't. I had other things planned and it was a secret I couldn't even tell him about. Even if it meant putting myself in danger.

CHAPTER 53: MOST WANTED

Susan was feeling apprehensive about her dinner with Benjamin. Since yesterday's conference and Benjamin's refusal to even consider meeting Dr. Glenn Wu, a chasm had opened up between them. They'd still spent the night in Boulder but it wasn't as romantic as Susan had hoped. Now she wasn't sure what their date would bring, but she was ready to find out.

Benjamin picked her up in his Toyota 4Runner and together they headed up the hill to a top-notch seafood restaurant in Genesee. Perched on top of a hill overlooking the city, they sipped white wine and stared at the twinkling lights below. They were a sea of stars. It was a magnificent distraction to remind Susan that despite their differences in opinion, Benjamin was still the man she had her eye on.

Susan keep the mood light and talked over an incredible meal as fresh as the ocean. Benjamin looked fantastic in his three-piece suit and Susan was never one to shy away from wearing her best. They flirted and laughed and spoke little about work until finally the hours passed and the inevitable arrived as soon as their plates had been cleared.

"How is Allison doing?" Benjamin asked sincerely.

Susan cast her gaze to her glass. "She's receiving genetic counseling."

"She's lucky they found the gene now, before there were any symptoms. It's still tough to swallow, but her prognosis is hopeful."

Susan knew Benjamin was right. Allison was one of the strongest women Susan knew, and selfless, too—never one to put the spotlight on her personal struggles. She also knew Allison might be masking her emotional struggles and putting on a strong face.

Susan lifted her gaze and locked her eyes on Benjamin's. "She's on the list for CRISPR gene therapy. Just like Dr. Wu was talking about yesterday."

Benjamin nodded. "Gene editing," he corrected her. "The goal is to target and correct the mutation in the single gene that causes Huntington's Disease. If it works, it could save her life."

Susan cocked her head to one shoulder and gave him a look that said, *Really? Now you're all for it? What's with this guy?*

"What?" Benjamin grinned. "Did I say something wrong?"

"No." Susan tucked her hands beneath the table. "Now you just seem to be for the same technology you were resisting yesterday."

She felt herself getting heated over something small. They should have talked through their argument yesterday but had avoided it instead. Now she felt silly for continuing the disagreement that should have ended the day it started.

"This is different," Benjamin said.

"How is this different than the couple looking to edit their embryo?"

Benjamin leaned back and looked to his left. Susan watched his jaw muscle bulge. Was it annoyance or frustration? She couldn't decide.

Lowering his voice, Benjamin turned back to Susan and said, "Correcting a gene to a disease like Allison's is good medicine."

"And in fertility it's not?" Susan lengthened her spine.

"The ethics of that same medicine begins to take on a different shape when a scientist pushes the boundaries of what is possible with an undeveloped embryo who has no say in the matter."

"But if the baby who is to grow from that embryo is susceptible to a disease—like cancer—or another life alternating illness, are we supposed to sit back and ignore it even when we have the tools and science to fix it?"

Benjamin's face tightened as he stared. "Maybe I'm not making myself clear."

Susan leaned back, crossed her legs at the knee, and tucked her hands deep inside her armpits. "No, I don't believe you are."

"My fear is not that a doctor will ignore the science or not make use of the tools he has available to treat illnesses. This technology is incredibly powerful, and with it comes great responsibility." Benjamin paused and sighed as he carefully chose his next words. His eyes were back on Susan when he continued. "My fear is that a research scientist will take the application of CRISPR too far and begin creating designer babies according to the parents' desires."

A pensive expression filled Susan's face. The thought had never crossed her mind, and now she was beginning to understand the ethical challenges attached.

"Blue eyes? No problem." Benjamin's hand waved through the air. "Want to ensure your boy is over six feet? Done. Muscular? We can do that, too."

Susan was beginning to see his point. She felt awful for the way she'd been treating him. "But why couldn't you have said this before?"

"Because I needed to make sure it wasn't already happening."

Susan's lips parted as a tiny gasp escaped her chest. "It isn't. It can't be." Susan reached for her pearl necklace and felt her brow crease with sudden worry. "Nobody in their right mind would take such risks."

A condescending smile tugged on Benjamin's mouth. "Darling, I wish I could say you're right. But I'm afraid that designer babies are already a reality."

"Why haven't I heard about this? If what you're saying is true, this would be big news."

Benjamin brought his elbows to the table and leaned forward. Staring at Susan beneath a furrowed brow, he asked, "Have you heard of a company named Phanes Biotechnology?"

Susan felt the blood leave her checks as she shook her head.

"Well, you should have." A glimmer sparkled in his eye. "After all, the founder of that company floated the idea several years back."

"What happened? Did a baby ever get designed?"

"That's just it; as soon as the idea was presented, the founder received immediate backlash within the medical, religious, and scientific communities. The door was quickly shut after that. Then, everything went quiet—which is what makes me suspicious."

"Who was the founder?" Susan's pulse ticked hard as she suspected she might already know the answer.

Benjamin's eyes widened. "Dr. Glenn Wu."

Susan took a sip of her wine to relieve her suddenly dry mouth. "What happened? Did the research go underground?"

"That's what I don't know."

"You didn't know any of this before the conference?"

"Didn't have reason to."

"But we heard Dr. Wu speak. There was no mention of Phanes Biotechnology." Susan played with her hair, shocked into disbelief.

"And we heard him highlight his work with embryos." Benjamin nodded.

Susan's gaze went distant as she thought back to their invitation to meet the man Benjamin now suspected of paving the way to living in a world where parents decided what kind of children they would have. She couldn't help but feel like they may have dodged a bullet. But, at the same time, her curiosity had been piqued.

"And you still think the conference was one big publicity stunt?" Susan asked.

Benjamin rolled his shoulders back and nodded. "If Wu has the support of the scientific and medical community, he can soon change the narrative and begin opening the road to riches and fame."

Suddenly, Susan didn't feel so hot as she watched Benjamin pull out his phone.

"It all started here." Benjamin produced an image taken from the *Journal of the American Medical Association*. The photo was taken five years ago. "Tell me, does this look familiar?" He pointed to the right breast of a close up shot of Dr. Wu.

Susan took the phone between her fingers and brought the screen closer. There, pinned to his chest, was a silver angel. "No, I can't say it does."

"They all are wearing the same pin. Why?"

Susan moved her gaze across the photo. Dr. Wu was standing shoulder-to-shoulder with a couple dozen colleagues—all of them wearing the same angel pin. But, beyond the pin, it was the headline that captured Susan's full attention. Her mind raced as she wondered if this could be the man behind the missing babies Samantha was trying to find.

"I'll tell you why—" Benjamin's eyebrows flickered. "Because Dr. Wu is making a go at it again."

CHAPTER FIFTY-FOUR

KING KISSED ME GOODBYE BEFORE SAYING, "GO HOME, Sam. Get some rest. You look exhausted."

"Gee, thanks," I teased, running a single hand over my unruly hair. "Really, though, you look like you could use some sleep yourself."

King rolled his eyes. "Sleep isn't in my cards tonight."

The life of a detective wasn't much different than the life of an investigative reporter. We were always on the hunt for our next clue. Whether it be a murder suspect or a witness to crack open my next big story, neither of us got the sleep our bodies deserved.

"I'll call you tomorrow." King blew me one last kiss and headed to his car.

Standing near my Subaru Outback, I flicked my bangs out of my eyes and watched King drive away. I didn't mention my plans for the night because I didn't want to have to tell him the truth. It was better he thought I was going home—and eventually I would. But first I needed to check out the address Cameron said would take me to the Guardian Angel's clinic.

Tucking myself behind my steering wheel, I plugged the address into my cell phone's GPS. My heart was pounding hard in my chest as nerves reminded me of the potential dangers of what I was about to do. As soon as the location registered, I started the car and pointed the wheels east, driving toward the city of Aurora.

There was no record that this place even existed—or at least to what I could find. If it hadn't been for Cameron remembering the cross streets, I might not have had the chance to check it out myself.

The tires hummed as they bounced over the road.

The radio was off and I was lost in my thoughts.

All I could think about was how I hadn't connected Dr. Glenn Wu to the NDRM clinic and Phanes Biotechnologies. My sister had been inside the clinic where he worked. Could she have spoken to Dr. Wu? If so, was he the one to steer her toward becoming a surrogate mother? The thought alone left me short on breath.

When I wasn't thinking about Heather, I was thinking of little three-year-old Tommy. I knew I was falling into the trap of drawing conclusions I wanted to see without enough information. I hadn't been to NDRM or talked to Dr. Wu, yet my mind was going to dark places.

Fifteen minutes later I pulled into an empty parking lot, imagining the babies born to Kate and Cameron. It was important we didn't forget about their existence. I wanted to believe that if we could find Tracey, we could also find the babies.

I circled around the inconspicuous looking office buildings, scoping the place out before parking. It was another unremarkable strip mall, not the normal inviting feel of a clinic.

I parked in front and shined my headlights through the front glass doors. It was dark, just as it was in much of the offices nearby. But something about this place was different—like a business that didn't need to be advertised.

My cell phone started ringing and I jumped in my seat.

Catching my breath, I put one hand over my fluttering heart and turned my phone off.

I glanced back to the front doors and concentrated on my mission ahead. With my heart racing and my mind focused on confirming I was at the right place, I slid my phone into my jacket pocket and pulled the hood over my head before stepping out of the vehicle.

Wind swept between my legs as I glanced around and pulled the zipper up to my neck.

There was no one here; a few empty cars like my own, but that was it. I was alone.

A flurry of nerves shook my insides as I found it difficult to pick up my heavy feet and move toward the dark entrance. Time seemed to slow with each step. I listened to only my heart thrashing between my ears in a heavy rhythmic battle. This was a bad idea. I didn't have a good feeling. No matter how many times I wiped my palms on my thighs, they continued to pour with sweat.

Turn around now. Get out while you still can. The voice in my head pleaded for me to forget about it and come back another time—with Erin for backup.

Beneath the canopy, there was no lit-up sign. Just a blank glass door with a stenciled logo of an angel floating above the words *Your Guardian Angel Women's Health Clinic.*

I stared in disbelief. The lettering was so small I practically had to put my nose on the glass to read it. But I'd found it. Cameron was right.

Lifting my hand, I brushed the tips of my fingers over the letters as if needing to believe my eyes weren't imagining things that weren't really there. They were smooth and precise, etched into glass forever. It couldn't get any realer than this.

The hairs on the nape of my neck stood on end. Electricity was in the air and I had the strange feeling that I was being watched.

Slowly, I twisted my spine and glanced behind me.

It was the same sight as when I'd arrived. Nothing but my vivid imagination getting the best of me. I sucked back a deep breath of air to calm my raging nerves and turned back toward the glass.

I was only here to request more information if anybody asked. I was doing nothing wrong—not breaking any laws—but that wasn't what it felt like. Besides, how many walk-ins did a place like this get? Probably more than I suspected.

Cupping my hands over my eyes, I pressed my nose against the cold glass and peered through the window. Inside, I saw a front desk with nothing more than a single computer monitor on top. To the left, a closed wooden door that seemed to open up into the back.

A blinking red light caught my attention.

It was a security camera aimed directly at the entrance and, I assumed, my pretty face was also in the frame. There was another lens pointed at the closed door inside, and one more at the desk. It reminded me of one of the many marijuana dispensaries popping up around town, but without the skunky scent attached.

Suddenly, my heart stopped.

In the last corner for me to look there was a single and rather large pastel painting of an angel. The angel took the form of a man's body with broad expansive wings. His muscular torso was wrapped in a flowing white cloak as he hovered over two small children running through an open flowery pasture.

A chill zipped up my spine and caused me to shiver. The

place gave me the creeps. I couldn't stop hearing Cameron's cries as she asked where her baby was. Was the baby here? I certainly thought it could be possible.

I tried the door. It was locked.

Needing to know what hid behind that closed door, I edged the building and jogged around to the back. That door was locked, too. There were no windows to peek inside. Something was going on here—something that someone wanted to keep hidden in plain sight. I headed back to the front when suddenly a beam of headlights illuminated the back wall.

Without hesitation, I threw my shoulders against the bricks and hid in the shadow.

I held my breath and heard the car park, the engine turn off, and a pair of dress shoes clack their way to the entrance of the clinic. Keys jangled and I heard the lock click over. Peeling the back of my skull off the wall, I stretched my neck with hopes of seeing who'd arrived without risking being seen myself.

The door closed and I was too late.

But whoever had arrived certainly saw my car.

This is your chance, Sam. See who it is. Do it for Cameron, Kate, and Tracey. Take the risk if it means finding the babies.

With a surge of adrenaline, I bounded toward the door, only to find it locked. I glanced behind me at the parking lot. A white BMW was now parked next to me. When I peered back inside, the door leading to the back was now cracked open.

A beam of light shined bright and lit up a path through the front office.

Dancing back and forth on my toes, I tried to see what was hidden behind the door but I couldn't see anything. It was an eggshell white hall and nothing more. I heard myself curse when falling back on my heels. Then my eyes bugged when suddenly a figure stepped into the frame.

Everything stopped.

I froze and stared.

The figure did the same.

It was impossible to make out a face because of the way the shadows fell in front of him, but I knew it was a man. His shoulders were broad, his thighs spread in a strong stance, and I guessed him to easily be over six feet.

Slowly, I reached for my phone and pulled up the one number I knew would confirm whether or not this was where Cameron had been held.

With trembling fingers, I pressed the green call button to Cameron's cell phone without ever bringing it to my ear. Even while the phone was at my side, I could hear the line begin to fill the silent void surrounding me.

There was no noise coming from inside, but I held my breath and waited.

The man stared—frozen stiff like a statue, unsure how to respond to my presence.

Cameron's cell continued to ring. Somewhere, it was on— the battery hadn't died—but where was it?

Then, without warning, the man flung his head to the side as if hearing the phone ring somewhere in the back. Suddenly, the lights went out. He was gone. My time was up.

I sprinted back to my car and sped away, hoping to make it home without being followed by the man who now knew who I was.

CHAPTER FIFTY-FIVE

I IGNORED THE SHARP PAIN IN MY KNEES AS MY FEET pounded the pavement and ran faster. It was senseless. Impossible to get away from the demons that I felt were chasing after me. But I picked up my speed, pushed myself to go faster, and watched Cooper beat me to the house.

I joined him on the steps, bending over to grip my knees as I caught my breath. "Good run, boy," I said, patting his head as soon as the pain in my lungs subsided.

Cooper panted—the satisfied look in his eye saying he would now spend the remainder of the day curled up on the couch—and wagged his tail quietly back into the house.

After a thorough stretch and a hot shower, I was turning on the morning news and booting up my laptop when I received a message from Dawson.

Samantha, where the hell is my story?

"Shit," I said, dropping my face into my palm. I'd completely forgotten my headline. Now it was too late. Midnight had come and gone while I'd been beating myself up for not taking the plates of the BMW at the clinic.

The story I'm telling is still developing, I messaged back, thinking it was safer than getting on the phone. *Sorry for dropping the ball.*

I wasn't sure Dawson was going to forgive me for my mistake, but I didn't have time to dwell on it. Suddenly, the news anchor on the tube was updating the public about Tyler Lopez.

"The manhunt continues and the police are asking for any information that can lead to Mr. Lopez's arrest."

I shook my head and hit the mute button. The entire situation was absurd. Instead of making a hero out of one of his officers, Chief Watts was going to get a hard lesson on the length a person would go to win. Campbell was a fool to take the bait. Why did it seem like I was the only one who saw through this scam?

Turning to my computer, I navigated to Tyler's Instagram feed and searched for the video I'd asked Allison's help in getting removed. It was gone. I couldn't find it. A smile curled my lips as I said, "Ali, baby, you did it."

Then it was on to my next task of drafting up a public letter addressed to Tyler Lopez. I planned to publish this straight to my website—knowing it would be against Dawson's wishes—and share it to my social media feeds with the hopes that Erin and my audience would help spread the word. As for getting it in front of Tyler's eyes, I would send him a direct link through his Instagram account as soon as I was finished and pray my plan worked.

Tyler, if you happen to find yourself reading this, please surrender. My fingers worked the keys like a pianist. *Don't do it because you are guilty, but because I know the police have you mistaken. And I have the evidence to prove it.*

Over the next several paragraphs, I made my case. I included the photos of Cameron's scar, presented a hypothetical to what actually may have happened to lure Tyler to Cameron, and even pointed out that Tyler had been hosting a party when he received a call from an unknown number—a call from Cameron on the nurse's phone just before giving birth.

Tyler, I believe you were set up. Made to take the fall. As for who actually did this to Cameron, I know who you are and I'm coming for you. Sincerely, Samantha Bell.

I reeled my fingers away from the keyboard and crossed my arms. The house was quiet with Heather and Mason still asleep. I wasn't certain my plan would work, but I needed Tyler to know that he had at least one ally out there in a sea of nonbelievers.

But did I really know who was behind this? Or was I only telling myself I did?

Cooper groaned next to my foot and closed his eyes. The bright orb of sunlight rose over the eastern horizon when I hit publish.

There was no turning back now. I was publicly teaming up with Denver's Most Wanted.

I stood and made my way to the counter to make another pot of coffee when my mind wandered back to last night. All night I'd tossed and turned with visions of the shadowy figure at the clinic hovering over me. This investigation was getting dangerously close to the edge. I could feel it breathing down my neck when suddenly I was struck with a thought.

I hurried back to my computer and tried a couple different variations of the name stenciled on the glass leading into the fake clinic—*Your Guardian Angel Women's Health Clinic*—until finally, once again, I admitted defeat.

Had the website been taken down? Or was the domain so obscure and unrelated to what I knew that I couldn't decipher the code? I had nothing and wished I had a way to contact Cameron without detective Campbell ever finding out.

My chin hit my chest as I shoved my fingers through my hair and yanked at the roots.

"Sam," my sister's voice said softly from behind, "I'm sure I don't have to tell you what you already know, but you work too much."

Heather had her hair tied up on top of her head in a messy bun when she came into the kitchen with sleep in her eye. "It's just this story. I'm so close to breaking it wide open," I said, knowing my sister was referring to my late night and now my early morning.

Heather joined me at the table and stared like I was crazy.

"Thanks for watching Mason."

"No problem. We had fun until I couldn't pull him away from his video games." Heather rolled her eyes. "Do you always work this hard or are you really that afraid of losing your job?"

"Both," I admitted.

"I talked to Mom."

I closed the lid to my computer, my interest piqued. "Did you tell her about your plans to become a surrogate?"

Heather gave me an annoyed little sister look. "She's equally worried about you, Sam."

Of course Heather talked to Mom about me because I was the only one with problems. I rolled my eyes without her noticing.

Heather settled her chin inside her hand and propped her head up. She batted her long lashes at me with that queen bee look of thinking she was always right. "Your job is getting dangerous—"

"It's always been dangerous," I said, trying not to sound as annoyed as I felt.

"Journalism isn't what it used to be." Heather stared. "And Mom agrees."

"Which is why it's more important than ever," I argued. "You know, I looked up NDRM."

"Christ, Samantha." Heather fell back into her chair and groaned. She turned her head and sucked her bottom lip into her mouth. "You just won't allow me to make a decision on my own, will you?"

"You should hear what I have to say."

"Do you not trust I can make this decision by myself?"

"It's not that."

"Then tell me, Wise One, what is it?"

"I wasn't following up because of you. I started looking more into it because of a call that came to Erin." Heather snapped her lips shut and I proceeded to sum up our visit with the Pattersons.

"And have you confirmed whether or not their suspicions are true? Did a doctor at NDRM use his own seed for Tommy?"

"We're working on it. But there is another link to the story that has also brought our attention to the same clinic."

"Care to share what that is?"

"I'd rather not." I felt the cords in my neck tense. "But who did you talk to there?"

Heather splayed her fingers and looked at her nails. "I don't recall."

"Was it Dr. Glenn Wu?"

Heather pursed her lips and shook her head. "I don't think so." She paused. "Sam, I've made my decision."

I felt my jaw clench, stifling the impulsive reaction I felt bubbling up inside of me.

"I'm not looking to *have* a child, only to carry one." Heather stood and paced to the kitchen sink. "I'm not getting any younger, Samantha. I want to have these life experiences."

"Don't force it," I said. "Everything happens for a reason."

Heather pinched the bridge of her nose and even I rolled

my eyes at the cliché. "Look, I've given it lots of thought, and I'm not going to do it."

I blinked. I was stunned before a wide grin spread across my face as the excitement poured through me, leaving me breathless. "That's great." I perked up.

Heather shook her head and laughed with me. "I picked up an application for Denver College of Nursing."

"Excellent," my proud sister voice sang loud. "You know I'll support you with whatever you decide."

"Maybe I'll even find myself working in the maternity ward one day." Heather's eyes beamed. "Anyway, I've looked at student loan rates and I have an appointment to meet with a liaison who is going to put me in contact with a recent graduate from the program so I can get a feel for what to expect. You know, to see if this is really something I can take on and if nursing is really meant for me."

I stood and padded across the floor, giving my sister the supportive hug she deserved.

"I hope I'm not overextending my stay," Heather said as she latched onto me tight. "I don't know how long this will take and, as of right now, I don't have a return flight back east."

"Of course you're welcome to say longer." I looked my sister directly in her eye and smiled. "You can stay for as long as you need." I pulled back and held her hands. "I like that Mason has another adult in the house he can talk to."

CHAPTER FIFTY-SIX

THE GUARDIAN ANGEL'S PLANS WERE DETERIORATING quickly. He could feel the walls closing in around him. Could still hear the knocks on his door as she demanded to be let inside a place only few ever stepped and, even then, by invitation only. But the thing that really kept him on edge was that the woman from last night now knew what kind of car he drove.

His heart pounded steadily—high on adrenaline and fear. He found it impossible to sleep.

The hours slipped by. Only when he was sure it was safe did he finally leave the office. Making a turn at his house, he switched out vehicles—for he had many—and found refuge at the nearby clinic he used for recruiting new patients. There, he remained hidden behind the locked doors, camouflaged by the cover of darkness. Now, only the light from his small desk lamp was on and he planned on keeping it that way.

It was morning, but time was irrelevant when he felt the world turning against him. The chair he was sitting in squeaked when he leaned back, yawned, and rubbed his eyes. He felt his energy fading but there was still work to be done.

He needed to stay nearby for Tracey, be present when his baby called. But, with each passing minute, his nerves grew more intense.

Tapping his computer mouse a couple of times, he streamed the local news through his computer once again.

His belly was in knots as he scrubbed a hand over his coarse face. It wasn't only regret that was keeping him reliving past events, but also his battle with the ignorance he displayed when choosing to neglect everything other than Tracey and the babies.

There was no excuse for Cameron's survival. Now she was the single most damaging threat to all he had worked to achieve.

"How is this even possible?" he muttered.

Squeezing his eyes closed, he shook his head. Flashes of bright light lit up behind his eyelids. After sending his tech out of the room, he himself had started the IV drip that contained the lethal dose of fentanyl. Did he get this wrong? Where was that bag now? The fentanyl should have put Cameron's lights out. If that didn't, the wound from the C-section he'd left open should have done the trick.

His eyelids clicked open. "I can't let that little whore live."

The Guardian Angel hunched over his keyboard and replayed the coverage of yesterday's press conference. He listened to the chief of police's words, looked for any sort of clues that this was all a hoax to make him believe he was safe. But he couldn't find any.

The entire squad was outside the house he had dropped Cameron off at only hours earlier.

A sharp smirk curled the corners of his lips.

He was convinced the police believed Tyler Lopez was responsible. He could see it in their smug eyes. But the Guardian Angel was smart enough to know that, soon, everyone would figure out it wasn't Tyler, but himself.

Would the police's stupidity buy him enough time to complete his mission? Doubtful, considering it was the *Times* crime reporter sniffing him out.

His security camera at the office caught her face in a frozen frame. It was the first thing he'd searched as soon as he knew she was gone. A quick facial recognition internet search produced a photo. Samantha Bell. Crime reporter for *The Colorado Times.* It was a name and face he promised to never forget—a face he promised to keep in his crosshairs for when the time came. *Because the time would eventually come.*

Springing to his feet, the Guardian Angel stirred the contents inside a cardboard box. The one he kept hidden in the back of his office; the one he wished he'd gotten rid of earlier.

Digging out Cameron's phone, he chucked it hard against the floor and stomped it into a couple dozen pieces while grinding his teeth. "You fucking did this. You told that bitch reporter about me and now everything is ruined!"

He dug the sharp part of his heel into the floor. The plastic and metal casing crushed beneath his weight. Then he picked up the pieces of the broken plastic and electronics, tossed it back into the cardboard box, and, with the searing rage still pounding in his chest, marched to the back exit of the clinic with a bottle of isopropyl alcohol in his other hand.

Dropping the box into an empty metal trash bin, he emptied the bottle's contents over the items and put a match to it. It instantly went up in flames, burning everything to a crisp. The cell phones. The clothes. The women's identification cards. Everything—all incinerated.

He stood there alone watching the flames die, planning his next move. He knew it was time to begin getting rid of every single piece of incriminating evidence that could possibly be traced back to him. They were coming for him and wouldn't stop until they found who was responsible for both Cameron and Kate.

You need to do something about Cameron, the voice inside his head told him.

Cameron knew his face, knew his voice, knew the location of his clinic. It was a triple whammy just asking for trouble. But what was he to do? How could he get rid of her? Cameron was certainly being watched by the cops now.

He narrowed his gaze and dug his curled fingers into the palm of his hand, forming a tight fist. He felt his hot blood pulse up his arm and across his chest, flexing his muscles tighter.

He was certain the police were already talking to her, learning about how she was recruited, what he'd done and what he was after. Now, it would only be a matter of time before his secret was revealed and everything was lost for good.

Panic wrapped a lasso around his throat, squeezing the last breath of air from him as he glanced around the empty corner. All this time he'd operated out in the open, taking the risk, hoping it would be enough of a disguise to march forward in his grand scheme to change the way parents decided on what children they would have. But now he didn't know who he could trust or who was working in nearby offices that knew his routine or, worse, his true identity.

Stomping out the smoldering embers, the Guardian Angel shoveled the heaping mess up and tossed it into a nearby dumpster, knowing today it would get picked up by waste management.

Running back inside, he prepared for his assistant to arrive and the office to open for work. All was quiet now, but soon it would be a different story. How much of that story he wrote himself was entirely decided by the choices he made now.

Back in his office, he pulled drawers open and hurried to forge documents and write fake prescriptions to cover his tracks. It was no longer if the police would come, but when. Suddenly, the front doorbell rang.

He snapped his head toward the front and stared at the clock. It was too early for his nurse, who wouldn't ring anyway, so who could it be? With his heart in his throat, his mind raced to form a conclusion. He wasn't expecting any visitors. He could only assume they were back for him.

Narrowing his eyes, he lowered his brow and prepared for battle.

This time, he wasn't going to let them get away without giving them a piece of the action.

CHAPTER FIFTY-SEVEN

"ARE YOU TELLING ME DR. WU USED HIS OWN SPERM?"

Detective John Alvarez's look of disbelief hid behind squinted eyes. He pinched his bottom lip and had the stunned look of a man who couldn't believe what he was hearing.

With one hand on the wheel, Alex King flicked his gaze to his partner and said, "What I'm saying is the mother believes she received an embryo that was missing her husband's half."

"And she thinks maybe the other half is the doctor's?"

"She has her suspicions."

Alvarez squeezed his eyes shut, snapped them open, and shook his head. Turning his attention to the road, he was quiet for a moment before muttering, "Christ. That's a serious allegation to make."

King's brow furrowed. "Apparently the mother went as far as doing her own testing."

"And?"

"Her kid is only half theirs."

Alvarez didn't even want to know how Samantha Bell learned all this. He knew she had her way of digging into the trenches better than any other reporter he knew—sometimes even better than the police department itself—but this was a story to be told if he had ever heard one.

Stroking his chin, Alvarez angled his head back to King and asked, "What is the margin for error for these kinds of treatments?"

"Can't say for sure," King put on his blinker and merged into the next lane, "but I would like to think it would be zero. You know how much money couples drop for IVF treatment?"

Alvarez turned his palm to the ceiling and shrugged.

"Tens of thousands of dollars, *per* try." They were heading north on I-25, taking the exit at E 58th Ave, and pointing the wheels toward North Denver Reproductive Medicine in Commerce City. "And that doesn't guarantee an embryo will result in a successful pregnancy. Some couples have to go through the procedure two or three times before anything materializes."

All night, King had poured through his notes, thought about his conversation with Sam, and anticipated his meeting with Dr. Glenn Wu this morning. To say he was excited to tackle this lead was a massive understatement. In a matter of hours, Dr. Wu had become his obsession. King was determined to know whether or not he had something to do with Tracey's disappearance.

"The reason I'm mentioning all of this," King continued, "is because the Pattersons were receiving their treatment at NDRM at the same time Wu told Keith Brown he was dismantling his research."

"So, say he's here—" Alvarez pointed out the front windshield. "Where do you want to start?"

King was quiet for a minute as he considered his approach. He had a few ideas for questioning, and each of them would set an entirely different tone. Flicking his gaze to Alvarez, he asked, "You take a look at that email I sent you?"

Alvarez raised a single brow. "About the biotech conference in Boulder?"

"That's the one." King pointed to the NDRM sign and took the next turn.

"Are you saying you want to start there?"

Weaving his way through the mostly empty parking lot, King applied the brakes and pulled into an empty parking space near the clinic's entrance. "No, I just want you to pay attention to how he reacts when I ask him about it."

The men swung their doors open, stood, and tugged on their jackets as they glanced around. The air was dry and the hum from the nearby street filled the air. Commuters were heading into work and King hoped Dr. Wu would be doing the same.

Stepping up to the front door, Alvarez pointed to the hours. "We're a few minutes early."

King tried the door. Locked.

Alvarez jabbed the doorbell with his stubby finger anyway.

"Hello, I'm coming," a woman's voice called out from behind them.

The sound of keys jangling got the detectives to turn. A woman dressed in scrubs approached with the unmistakable morning hustle of an employee running a bit behind schedule.

"Sorry I'm late," she said, balancing a coffee cup in one hand and a tote looped over the forearm of the other.

King shared a quick look with his partner. "Can I help free your hands?" King asked the woman.

She handed him her coffee and smiled. "Car trouble." She

rolled her eyes. "Lucky for me my neighbor was able to give me a jump."

The woman fumbled with the thick set of keys just as someone inside appeared out of nowhere. He unlocked and opened up, leaving a look of surprise stamped on King's face.

King stared at the man intently. He was well dressed, a pressed blue collared shirt and red tie, but his hair was all over the place. He appeared to be somewhat disheveled in his actions.

"Good morning. Good morning," the nameless man greeted everyone, welcoming them inside. "I guess I forgot to unlock the door after opening it."

"Not a problem." Alvarez followed King inside.

"I'm just heading out," the man said. "Johanna will get you checked in."

King handed the coffee back to Johanna, stepped forward, and held one finger up in the air. "Actually, we're here to speak with a Dr. Glenn Wu; is that you?"

The doctor pulled back and volleyed his round eyes back and forth between the detectives. "Yes, that's me. I'm Dr. Wu." King introduced himself and Alvarez. The crease between Wu's brows deepened with visible confusion. "Can I ask what this is about?"

King glanced to Johanna. "Is there someplace more private we could talk?"

Dr. Wu inhaled a deep breath through his nostrils and sighed as he flicked his wrist and glanced at the time. "I have an appointment with a patient at Presbyterian St. Luke's Medical Center which I really should be leaving for."

"This shouldn't take long." King took a step forward, not about to let Wu squeeze his way out of this.

Alvarez nodded, tucked his padfolio beneath one arm, and buried his hand in his pants pockets. "We just want to ask you a couple of questions."

Dr. Wu rubbed his nape and asked, "About what, detectives?"

"Fine. We can do this here," King said.

Johanna paused and looked up from behind the front desk. Dr. Wu felt the air still and glared at her before waving his hand at the men, asking them to follow him to the back.

Together, they glided through the front lobby and headed down a back hallway. The air was stale and sterilized, the quiet sounds of a doctor's office that King never did appreciate. Rounding the corner, the three men entered a small office with a nice large window spilling the morning sunlight over Wu's expensive mahogany desk.

King took a moment to glance around the room. There were journals and books on neatly organized wall shelves next to professional certificates and licenses that could only be explained as something to feed a professional man's ego.

"May I?" King pointed to the cushioned seat across from Dr. Wu's desk.

Dr. Wu extended his hand and nodded before sitting himself. "Please."

King sat and crossed one ankle over his opposite knee while Alvarez roamed the walls behind. King stared at Dr. Wu and watched him nervously keep one eye on what Alvarez was doing while keeping the other firmly locked on King. The detective kept it purposely quiet to really make Dr. Wu feel on edge. It seemed to do the trick. The doctor finally squirmed in his seat and asked, "So, what did you want to ask me?"

King's fingers stopped drumming. "We're investigating the homicide of Keith and Pam Brown."

"Homicide?" Dr. Wu's eyes flashed as he glanced quickly at Alvarez. King stared and watched the doctor press the tips of his fingers together while his eyebrows knitted.

"You know them, don't you?" King asked, hearing his partner pull a book off the shelf.

"I do. I was told they had been found dead, but didn't realize they had been murdered."

King stared, looking for signs of guilt. Dr. Wu's color never flushed, though King felt the doctor was struggling with keeping his gaze steady.

"With their deaths conveniently timed the day before your trial was to begin, you naturally became a person of interest." King kept his gaze forward but felt Alvarez turn and hover over his left shoulder.

Dr. Wu immediately gave an alibi for the night the Browns were found murdered. King jotted it down and promised to check it out after. Then Wu continued. "We should have never allowed it to go to trial."

"Then why did it get that far?"

"Neither party could agree on a settlement." Wu shook his head. "Not surprising, since it all began because Brown said I broke our original contract."

"And did you?"

"There was a difference in professional opinions." His Adam's apple bobbed in his throat. "Keith was an early investor in my company, Phanes Biotechnology, and I can tell you that I didn't do anything that any of my colleagues would have done differently."

King glanced to the doctor's diplomas and certificates on the walls. "What is it exactly your company does, Dr. Wu?"

Wu's spine straightened as he brought his elbows to the table. Perking up, he said, "We study the possibility of CRISPR gene editing." Excitement flashed in his eyes.

"And yet, you're here at a fertility clinic," Alvarez said, looking around the room.

"Yes," Wu said in a confident voice. "Ground zero for

much of my work. It's been an incredible partnership between Phanes and NDRM."

"I'd say so, seeing as they gave you the corner office."

"Yes," Dr. Wu agreed.

Over the next several minutes, King asked when the partnership began, what his current work was like, and if the Browns' lawsuit against him slowed him down. Dr. Wu answered every question he was asked and ended by saying, "I really am pressed on time, Detectives."

"Tommy Patterson," King said, getting the air to stop. "The son of Tony and Kristi Patterson. Ring a bell?"

Dr. Wu's eyes blinked as if stunned by what he assumed was coming next.

"No?" King raised his eyebrows. "Well, maybe this will jog your memory." He brought both boots to the floor and tipped his broad shoulders forward. "Tommy Patterson's mother believes the embryo your team implanted inside her womb contained another man's sperm—"

"Perhaps the doctor's sperm," Alvarez said for added emphasis.

"And, you know what I think?" King said. "I think maybe Mrs. Patterson is right."

Dr. Wu wiped his mouth. He was frozen to his chair as he cast his gaze to his desk. That's when King noticed something hiding behind a framed photo. A silver angel paperweight.

"I'm sorry," Dr. Wu said, "but I thought you were here investigating the Browns' deaths?"

King hooked his pinchers over the photo and took the metal angel into his hands. "We are." He grinned. "But now that we're here," he looked to the angel, "I'm thinking NDRM—and maybe even you—" he swept his eyes up to the doctor's and held his gaze, "might have connections to other open cases our department is currently investigating."

"This is a witch hunt," Dr. Wu snapped. "How dare you come into my place of work and accuse me of doing something for which I most certainly did not do."

"Does the name Kate Wilson sound familiar, Dr. Wu?" Alvarez asked.

Dr. Wu shifted his weight around. King watched his knuckles go white when he latched his fingers together on top of his desk.

"Or how about Cameron Dee?"

Sweat glistened on Wu's upper lip. "I've seen the news. I'm sorry for what happened to those women, but I don't see how Kate's death or Cameron's assault have anything to do with me."

"But they were patients of yours, correct?"

Dr. Wu's fists went back beneath his desk. His face went so red King was certain a vein would explode any second. "You know I can't share patient information without a warrant."

Alvarez chuckled. "Hear that, Detective? Dr. Wu thinks that we haven't spoken to the judge already."

"What my partner is saying," King applied the pressure, "is it would be easier for both of us if you would cooperate and answer our questions fully."

Dr. Wu's eyes hooded as he glared from beneath his sunken brow.

"Or we could take you down to the station and finish our conversation there." Alvarez jiggled his hands in his pockets and rocked back and forth on his heels. "Whichever you prefer, Doctor."

King lifted himself out of his chair and placed the paperweight back where he'd found it. "Let's talk about your alibi. You said you were meeting with colleagues over dinner the night before the conference in Boulder."

"That's right. I was the keynote. Would you like a quick

overview of what I presented?" The doctor's tone sharpened and King caught a hint of sarcasm. "Or should I just wait to receive a subpoena for that, too?"

"That depends," King said, falling back into his chair. "Does it have to do with modifying a woman's embryos?"

"It certainly does," Wu said proudly, freely sharing what his speech was about. "It's my work. It's what I do."

King's eyes drifted around the room as Wu summed up how the recent biotech conference in Boulder brought together the region's top doctors and scientists with a long list of wealthy donors.

"Wealthy donors." King flicked his gaze back to Wu. "That's interesting."

"Not really, Detective. Our research is expensive and, without donations or investments, modern medicine wouldn't be what it is today."

"Was that also who you had dinner with?"

"Some, yes."

"So, help me understand something." Alvarez took one hand out of his pocket and rubbed his brow. "You parted ways with your original investor, Keith Brown, and he just so happens to get knocked within hours of you being in Boulder pitching your sales speech at new fat wallets to make up for what you lost. Is that what I'm hearing?"

"What are you suggesting? That I planned this?" Wu chortled. "I had nothing to do with Keith's death. You can ask anyone who was with me that night. They'll tell you I wasn't anywhere near Congress Park."

"It just seems...what's the word?" King tapped his forefinger to his forehead.

"Convenient," Alvarez said.

King snapped his fingers. "Convenient."

Wu tucked his chin into his chest and shook his head.

"Not only that, but the Browns' daughter, Tracey, also

vanished that same night." King stared intently into Wu's brown eyes. "Did you know the Browns had a daughter, Dr. Wu?"

"I think he did." Alvarez cast his gaze down to King. "And I'm also willing to bet that he knew she was pregnant."

The doctor's eyes darkened. "This conversation is over."

"I thought you might say that. Because this is how I see it." King scooted to the edge of his chair. Tipping closer to Dr. Wu, he wanted to make sure he saw the seriousness swirling in his eyes. "You were inside the Browns' house the night you killed them. Tracey came home and saw that it was you, and you took her, knowing that she would recognize you."

"This is ludicrous." The doctor fumed. "You can't prove any of this." Dr. Wu stood and spoke animatedly. "My research benefits everyone, and here you are, nailing me to the cross all because of what? You don't approve of the science I preach? Is that it? You're no different than everyone else who has fought me on this—blocked the science that is giving life to people who otherwise wouldn't have it."

King stood and rolled his shoulders back, satisfied that he had cracked his suspect. "Let's just hope that we don't connect those other women back to you or any other organization you're affiliated with, Doctor." King paused and stared. "But now you understand why it is we're here and what we're after."

Dr. Wu put his hands on his hips and breathed heavily. "If you're not going to arrest me, I really do need to be going."

"We're not arresting you today, but it's a good idea to let us know if you plan to leave town."

Dr. Wu snagged his coat off the back of his chair and gathered his things as he headed to the door.

Before he could get too far, King said, "Just one more thing."

Dr. Wu hit the brakes, turned his head, and raised a single brow.

"Do you know a Dr. Cherub?"

"Is this some kind of joke?" Wu squinted his beady eyes. "You men disgust me."

King tipped his head back. "Do I look like I'm laughing?"

"Yes, I know a Dr. Cherub. In fact, I know many." Dr. Wu paused. "That was the nickname we gave the group of original scientists who developed our revolutionary technology."

CHAPTER FIFTY-EIGHT

IT WAS AFTER NINE BY THE TIME ERIN ARRIVED AT THE house to pick me up. I jumped into the front seat of her car and we hit the road. With everything that was on my mind, I hoped the Mile High Health Clinic would provide some clues to just who this Dr. Cherub really was. I'd left a message with King but hadn't heard back.

"I saw your letter to Tyler." Erin pulled down her visor and flicked a quick glance in my direction.

"You don't think it was too direct, do you?"

"I understand what you're trying to do, Sam," her eyes were back on the road, "but I'm not sure that King or the department will like what you did."

"What's new?" I shielded the sun's glare with my hand, tapping my foot on the floor in an attempt to rid my body of its nerves.

"Sounds like a lot." We locked eyes. "Do you really know who is behind this?"

I pushed my spine straight, suddenly realizing I hadn't told Erin about my date with King. "Shit. I should have called," I apologized.

"I could see it in your tired eyes." Erin smiled. "Did you find the website? Is that what makes you believe you know who is behind this? Because I didn't have any luck."

"No, it's not that," I said, diving into the conversation I'd had with King.

Erin kept her questions for the very end. I told her about the civil trial that the Browns had against the founder of Phanes Biotechnologies and how it was scheduled to begin the day after they were found dead. "But here is where it really takes a turn," I said. "Dr. Glenn Wu parted ways with the Browns about the time Tommy Patterson was conceived."

Erin was shocked speechless. She kept the wheels straight as she processed everything I just unloaded on her. I gave her time to think before I said, "Now I'm wondering if Dr. Wu is the doctor we're trying to connect to MHHC."

"Sam, if this Dr. Wu happens to also be the Dr. Cherub we're looking for, and he happens to read your plea to Tyler, we might lose him before ever proving he's the one who killed Kate, injured Cameron, and who might still have Tracey."

I felt my breath catch in my throat. Erin had a point. It had been something I had thought about myself, but I needed to also convince Tyler that I knew he was innocent of Cameron's injuries.

"I just want to see Tyler come in so we can hear his side of the story," I said. "Maybe he saw something that has him fearing for his own life. But let's also not forget that if Cameron called him the night she gave birth, Tyler will have a record of that number on his phone."

Erin bounced in her seat with the same amount of energy packed into a double espresso. I, too, was feeling anxious, though I kept my lid on the excitement rushing through my veins, not wanting to get too far ahead of myself.

As the wheels bumped along, I kept squeezing my hand

into a tight fist and letting it pop open with the force of a spring trap. If I had this wrong and something happened to Tracey, I didn't know how I would be able to ever forgive myself.

"There is something else you need to know." I rolled my neck toward Erin. "Last night, after my dinner with King, I went to the address Cameron told us about."

"The Guardian Angels clinic?"

My head nodded slowly.

Erin's expression pinched and she stared at me long enough for me to fear she might rear-end the car in front of us.

"Shit, Samantha." Erin smacked the steering wheel and turned her eyes back on me. "You went without me?"

"I had no choice. Not after everything King told me."

"Why didn't you bring King?"

"I had to see if it actually existed first, and he has parameters to work within that I don't."

Erin's blonde bangs swished across her forehead and she shook her head at me. "Well, what did you find?"

I paraphrased my encounter, telling her the name on the door and the guardian angel painting inside. I heard her gasp when I mentioned how someone arrived when I was snooping around back. "I saw him, Erin."

The color in Erin's face drained.

"His face was blocked by a shadow, but we were staring at each other." I rubbed my arms as if feeling the same creepy prickles that fell over me last night. "He knows who I am."

"This is worse than I thought." Erin ran a hand over her head. "Your letter doesn't mean jack now that he knows your face."

Erin apologized. She was heated from everything I'd just shared. "You're right," I said. "It was stupid. But it was him, Erin. I know it."

"How can you be so sure?"

My eyes lit up. "I called Cameron's phone, and I swear it was inside his office. I saw him turn his head as if hearing it ring."

"My god." Erin reached for her coffee and wrapped her lips around the rim, taking a big swig. "Well, thank God you told me this before we barged into the clinic riding on our high horse. Now at least I know where we stand."

A wave of pain moved across my chest. I could feel my heart knocking and I realized just how much danger I might actually be in. I sat there with tingling limbs, quietly thinking about the white BMW and the security cameras I was sure captured my face.

What else did he learn about me? He certainly knew my car, maybe even knew the license plate number. But what was someone doing there that late at night if it wasn't our suspect? It didn't make sense. Not the secrecy, nor the fact that no one could find their website.

Erin pulled into the Mile High Health Clinic parking lot and I was about to step out of the car when suddenly my cell phone's ring sliced through the silent air. It was Susan.

"Hey, girlfriend," I answered.

"Sam, Benjamin figured it out." She sounded frantic. "I've been calling to try to tell you."

"I'm sorry I didn't call you back," I said, thinking how I forgot to turn my phone back on last night. "What do you mean, Benjamin figured it out?"

"Sam, he knows the person you're looking for. You know, the one who *only* wants babies."

CHAPTER FIFTY-NINE

I FELT MY HEART STALL IN MY CHEST. SUSAN'S WORDS FIRED fast into my ear. I was stunned by Benjamin's theory. The story was nearly identical to my own, the only difference being Benjamin actually had proof to support his argument.

"I'm sending it over to you now," Susan said.

The line rustled as I stared at Erin, relaying the message in a whispery tone while keeping one ear with Susan.

"Don't tell Benjamin I told you this. I don't know if he knows what he stumbled upon. He was only trying to learn more about what Dr. Wu is doing. But it makes sense, right?"

"Completely," I said, knowing Benjamin just confirmed the theory I'd originally considered too far-fetched to believe.

I doubted myself when I shouldn't have, and now we were at least a day behind whatever our perp had planned next. Anger boiled up inside of me. What happened to Cameron was unforgiveable. I felt a surge of power shoot through my fingers when I thought about how I could redeem all of this by simply saving Tracey from this creep's experiment. Not only was Dr. Wu a founder of the designer baby idea but, according to Benjamin, he was pitching his idea once again to the public with hopes of restarting it.

"Oh, I'm so happy you agree with me." Susan sighed. "I stayed awake all night doing research on my computer, thinking I was crazy."

"You're not crazy." I pinched the bridge of my nose and closed my eyes. "Benjamin was right to have his hesitations."

"He doesn't know about your investigation."

"He doesn't need to."

"But he knew, Sam. Knew before any of us that something wasn't right about Dr. Wu."

"He has a good instinct," I said. "You're lucky to have him."

I lifted my head and swept my gaze over to Erin. Covering the mic with one hand, I whispered, "Phanes Biotechnology. That's what this is about. Benjamin thinks Dr. Wu might be creating designer babies."

Erin's eyebrows shot to the top of her head.

"Did you get the message I sent yet?" Susan asked.

I pulled the phone away from my ear and glanced to the screen. "I did. Give me a minute to look at it."

"Make sure to take a look at the headline," Susan called out as I pulled the phone away from my ear.

The link Susan sent was to the *Journal of the American Medical Association*. A second later, an image popped up on my screen. I pinched my fingers and zoomed in as Erin leaned her shoulder into mine.

"Is that who I think it is?" Erin's words floated into my ear.

"That's Dr. Glenn Wu," I said.

She looked me in the eye. "Was that the man you saw last night?"

I bit my lip and murmured, "I don't know."

"Send me the link," Erin said, retreating back to her side of the car.

I quickly forwarded the link, took a look at the headline, and brought the phone back to my ear. "Good work," I said.

"You can thank Benjamin when this is all over. But Dr. Wu's there in the picture and he's part of the group who called themselves the Guardian Angels."

Once again, all signs pointed at one man and it didn't make me feel any better about what we were about to walk into. I stared at the front entrance of the Mile High Health Clinic, feeling my palms go damp. A part of me hoped that this was it—our last stop—and we could finally connect Wu to the referrals sending women to Your Guardian Angel Women's Health Clinic. But that still didn't answer how the women got pregnant with his babies.

I ended my call with Susan, promising to keep her in the loop, and found Erin still staring at her phone. We both knew we were close to solving this case, but we also weren't ignorant to the fact that this was the time when things almost *always* got dangerous.

"Stay close and keep an eye out for anything unexpected," I warned Erin just before we both swung our doors open and entered the clinic with our heads held high.

"Do you have an appointment?" the woman working the desk asked.

I took in the décor—a picture of the city and a bubbling fish tank—noting the closed thick wood door leading to the back that vaguely reminded me of what I saw last night. Security cameras were in nearly every corner of the ceiling and we were most certainly being watched.

We identified ourselves and the woman grew defensive.

"We're not opposed to reporters, but you will need to schedule an appointment."

It was clear she didn't like surprise visits. "The story we're working isn't about the clinic," I assured her, "but a woman who was found dead the other night." *Kate*.

The woman apologized half-heartedly. "It's not uncommon for us to receive bad publicity, and threats are made against us on a weekly basis. As you can see from our security, there are many who don't agree with what we do here."

"We don't have an opinion either way," Erin said.

"Then what can I do for you?"

I took a step forward. "We're looking into a possible connection between MHHC and a facility that goes by the name Your Guardian Angel Women's Health Clinic."

"I'm sorry, I've never heard of it."

"How about a Dr. Cherub? Ever heard of him?" Erin asked.

"Maybe he works here?" I added.

"No. Again, that's a name I've never heard before," the woman answered without hesitation and I believed her. "But I see what you just did there." She pointed her finger at us and smiled—*Dr. Angel*. The woman was clever, if not helpful. "You said this had something to do with a woman who was found dead?" She paused and watched me nod. "Was she a patient of the women's clinic you mentioned?"

"Actually, we were told that someone who worked here maybe referred her to the women's health clinic—offering money and medical treatment."

The woman tipped her head to the side and acted surprised. "No one here would do that without the director's approval."

"Could we get a list of who is on your staff?" I asked, thinking of how Kate's father thought a doctor here convinced her not to have an abortion.

"A detective called the other day asking similar questions. Like I told him," the woman finally stood and placed her hands firmly on her desk as she tipped forward on her toes, "you'll have to make your requests through our attorney."

A man wearing a collared shirt and slacks emerged from the back. He approached the desk and picked up a couple of charts. I kept an eye on him, wondering if he could be the infamous Dr. Cherub we were after. The stethoscope around his neck certainly made me think it was possible. Suddenly, he looked me directly in the eye and I felt my heart stop. His face was familiar. I knew him. But where had I seen him before?

"Here is the card to our director." The woman pushed a business card toward me. "She'll be in at eleven if you would like to wait. If not, I suggest you call and make an appointment."

I snatched the card off the desk and left the office in a hurry. I didn't want to forget the face I'd just seen. Back in Erin's car, I pulled up the link Susan sent and the image of Dr. Wu's group of guardian angels. I scrolled across the many faces before landing on the man from inside.

"There," I said. "That's him."

"Who?"

"The doctor we just saw."

Erin leaned closer. "What's it say his name is?"

"Dr. James Andrews." We shared a knowing look. "What if they're in on this together?"

"You mean, like Andrews is recruiting the girls here and sending them to Dr. Wu's clinic?"

"That's exactly what I mean." I turned my focus back to the image. "There is no denying they don't already know each other."

Erin swallowed hard. "Was he the one you saw last night?"

I wasn't sure. "It might have been."

Then my phone blew up when King called. I answered

and told him where I was. "Dr. Cherub isn't a made-up name, Sam."

My ears perked. "Do you know who it is?"

"Not who it is. But who *they are*. Wu had a research team who called themselves the Guardian Angels and they gave themselves the nickname Dr. Cherub." I snapped my neck to Erin. Susan had already told us the first piece of the puzzle, but King just connected another important link. "It's his original team of scientists. Each of them calling each other Dr. Cherub, members of the Guardian Angels."

"But why not call each other by their real names?"

"Maybe to hide their true identities." King explained how he learned all this, how Dr. Wu had an alibi that still needed to be checked out for the night the Browns were killed but seemed nervous enough to still be hiding something. My head was spinning so fast, I was forced to close my eyes to find my balance.

"Did you at least follow him?" I asked King, hoping Dr. Wu could lead us to Tracey.

King's gravel voice came through the line. "No. But we know where he's heading."

My head snapped up. "You know where he's going?"

"Said he had a meeting at Presbyterian St. Luke's. We have no reason to believe he's lying."

Everything stopped.

"King. Oh, shit. No, no, no." I motioned for Erin to start the car. She put the car in reverse and pointed the tires south after I told her where to go. "King, don't you see what's happening?" I told Erin to punch the gas. "He's going after Cameron."

CHAPTER SIXTY

HEATHER GARRET TUGGED ON HER CLOTHES AND RELEASED a deep, heavy sigh when checking the time on her phone again. Her black coffee was getting cold and she was beginning to doubt the nurse, Carly Jo, who promised to meet with her would show at all.

Stretching her neck, Heather glanced over her shoulder and let her eyes bounce around Starbucks, looking for a woman who could potentially be Carly.

A man with thick glasses had his attention glued to his laptop computer. The woman next to him stared into her phone, completely oblivious to what was happening around her. It seemed everyone was plugged into their electronic devices. No one looked like they were waiting for someone to arrive.

Heather had messaged Carly over fifteen minutes ago and still hadn't heard back. She turned her attention back to her phone, giving Carly another five minutes before calling it a dud, and pulled up her sister's blog, *Real Crime News*, to help pass the time.

Heather was still thinking about the conversation with

her mother last night and how both of them were concerned about Samantha's job growing increasingly more dangerous in a polarized world when suddenly her eyes stopped on her sister's last blog post.

Heather checked the time stamp in the upper right-hand corner.

"You published this this morning. Why didn't you tell me?" she whispered to herself, but was intrigued to continue reading.

Heather felt her heart race the further she read into Samantha's story arguing for Tyler Lopez's innocence. It was nothing short of convincing and Heather knew Samantha was hot on the trail of who was actually responsible. Heather wanted to help.

Giving up on Carly Jo, she pushed her arm through the strap of her purse, dropped her feet to the floor, and weaved her way to the exit when suddenly a woman stepped inside.

Heather hit the brakes and paused to question whether or not the woman she was staring at, and who looked like she'd had quite the morning, could actually be Carly.

The woman removed her sunglasses and locked eyes with Heather. A flash of recognition sparked between them.

"Carly?" Heather asked.

The woman's eyes brightened. "Heather."

Heather smiled and nodded, wishing she had waited only a minute longer so she wouldn't look like the fool who was about to walk out on the meeting she'd requested.

"Sorry I'm late." Carly folded up her sunglasses and stuffed them into her purse. "My one-year-old has been sleeping like a newborn."

"That's okay. I was just about to step outside for some fresh air." Heather played it cool. "Do you have a boy or girl?"

"Girl." Carly smiled, stepping in line at the counter.

Heather offered to pay for their drinks and Carly happily

accepted. Soon they found themselves sitting at the same table she had been waiting at and, over mocha lattes, Carly summed up her nursing experience.

"So, what makes you want to become a nurse?" Carly settled in, taking off her jacket.

Her hair was still wet from her morning shower and Heather felt a little guilty for taking up her time on what was obviously her day off. "I've been working an office job for the last five years on the east coast and now I want to make a switch and start working with people—more specifically, I'd like to work with babies."

"Do you have any of your own?"

Heather cast her gaze to the table and shook her head.

"Honey, enjoy your sleep while you still have it." The women shared a laugh. "But the east coast to Denver? That's a big move."

"My sister and her teenage son live here and I'd like to be closer to them."

"I can understand that. I moved from Ohio three years ago. Denver is a great place. I mean, look at this sunshine." Carly extended her arms and soaked in the bright warm light.

"I've always liked it here," Heather admitted as she wrapped her lips around her coffee. "Did you have any trouble finding a job?"

"In this market? Are you kidding? Talk about a career with job security." Carly sipped her coffee. "I assume by your email you wanted to get a feel for the intensity of the program."

Heather nodded and Carly jumped in head first explaining the class load, how the first year was much harder than the second, but all worth it. "Many of the students in the program are in a similar position as yourself. I'm sure you'll fit in no problem."

Carly clearly had a passion for nursing and was an intelligent young woman. Heather liked listening to her speak and got sucked into the stories from Carly's clinical hours. The field of nursing sounded like the exact type of adventure Heather was looking for and couldn't wait to get started. But there was something Heather wanted to hear more of, something Carly seemed to have forgotten. "Tell me more about what your job is like now."

Carly cast her gaze to her fingers ironing up and down her cup. "I am lucky to have what I have." She swept her eyes up to Heather. "Don't take this the wrong way, because I love what I do, but my work isn't what I imagined it would be."

"What do you mean? I thought you liked what you did?"

"I do. And I certainly wouldn't trade it for the world, but it's a lot harder than I ever imagined it would be." Carly paused as if needing a moment to collect her thoughts. "And I'm not talking physically hard. It can be emotionally draining some days." Carly went on to explain how she would cry herself home, only to pull herself together to appear strong in front of her family.

"I guess I never really thought of that," Heather murmured.

Carly shrugged. "It's not always like that. There are good days and bad, but the clinic I work at is a bit different than those I experienced during my clinical hours."

"Really? How so?"

"For starters, we're more like a research facility with one doctor at the helm." Heather asked what kind of research and Carly said, "We monitor the pregnancy of a select few first-time mothers."

Heather felt her brow twist when seeing the sad look fall over Carly's face.

"In just this last week, I've witnessed more births than I ever imagined I would."

"Sounds like you found yourself a great place to work."

"Yeah. I guess so," Carly whispered into the table. "It's an experience builder but, like you," Carly fixed her eyes on Heather's, "I would also like to get into maternity care at a hospital someday." Heather smiled. "But I can't complain. It pays my bills and, as my boss says, he'll never let me leave."

Heather finished her coffee and perked up. "Would it be possible to give me a tour? I'd love to see it firsthand."

Carly looked at her sideways and grinned. "I'm afraid not. Not without prior authorization—which I did not ask for considering the kind of week we've been having."

Heather's shoulders sagged. She wanted as much information as possible. Without knowing where Carly worked, she wasn't sure she'd get a firsthand view now.

"Sorry," Carly said taking a call, "it might be my boss. He does this sometimes."

Only a moment into Carly's call, Heather watched her entire expression change. Not wanting it to seem like she was eavesdropping into Carly's private conversation, Heather peered out the window and strained one ear toward Carly's phone. If it was Carly's boss who was calling, Heather was interested in hearing what kind of man she worked for.

"Look, creep. I never called you. Not from this phone. Not from any phone." Heather could feel Carly's blood pressure rise. "What did you say your girlfriend's name was? Uh-huh. Cameron Dee. Well I don't know a *fucking* Cameron Dee." Carly slammed the phone down and apologized to Heather.

A sudden rush of adrenaline spiked Heather's veins as Carly locked eyes with her. "Did I hear you say Cameron Dee?"

"Yeah." Carly's brows knitted. "You know her?"

Heather lunged forward. "Have you not paid attention to the news?"

"The news is depressing." Carly swiped at her bangs and slurped her drink. "Why has she been on it?"

Heather remembered the conversation she'd overheard the other night around Sam's dining room table and wanted to strangle Carly for being so dense. "That's the woman whose boyfriend allegedly cut her baby out of her womb. Her face is all over the news and the police are still looking for the man who they say did it."

"Jesus." Carly's face went pale. "Do you think that could have been him?"

Heather could feel her sister breathing down her neck as if standing over her shoulder. "Was Cameron a mother at your clinic?"

"We don't know the names of our patients. It's against policy."

"You don't know their *names*? What kind of clinic are you working at?"

"Your Guardian Angel Women's Health Clinic." Carly clicked her eyelids a couple of times and had an oblivious look on her face that told Heather she was clueless to the manhunt underway.

Heather dove her hand into her jacket pocket and pulled up a photo of Cameron on her cell phone. "This is Cameron."

Carly stared and covered her mouth with a trembling hand. "Oh my god."

"You know her?" The words left Heather's mouth in a breathless gasp.

Carly nodded, saying, "What have we done?"

Heather couldn't believe what she was witnessing. Lunging forward, she stole Carly's phone off the table and hit redial.

"Hey, what are you doing?" Carly reached for her phone, but was too late.

Standing firmly on both feet, Heather held the phone to

her ear and listened to it ring. To Carly, she said, "The man who just called was probably Tyler Lopez calling to ask you who was responsible for nearly murdering his girlfriend."

When a man answered, Heather didn't even greet him. "I know who set you up. And I know where to find him."

CHAPTER SIXTY-ONE

ERIN'S HEAVY FOOT KEPT THE PEDAL FLOORED AS SHE SPED through traffic. My heart was in my throat and I kept thinking there was no way in hell we would get to the hospital in time.

"God, I hope Campbell is still there," I kept saying to myself, surprised by my own wishes to support the one cop who clearly had it out for me. I kept wondering how far King was and who would get to Cameron first.

Erin drove with both hands on the wheel, and I had my right hand securely clamped to the chicken handle above my head, helping Erin keep an eye on any unexpected obstacles coming for us. As she raced, she casually turned to me and said, "There is something I still don't understand." I barely had time to look. "Say our theory is right and Dr. Andrews is sending referrals to Wu's sham clinic, how are they implanting their designer embryos into these women?"

I had asked myself the same question but wasn't sure we knew enough to have an answer. But when I thought back to what Cameron said about her own experience, there could only be one explanation. "Dr. Andrews must have done it at MHHC."

The engine shifted gears and Erin yanked on the wheel as she swerved past a slow commuter bus. Breathing in its exhaust, we discussed the timing of Cameron's blood work and the need for an ultrasound. "If it wasn't for Cameron's original request for emergency contraception, I would have said it was excessive. But maybe it wasn't?"

Erin's spine was straight, her focus on her driving, but her head was somewhere else. "How could she not know an embryo was put inside of her?"

I felt my stomach harden with thoughts of us crashing before we ever got to the hospital. "MHHC attracts vulnerable women. They're scared and trust the opinions they are receiving. The women who go there probably don't ask why a doctor is doing what they are doing as long as it seems legit."

"Still," Erin flicked her gaze in my direction, "she would have had to allow someone access."

The hospital came into view and this time we didn't even bother taking the time to find a parking spot. Erin slammed on the brakes near the front entrance and took the first handicapped space she saw without remorse. We kicked open our doors and booked it up to Cameron's room.

The elevator couldn't travel quickly enough. As soon as we jumped off, I pushed my way past the people filling the busy hallways and continued to pray Campbell assigned an officer to watch over Cameron.

Rounding the corner at full speed, I heard the soles of my shoes squeak on the floor. When I came within sight of Cameron's room, my worst nightmares became reality. There was no one standing guard. Her door was cracked open and I wondered if maybe we were too late.

"Miss, you need to check in at the desk." A nurse came out of nowhere and chased after me after blowing past the desk. Erin took off in the opposite direction, saying she was going to sweep the halls looking for Wu.

"I won't be here long," I called back to the nurse.

"That's not the point." She grabbed my arm and spun me around. "Visiting hours haven't started."

"You don't understand." I pointed a straight arm at Cameron's door. "The woman in Room 52 is in danger."

The nurse squinted her eyes at me. Ms. Dee must have heard my voice because she came flying out of the room. "Samantha? What's this about?"

Taking my eyes off the nurse, I swept them over to Ms. Dee. "I think I know who left your daughter for dead." Air was sucked out of the entire hallway. "It might have been a doctor she knew."

"That's it." The nurse hurried back to her desk. "I'm calling security."

Ms. Dee stood there with wet eyes, wondering if I could be right.

Ignoring the nurse, I nodded and added, "And I think he might be coming to finish what he started."

CHAPTER SIXTY-TWO

"Have any doctors recently stepped foot inside Cameron's room?"

Ms. Dee had her arms folded across her chest as she glared at the back of the nurse's head. She flicked her gaze back to me. "No."

A sudden lightness lifted off my chest. Pulling out my phone, I showed Ms. Dee a photo I had saved of Dr. Glenn Wu. "This is the man. Are you sure you haven't seen him here?"

Ms. Dee stared into my cell phone's screen. "I haven't seen him. But all this talk on the news is making me nervous."

We locked eyes and I could see the uncertainty swirling around her dark pinpricks. "What about Campbell; where is he?"

"He hasn't come back since he threatened to arrest you."

I clenched my jaw and turned my head away. Campbell's showmanship was grating on my nerves, but I refused to allow my criticism of how he conducted his police work to stop me from making sure Cameron stayed safe. "What has Detective Campbell been telling you?" I asked.

Ms. Dee dropped her arms and leaned her face closer to me. Shaking her head, she said, "Maybe you can tell me what's going on because Campbell is keeping me in the dark."

I could feel the clock ticking. There wasn't enough time to explain everything in great detail, but I told Ms. Dee enough for her to understand the importance of speaking to her daughter immediately.

Without hesitating, Ms. Dee hooked her arm through the crook of mine and tugged me into the room. Cameron met my eye and I smiled. Then I watched her smile fade as she flicked her gaze over my shoulder.

"That's her," I heard the same nurse who threatened me earlier say. "That's the one."

I turned on a heel and saw the nurse pointing directly at me. Her scowl was fierce but not as intimidating as the six-foot-two linebacker security officer she had brought with her.

"Ma'am, I'm going to have to ask you to leave." The officer's heavy boots stopped at the door.

I debated my options, knowing I had no choice but to stay with Cameron. Ignoring the officer's calls for me to leave, I said, "I don't have time for this. Her life is in danger."

When the officer stepped for me, Ms. Dee stepped in front of him and blocked his pursuit. "You're going to let her stay."

Everything behind me suddenly went quiet. I heard Ms. Dee demanding he give me five minutes to speak with her daughter. I didn't wait for permission. I reached for Cameron's hand and gave it a firm squeeze before lowering my tail to the edge of her bed. "I visited the clinic you told me about."

Cameron's brow wrinkled. "Did you find my baby?"

"No." I choked on my own words. "But I haven't stopped

looking." Cameron dropped her gaze to our hands still locked together and I shifted the conversation to Dr. Wu. "I was hoping you could identify someone for me."

"I'll do anything to get my baby back in my arms."

I smiled and patted her hand. Then I showed her a picture of Dr. Wu. "Is this Dr. Cherub?"

Cameron took my phone into her hand and brought it close to her face. "No. That isn't him."

I was knocked to the floor with surprise. If it wasn't Wu, then who was Dr. Cherub? "Okay, but have you ever seen this man before?"

Cameron glanced to the image of Dr. Wu for a second time. "He doesn't look familiar," she said, placing my phone back into my palm.

Ms. Dee stood quietly on the opposite side of the bed with her arms folded across her chest, waiting to see where I was going with all this. I wasn't so sure myself now that Cameron hadn't recognized the man King said was heading our way. But there was one last person it could be.

I swiped over to Dr. James Andrews's image and turned the screen back to Cameron. Her eyes widened the moment they landed on his face and I heard her lungs suddenly freeze. There was no doubt in my mind she knew him, but I asked anyway. "Is this Dr. Cherub?"

Her shoulders fell in on themselves as she nodded. "That's him. That's Dr. Cherub."

"Is that who took your baby?" Ms. Dee asked.

Cameron flicked her gaze up to her mother and I watched as tears pooled in the corners of her brown eyes. "I don't know. But he was my doctor. The doctor that would only visit occasionally. The doctor who delivered my baby."

Ms. Dee fixed her intense gaze on me. "Is this who has my granddaughter?"

"I'm not sure." I swallowed. "Here is what I believe is

happening." I explained what Erin and I discussed on our drive over; how it was possible Cameron might not have been pregnant until the doctor implanted his own embryo inside of her. I left out the part about Erin and me wondering if Wu and Andrews were working together. There was little doubt left in my mind, now, that they were both involved.

"That's disgusting," Ms. Dee snapped. "Cameron, is what she is saying true?"

Cameron nibbled on the inside of her cheek as she muttered, "I don't know, Momma. Maybe."

"We'll of course have to confirm it," I said. "But first we need to find your baby."

"I'm going to kill him," Ms. Dee fumed.

"Is the baby even mine?" Cameron asked me.

I stared into her eyes, not sure I had an answer to give.

"Of course it's yours, Cam, baby," Ms. Dee said with conviction. "You carried it for nine months. That girl is yours no matter what anybody says." Ms. Dee's hands balled at her sides as if she was gearing up to start swinging.

Standing, I explained the Pattersons' story and how Dr. Andrews and Dr. Wu were original founders in a biotech company that created designer babies through a complicated process known as gene editing. Ms. Dee stayed with me the entire way as Cameron seemed to drift off into her head.

"They took advantage of my baby because her womb was ripe." Ms. Dee spit fire. "Is that what you're saying?"

"Basically." I nodded. "I'm certain Cameron wasn't the only woman they took advantage of. There are more, and I think they might be housed at the private clinic they had Cameron at."

"The women the police mentioned in the news? Is that who you're talking about?"

"Yes." I looked to Cameron. "It seems to me like it might have been an elaborate scheme to impregnate women and then convince them to seek assistance at a private clinic the corrupt doctors also managed."

The whites in Ms. Dee's eyes were the size of headlights as they stared openly at me. I could understand the confusion, the heartbreak, and the desire to make sure these men received the justice they deserved. But I still had to confirm whether or not Cameron believed her baby—and Tracey Brown—might still be at the Guardian Angel clinic.

"Tell me, Cameron," I reached for her hand, bringing her focus back to the present, "was I at the right place? Is that where I should look for your baby?"

"What about the man you said was coming to finish what he started?" Ms. Dee asked sternly.

I fixed my eyes on Ms. Dee. "As long as that officer comes back, Cameron is safe here."

"Samantha," Cameron's voice was small when I turned my attention back to her, "you were at the right place. That's the clinic. If my baby is still alive, that's where you'll find her."

CHAPTER 63: LET ME OUT

DETECTIVE ALEX KING RAN TO THE EXIT OF THE NORTH Denver Reproductive Medicine office and stiff-armed his way through the glass door. The warm spring air hit his face as Alvarez hit the brakes behind him.

"Do you see where that bastard went?" Alvarez shielded the sun from his eyes with his hand.

King continued to scan the parking lot. He looked through windshields and popped over the hoods of cars. There wasn't movement anywhere he looked and he feared that they had let Dr. Wu get a head start on them.

"Any idea what kind of car he drives?" Alvarez asked.

Neither of them knew.

"C'mon, let's go," King said, running to their car. "We have to catch up with him."

Not more than a minute later, they were speeding south. The siren wailed over their heads and Alvarez was on the radio speaking with Dispatch when King had to cut the steering wheel sharp. The tires squealed on the pavement when blasting through the traffic light, and the car they nearly collided with honked in a rage of anger. King kept his hands firm while straightening out the wheel and driving as fast as the road allowed.

Without breaking a sweat, all he could think about was how he missed the connection between Cameron and Dr. Wu. If it weren't for the call from Sam, who knows what would have happened. But now, at least they had a chance to stop Wu in his tracks before anything worse could happen.

Alvarez clutched the radio mic inside his grip and said, "Dispatch is directing a couple patrol cars in the area to head this way."

King kept glancing at the clock and the minutes felt like they were frozen in time. To the detective, it seemed to take them forever to cut across town to Presbyterian St. Luke's. Finally, they arrived, after what felt like an eternity, and King parked near the entrance in the emergency vehicles only area and sprinted inside.

Alvarez followed as they pushed through the knots of people impeding their rush to the elevators. The hospital seemed especially busy with both visitors and patients, not to mention the staff filling the halls.

King kept an eye out for Sam, and was convinced they would collide with Wu at any moment. He saw neither person before they tumbled into the elevator and jabbed at the buttons to be whisked up to Cameron's floor.

King stared at the floor numbers climbing up and cursed every time the car would suddenly stop on an unexpected floor. He felt his heart race the closer they got to their landing. As soon as the elevator stopped and the door opened, the two men wedged their way through and sprinted toward the front desk, holding up their badges.

The nurse working the desk stood and nodded without speaking.

King hurried down the hall and was surprised that hospital security was already standing guard.

"Have you let anyone past?" he asked the security officer.

The man leveled his gaze with King. "No one who hasn't been authorized by the patient or the patient's guardian."

Cameron's door was closed. After having the officer confirm the safety of the patient inside, King spun around and asked his partner, "Why the hell isn't Campbell here? Or someone he posted here?"

Alvarez turned and faced the front desk when he heard boots clacking toward them. "Looks like you got what you wished for."

Two uniformed officers joined them and Alvarez was filling them in on the situation when King took out his cell and dialed Campbell.

"King, where the hell are you?" Campbell answered.

King's brows squished. "Me? I'm at the hospital guarding Cameron. Where the hell are you?"

"Haven't you heard? A tip came in and we have eyes on Tyler Lopez."

King turned to face Alvarez.

"Lopez is driving east and just crossed the line into the city of Aurora." King could hear Campbell practically smiling with elation. "I suggest you hurry and get your ass down here before the party is over. That is, if you want to be part of the arrest."

CHAPTER SIXTY-FOUR

TRACEY BROWN'S STOMACH GRUMBLED WITH HUNGER PAINS as she pushed herself up and tried the TV. Again, it didn't turn on. She was tired of being held against her will, and exhausted from not eating. Something wasn't right. It was time for her to figure her way out of here.

Her bare feet hit the cold floor and she padded lightly to the door only to find she had been locked inside. Panic squeezed her ribs as she jiggled the unforgiving door handle. The lock didn't budge no matter how hard she tried. Slapping her hand against the hard wood door, she screamed, "Let me out! I'm starving in here."

After calming herself down, she pressed an ear against the door. She heard nothing. It was completely silent which only made her worries grow. *Where did everyone go?*

Balling her hand into a fist, she punched the door with the sharp point of her knuckles before jumping back into her bed. Tracey pulled the covers over her cold skin, sure she had missed at least two meals and was close to missing a third.

She wanted nothing more than to bust her way out. With the door securely locked, she didn't know how that would happen. Tracey reached for her water bottle and sipped it down until it was nearly empty. At least she had access to a tap in the bathroom. It was the only relief for her stomach.

The young woman sat quietly, not sure what to do about the situation she was in. Suddenly, Tracey was hugging her knees to her chest, rocking back and forth, and found herself humming a song her mother used to sing to her as a child.

Closing her eyes, a smile lifted the corners of her mouth.

She missed her parents, wanted to talk to her best friends, and most of all to apologize to her dad for being such a brat. She would do anything to take their advice now. That was the deepest regret she had—knowing how she'd left things before disappearing.

Her belly grumbled. She weighed it down with more water, but after having Dr. Cherub be so adamant about her eating healthy and religiously taking her prenatal vitamins, she imagined something must have happened to him.

Turning her head, Tracey glanced to the bathroom and found herself grappling with the same dark thoughts that crossed her mind once already. There, inside that small tile-wall room, she could end this, take her own life, end the suffering. She might have if it wasn't for the baby growing inside of her—the one she was now responsible for.

Instead, as soon as that door opened, Tracey knew she would make her escape and choose to live.

Then she heard a noise echo off the hallway walls.

Tracey stared through the darkness and opened her eyes wide as light spilled beneath the door. Her blood ran hot as the footsteps got closer.

Tossing her covers, she dropped to the floor and crouched low near the door.

Her heart pounded like a hammer driving a nail into thick wood. She waited. The footsteps stopped and she listened as the lock gently clicked over. The door cracked, spilling in light, and Tracey sprang between the thick leg stepping into her room and the doorframe, making her escape.

"Not so fast." A strong hand caught her ankle. "Where do you think you're going?"

"Let me go." Tracey twisted onto her back and kicked her legs at the doctor. "I need food."

Dr. Cherub pulled her to her feet easily and tossed her back into the room. Tracey watched as he threw down a plastic bag of clothes onto her bed. She glanced to it and covered her chest with her hands.

"Get dressed. We're leaving."

Tracey stared and gaped, frozen with fear.

When Tracey didn't move quick enough, the doctor lunged one foot forward and let his open palm swing across her face. *Smack!* Tracey cried out as if getting stung. She covered her face with both hands and keeled over as she felt tears prickle the backs of her eyes.

"Hurry up," the doctor said. "We don't have much time."

Scared he might take her life, or do something much worse while she was alive, Tracey slowly stood and removed her hospital gown. With her back turned to him, she stood on trembling legs and slipped her feet through the grey sweat pants Dr. Cherub provided and pushed her arms through the navy blue hoodie.

Dr. Cherub stood and watched with a glint in his eye that made Tracey nervous. Once she was fully clothed and had her shoes laced up, he clamped a strong hand around her arm and tugged her into the hallway.

"Where are you taking me?" Tracey asked, turning her body into dead weight.

Dr. Cherub dragged her heels across the floor and marched forward without responding.

Tracey could see the determined look in his eye. It was different than any other expression he'd worn. *What happened to make him so angry? But, more importantly, what could she say to make him relax?*

They passed one open door after another. Each room was set up exactly like hers, but were empty. "Where did the other women go?" she asked.

The doctor tugged on her arm and grunted.

Tracey's eyes lit up when she heard a baby begin to cry.

Dr. Cherub squeezed tighter and the baby's cries grew louder. When they turned the corner, Tracey found herself staring into the eyes of a man she had never seen before. The stranger turned, bringing the crying child to his chest. Confused to what was going on, Tracey looked to Dr. Cherub and she swore she could see recognition flashing over his eyes as he grinned at the other man staring back at him.

"Dr. Wu," Dr. Cherub said. "I was wondering when you would decide to show up."

CHAPTER SIXTY-FIVE

I'D WANTED TO STAY WITH CAMERON BUT HAD TO KEEP going. The security officer—realizing I wasn't the person he should be removing—agreed to stay with her until the police arrived and I'd left to find Erin. I hoped Campbell would be back within minutes of my departure. Every second counted.

I raced to the elevators and found Erin jogging toward me. "Sam, I didn't see Wu anywhere."

"He's not here," I said, jabbing the button with my finger.

Erin looked stunned by my statement. "What happened? What did I miss?"

I caught Erin up to speed. "Wu isn't Dr. Cherub. At least not the Dr. Cherub that Cameron was familiar with."

Erin placed a hand to her forehead and turned to glance over her shoulder as if needing to see it to believe it.

"Cameron had never seen Wu in her life," I added.

"But that doesn't mean that Andrews and Wu aren't still working together." Erin locked her eyes on mine. "We can't leave. Not until we can be sure Cameron's life isn't in any kind of danger."

The elevator doors opened and I stepped inside. Erin

remained in the hallway with a confused look pinching her forehead. The doors tried to close and I stopped them before they could. I heard my teeth grind with sudden impatience. We didn't have time to play spin the bottle on whose life was in more danger.

"Wu isn't coming here," I held up one hand and pleaded. "We would have seen him if he was."

"If he's not coming here, then where is he going?"

"The Guardian Angel clinic." I kept one hand on the doors to keep them from closing. "I don't have proof that what I'm saying is right, but it makes sense. We already know Wu and Andrews know each other. If Wu got nervous after speaking with King, what would you do if you were him?"

"Assuming I'm not a killer and didn't want to silence the only witness who I knew was talking to the cops?" Erin raised her eyebrows as sarcasm soaked her words. "I would cover my tracks."

The elevator alarm buzzed.

"Exactly. Now c'mon." I reached for Erin's hand and yanked her inside the metal box. "If Tracey is still alive—and my god, I hope she is—Wu will want to make sure she doesn't become another material witness like Cameron. But, more importantly, he'll want to protect his investment."

"Which is?"

"The baby he has growing inside of her."

"Sam, we have to warn King," Erin said as soon as my cell started ringing from my hip. "There are still two babies unaccounted for that we can't forget about."

Surprised I had service inside the elevator, I answered the call from my angry editor.

"Samantha, where the hell have you been?" Dawson barked into my ear. "I was expecting a story from you and I have nothing."

"Dawson, I'm still working the headline story. You're going to need to give me more time."

"If you mean that open letter you wrote to Denver's Most Wanted, I don't want it. Are you out of your mind? I told you to stay off your blog this week."

Dawson wasn't the only one asking himself if I was out of my mind. The further down this rabbit hole of conspiracy and murder I went, the more out of my mind I felt. I could be wrong, but something told me I wasn't.

"Dawson, these women were used as incubators to grow a doctor's designer babies." I could hear Dawson open and shut his mouth. "We're on our way to the clinic now to find out if my story checks out."

"Jesus, Sam. Designer babies?" His tone was more disbelief than anger and I was happy to have him listening again.

"You wanted a headline story. Well, this is it."

As soon as we jumped off the elevator, we sprinted to Erin's car. Despite being parked in handicap, it hadn't been touched. No ticket. No boot. No tow truck hooking it up to the back. We slammed our doors shut at the same time, considered ourselves lucky, and buckled ourselves inside. Erin punched the gas and drove like the car was stolen.

Recalling my journey last night, I guided her the entire way, telling her where to turn and the quickest route to get to where we needed to go. When we finally came within sight of the building, I pointed over the dash and said, "There."

Erin dropped the gear and sped forward.

We arrived to a full parking lot. Men and women were filing in and out of adjacent businesses but I didn't see the white BMW from last night anywhere. When everywhere else was ripe with activity, the Guardian Angel's clinic looked completely dead.

I suggested Erin park off to the side but stay near the front. We needed to play this safe and calculate our risk.

There was no telling what was waiting for us inside—if anything at all. But if Wu and Andrews were here, like I thought they were, there was no doubt in my mind the one who saw me last night would know I would be coming back for more.

"Erin," I whispered, "you go around back and I'll go through the front."

"Shouldn't you call King first?" She breathed heavily and I could feel her nerves zapping the air between us.

"Yeah," I breathed. Swiping my phone awake, I pulled up King's contact and was about to hit the green call button when suddenly we heard shots ring out from inside the clinic.

CHAPTER SIXTY-SIX

I HAD TUNNEL VISION AS I SPRINTED TOWARD THE entrance, focused on making sure I not only came out alive, but also had Cameron's baby and Tracey with me when I left. Everything was moving so fast it was a complete blur. We didn't have time to debate options or sit around and wait for the police to arrive. Gun shots had already been fired. We were the first ones on scene.

Erin edged around back to make sure we had all exits blocked in case someone was trying to flee. We didn't have much of a plan—we were operating on adrenaline alone—but we knew we couldn't let whoever was responsible for Kate's death get away.

The front door rattled on its hinges as I swung it open. The glass smashed as I passed the same empty desk I'd stared at last night and yanked open the wood door that brought me to the back of the clinic.

My eyes were wide and I was on high alert as I moved swiftly down the hall like a commando on a mission to take out her target. Everything about this place reminded me of my own doctor's office. The sterile smell. The bright lights and white walls. It didn't seem like the scam I knew it was. Ironically, the further I moved inside, the more legit it felt.

Walking on my toes, I heard a man groan. The noise wasn't near, but loud enough for me to hear. My pulse ticked hard and fast in my neck as I continued clearing rooms. I wasn't sure what I was about to find but I kept moving closer to the sound, thinking that Tracey couldn't be far.

When I reached the room the groans were coming from, I found Dr. Glenn Wu on the ground holding his neck where he had been shot. The pistol lay next to him.

I reached for the doorframe and steadied my stance when a sudden wave of dizziness twirled my head. I wasn't sure what I was looking at—other than that Wu was shot and had a serious, life threatening injury to his neck. He was still conscious as I tried to make sense of what could have happened.

Too afraid to move, I raked my gaze over the dozens of documents scattered across the floor. In the far corner, a baby crib was set up beneath a mobile. In the opposite corner, another. I couldn't believe I was standing at the entrance of a nursery. It seemed that Dr. Wu had come here—to his research facility—to kill himself, knowing King and the rest of the department were on to him.

Wu lifted his head and coughed up blood.

When my eyes landed on him, he was staring directly at me.

"Call an ambulance," he muttered through a wheezy breath.

I blinked and couldn't believe the words I was hearing.

"I'm losing too much blood."

A spike of adrenaline had my phone out of my pocket and into my hand in a flash. "Where is Dr. Andrews?"

"Put the phone down, Samantha," a man's calm voice said behind me.

I turned slowly, hearing Wu continue to gurgle and choke on his own blood filling his throat. I found Dr. James Andrews pointing his gun directly at my head. "You ruined my plans."

"Are you sure it wasn't him," I nodded to Dr. Wu, "who ruined your plans?"

"True." Andrews's head nodded. "But I was going to make it look like a suicide. Now how am I supposed to do that with you here?"

Dr. Wu spat at Andrews. "Fuck you."

Andrews peeked over my shoulder and laughed. Then it hit me.

"It was you," I said, standing. "You killed the Browns." And he was about to do the same to Dr. Wu.

"No, fentanyl killed them." Andrews sneered. "Prescribed by the doctor bleeding out behind you."

Wu gasped for air, his eyes popping open with each pulsating beat from the heart that was struggling to keep him alive. I wasn't sure he was going to make it. He was in bad shape, and for what? Because his partner wanted to take the glory of what they'd created together for himself?

"A look through these documents will prove it, too." Andrews nudged the muzzle of his revolver and aimed it between my eyes.

"What about Tracey? Where is she? I know you have her."

I could hear my own heart drumming loud in my chest. I was afraid that if I pushed Andrews too far, he wouldn't hesitate to pull the trigger on me. With my palms pointing at Andrews like large stop signs directing traffic, I looked around the room for any signs of Tracey. I couldn't see any, but my focus was distracted by what Andrews was planning to do next.

"Did you kidnap her?" I asked.

"If only it were that easy." Andrews wiped the sweat

beading off his upper lip with his free hand. "No, I had nothing against the Browns."

"Are you sure about that? Because the story of Phanes Biotechnology tells me you had every reason to want to kill them." I turned and looked at Wu. "Both of you did."

Andrews waved his gun at me. "I knew when I saw you last night that you would be trouble."

Him. It was Andrews I saw. That bastard was cleaning up, knowing I would be coming back.

"But it wasn't me who was set to go to trial with them over a stupid breach of contract." Andrews's eyes went to Wu. "No, Tracey found her way to me when she showed up at Mile High Health Clinic and I mistakenly implanted one of my embryos inside of her."

"You mean when you seeded her with one of your designer babies."

"You're smarter than you look, Samantha." Andrews's eyes narrowed. "After seeing the look in your eye last night, I knew you would be the one to figure this place out. I just didn't think you would do it so soon."

"I get underestimated a lot."

"The irony of it all is that Wu had beef with the Browns. So when I learned of my mistake, several new opportunities opened up. They knew about Phanes Biotechnology so were too close to it all. And with Wu already involved in a civil suit with them because of his *morals*, it was just too easy to get rid of them and Wu at the same time."

"But you were in this together. The Guardian Angels of gene editing technology."

"We *were* in this together."

I gave him a questioning look.

"He," Andrews pointed his gun at Wu, "let his conscience get the best of him. As a result, he got sued over a stupid breach of contract after backing out on what he promised to give so many."

"And you never let it go."

"Designer babies was what it was always about. From the beginning, we set out to bring real change to the future of medicine. And you know what? I did it. You're right," he snapped his teeth. "I never let it go. And neither should he have."

"That's why you shot him?"

"He was going to turn me in. I had no choice."

Now that I had Andrews talking, all I could think about was getting to the pistol lying next to Wu and hope it was loaded with at least five more bullets. Andrews circled around me and moved to Wu. When he stomped his foot, I snapped my focus back to him and kept my hands held high in the air.

I watched as Andrews knelt next to Wu and stared into his fading eyes. He kept his gun pointed at the doctor and began to speak. "You stopped right when we were closing in on actually figuring it out."

Wu coughed up more blood.

"We could have done this together. A healthy baby girl was born." Andrews smiled through misty eyes. "The future is now, Dr. Cherub." He reached for Wu's forehead and set a hand on his head. Stroking Wu's face, Andrews titled his head to the side and continued speaking. "Your idea will now be my legacy."

In that split second, I saw my window of opportunity and lunged for the pistol near Wu's head. The cold metal suctioned to my hand as I jumped back and pointed the gun at Andrews. "Where is Tracey?"

Andrews slowly moved his hands away from Wu's face, but remained kneeling. His eyes darkened as he stared up at me. "Don't be a fool, Samantha. Put that gun down."

I squeezed my grip tighter and locked my elbows. "Where is she?"

"My god, woman, don't end up like him." Andrews flicked his gaze to Wu and his words made me believe Tracey was still alive.

"Tell me where she is, dammit." I stepped around Wu and motioned for Andrews to stand up.

Andrews slowly stood and stepped away from Wu. Giving me a pathetic sorry look, he shook his head and said, "What am I going to do with you?"

I took one step forward and cornered him to the door.

Suddenly, out of nowhere, a foot flew between his legs and slammed into his privates. Andrews's fingers snapped open as he released the gun he was holding. I watched it drop to the floor in slow motion, praying it wouldn't fire, when Erin laid another swift kick to Andrews's torso and knocked him on his side.

I kicked his gun away and held mine to his head. "You move and I'll shoot you."

Andrews held his hands between his legs and moaned in agony.

Then, as if hearing a call to prayer bellow out into the sky, I heard the sounds of sirens outside.

It was over. We'd got him.

CHAPTER SIXTY-SEVEN

EVENTUALLY, DR. ANDREWS FLOPPED TO THE SIDE AND curled into a small, pathetic ball, having completely given up. There was a distant look in his eye that I couldn't shake. It was one of despair, loss, and perhaps even regret that seemed to deepen the longer he lay on his side facing the two cribs that were meant to house his creations.

I kept the gun pointing at his chest in case he tried to make one last stand, but he never did. I was thankful for him not forcing me into shooting him. The thought of him doing a death by cop suicide certainly crossed my mind.

I didn't feel bad for him. Not after what he'd done to Kate, Cameron, Tracey, and Wu. Everything he worked so hard to achieve was finished, and a part of me hoped that the idea of designer babies was, too.

Erin was breathing heavily as she applied pressure to Dr. Wu's neck wound. She kept telling him to keep his eyes open, that help was on the way. But we both knew that Wu was fading fast.

An army of heavy boots filled the hallways as I heard the police storm through the building and work to clear each room on their way to us. Sweat scurried down my spine and I kept my gun on Andrews until I felt a half-dozen muzzles suddenly aim into my back.

"Gun!" an officer shouted. "Police! Drop the gun!"

Slowly, I raised my hands, removing my finger from the trigger, and dropped to my knees on the floor. Setting the gun on the ground next to me, the officers swooped inside the nursery and restrained my hands behind my back. They did the same to Erin and Andrews and called for EMTs to assist with Wu. EMTs rushed into the room and immediately began working on Wu's injuries.

As I sat there on my knees watching the final scene unfold, I started shaking. Soon, tears prickled my eyes when reality began to sink in.

"Tracey Brown," I said to one of the officers. "She might be here. Have you found her?"

"And a baby, too," Erin added.

Our pleas to search for the missing victims fell on mostly deaf ears. Wu was a top priority, and the police didn't know who was good and who was bad. And frankly, neither did I. I was sure most of them had no idea what kind of jackpot they had just stumbled upon.

"Sam." I heard King call my name from behind.

I closed my eyes and cried harder.

King announced himself before lifting both Erin and me to our feet. After a short conversation with the arresting officers, King escorted us out of the nursery and headed for the exit. He didn't ask questions, and certainly didn't seem too surprised to find us here.

He released our restraints as we walked and, as I began rubbing the raw pain out of my wrists, a female officer rounded the corner, escorting a beautiful young woman strapped to the EMT gurney. And she was holding a baby.

"Tracey?" I said as we let her pass.

The young woman flicked her eyes to me. Fear flashed over her colorful irises but her face twisted with confusion. I smiled and said nothing.

The gurney wheels rolled ahead of us and I breathed deeper. Erin shared a questioning look with me as we exited the building, knowing there should have been two babies.

"King, there should be another one. Kate and Cameron both had babies here."

Tightening his grip on my arm, he lowered his head and kept walking. Dropping his voice to a whisper, he said, "One didn't make it."

"Which one? Kate's or Cameron's?" I asked as we stepped outside.

He shook his head, not having an answer for me.

"Tell me," I said, "how did you know where to find me?"

The dark sky flashed with red and blue when I spotted another familiar face peering out from the back window of Detective Campbell's unmarked sedan.

"I didn't." His hand was on my arm and a part of me knew he was afraid of letting me go. King jutted his jaw to Campbell's car. "We were following Tyler Lopez and he just happened to lead us to you."

Campbell caught sight of me and grinned—a knowing glint in his eye—as he stood guard of his prize in the backseat.

"What was Tyler charged with?" I asked.

"Nothing yet," King said. "He surrendered as soon as we cornered him here."

"Has he talked?"

"Nothing specific about Cameron, only that he was coming here to confront the man who set him up."

"Everyone was coming for Andrews, it seemed," Erin said.

"Tyler will be taken to the station and interrogated until his nose bleeds." King stopped at his car and turned to face the Guardian Angel clinic. "If he's smart, he'll lawyer up before answering any questions. As long as he answers truthfully and is innocent like you think he is, Campbell will have no choice but to release him."

I stared at Campbell, thinking how he got what he wanted. If he squeezed a confession out of Tyler, Chief Watts would have no choice but to celebrate Campbell as the hero who collared Denver's Most Wanted. But, in the end, it didn't matter who got the victory lap. We found Tracey and the baby girl I hoped was Cameron's.

News vans arrived and a police helicopter's rotors shook the sky above. We stood by King's car and watched Dr. Wu get whisked away in an ambulance.

"Alex," I turned to my boyfriend, "Andrews confessed to murdering the Browns." Then I told him about his designer baby scheme. "He did it. He's your man."

King's hand moved to the small of my back. "C'mon, let's get you two down to the station to give your official statements." King opened the back door of his sedan and motioned for Erin and me to get inside.

Erin ducked her head and got inside first. I stepped forward, but before I got inside, Alvarez said, "Sam—" I lifted my head and turned to face him. "You should know it was your sister who tipped us off on Tyler's whereabouts."

I felt my eyebrows pinch.

"If it wasn't for her call, we wouldn't have arrived when we did."

Staring at Alvarez with a surprised and unwavering gaze, I said, "I'll be sure to thank her."

Alvarez nodded. "Good sleuthing must run in the family."

I glanced to King. "Let's get this over with. I'd like to get home to my son."

CHAPTER SIXTY-EIGHT

Two months later...

The four of us girls were sitting outside on the patio of The Rio with the sun beating down on our backs and sipping margaritas listening to Erin entertain us all with the story of how she saved me from Dr. James Andrews.

Erin had her voice low as she told her side of the story. Her hand was over her heart as she imitated how it had been racing that day. "I could hear Sam demanding to know where Tracey was and the moment I came around that corner and saw Dr. Andrews pointing his gun at Sam, I thought I was going to be witness to my friend's death."

I rolled my gaze to Susan, flicked my eyebrows, and grinned.

Erin's spine straightened. Her voice raised. "And you know I wasn't about to let that happen, so I wound my foot back and kicked that son of a bitch square between the legs."

"Got 'em in the crown jewels," I said.

Erin jumped off her stool and landed on her feet. She brought her fists up in front of her face like she was readying to fight, and swiftly kicked her leg through the air mimicking her amazing moves from that day.

We clapped and cheered, just like we had done the previous times Erin needed to relive her moment of glory. With each new telling, our cheers became more enthusiastic and Erin's moves tighter, more controlled, and more dramatic.

Allison jumped to her feet and was punching the air in front of her. I was laughing along with Susan, thinking how lucky I was to walk away from that day without being seriously injured.

In the end, it all worked out. Andrews was indicted by a grand jury and was set to serve life in prison without parole. He went down for the murders of Keith and Pam Brown, Kate Wilson and her baby girl, and attempted murder of Cameron Dee and a whole list of other charges related to his elaborate scheme that was supposed to make him rich. He never did confess to the police like he did to me, but that was all right because the evidence against him was overwhelming.

As for Tyler Lopez, he was cleared of all charges and, though Cameron's baby girl wasn't his, he remained a friend to Cameron until going their separate ways. Ms. Dee took her role as matriarch and was doing what she could to help her daughter bring up the child right.

Tracey Brown was released from the hospital three days after Andrews was arrested and she and I became close friends. Though she never said it, I knew she liked having someone to talk to. In the end, I helped her put her parents' house on the market and it sold astonishingly fast. It was hard for her to say goodbye, but she knew that it wouldn't be a house she could stay to raise her child in without constantly thinking about past memories of her parents.

It was revealed that Tommy Patterson was Dr. Andrews's

son. We never did learn how, or why, but Kristi said it was for the better. Tommy would always be theirs, no matter what DNA he shared. But I suspected as Tommy grew older, it would always be in the back of her mind that her son shared the genetics with a psychopath.

Whether I agreed with it or not, designer babies were in our future for those who could afford it. As for me, I had already moved on and was a solid six weeks into an investigation that was sure to make the front page.

"Sam, how many times did I kick him?" Erin asked.

"About a dozen."

Erin puffed out her chest and nodded.

I dropped a twenty on the table and said, "That's it for me."

"No. Sam, stay. We're having fun."

"I'd love to, but really, I have to run."

Allison pushed my twenty back. "Keep it. Tonight's on me."

I flung my arm around her neck and we hugged. She felt warm and strong and though I knew she had begun her treatment, it was impossible to tell. Allison hadn't let on to any of what she was going through and I admired her strength.

"Stay," Susan suggested. "You know the rules."

"Not tonight." I chuckled.

"She's right. Not one of us has been asked out yet."

I turned to Erin. "Walk me to my car?"

"Certainly." She held her arm out and I looped mine through the crook of hers.

"There," I said. "Erin just got asked out."

Allison slapped her hand down on the table and laughed.

Susan crumbled up a napkin and tossed it at my head.

"I love you all, but this girl is on deadline," I called over my shoulder as I walked Erin to my car.

"You know, Susan will eventually find out what you're writing," Erin said as soon as we were at my car.

"I know."

"You should tell her before it gets published."

"I will."

Erin held my gaze for a long pause before saying, "Sometimes the truth hurts, but sometimes it's exactly what we need to hear."

I turned my head and stared up the block watching the cars go past.

"When does Dawson want to run it?"

"In Sunday's paper." Besides Dawson, Erin was the only other living soul who knew the depth of my investigation and the lengths I had to go to in making sure I had my ducks in a row, but there was something that even Erin didn't know.

"Are you ready for the world to read it?"

I stared into her eyes and shook my head, no.

"You believe it's true?"

"I do."

"Then that's all that matters."

I wet my lips and swallowed. "Someone else knows what I've been investigating."

Erin's eyebrows pulled together. "Someone like who? I thought you've been keeping this a secret?"

My head was light from the drinks, but the alcohol was also making my nerves feel extra jittery. I pulled out my phone and opened the email I'd received earlier this morning. I turned the screen to Erin so that she could read it. I'd read it so many times this morning I knew it by heart.

Be warned, Dearest Bell, you're barking up the wrong tree. If you publish even just a piece of the fabricated story you're investigating, there will be hell to pay.

Erin's head snapped up and I watched fear flash over her eyes.

"It was sent to me about two this morning through the email linked to our website. It's him, Erin, and I'm afraid of what he might do to make sure his story never gets out."

Continue the series by reading Bell to Pay. Click here and start reading today!

AUTHOR NOTE:

*Thank you for reading BLOODY BELL. If you enjoyed the book and would like to see more Samantha Bell crime thrillers, **please consider leaving a review on Amazon**. Even a few words would be appreciated and will help persuade what book I will write for you next.*

One of the things I love best about writing these mystery thrillers is the opportunity to connect with my readers. It means the world to me that you read my book, but hearing from you is second to none. Your words inspire me to keep creating memorable stories you can't wait to tell your friends about. No matter how you choose to reach out - whether through email, on Facebook, or through an Amazon review - I thank you for taking the time to help spread the word about my books. I couldn't do this without YOU. So, please, keep sending me notes of encouragement and words of wisdom and, in return, I'll continue giving you the best stories I can tell.

ABOUT THE AUTHOR

Waldron lives in Vermont with his wife and two children.

Receive updates, exclusive content, and **new book release announcements** by signing up to his newsletter at: www.JeremyWaldron.com

Follow him @jeremywaldronauthor

facebook.com/jeremywaldronauthor

instagram.com/jeremywaldronauthor

bookbub.com/profile/83284054

Made in the USA
Middletown, DE
05 December 2023